Captivating in Love

~ The Maverick Billionaires ~

Book 6

Bella Andre &
Jennifer Skully

CAPTIVATING IN LOVE

~ The Maverick Billionaires, Book 6 ~

Gideon Jones came back from war a changed man. Though the Mavericks claim he's one of their own, he doesn't believe he deserves to be part of their tightly knit unit. Just like he doesn't deserve Rosie Diaz—an amazing mother...and an utterly captivating woman he can't stop dreaming about.

Rosie Diaz pulled herself out of the foster care system and made a great life for herself while raising Jorge, the son she adores. Only one thing is missing—a good man, one she can respect and love with her whole heart. A man exactly like her best friend's older brother, Gideon.

When Rosie and Gideon agree to take care of Matt and Ari's son, Noah, while the couple are on their honeymoon, they have no idea of the havoc two matchmaking little boys can create. Not to mention the steamy kisses that Rosie and Gideon can't help but steal from each other as their connection deepens and grows. But when mother and son are threatened, Gideon will stop at nothing to protect them. Will he finally believe that he truly is Maverick material...and worthy of Rosie's and Jorge's love?

A note from Bella & Jennifer

Thank you for your outpouring of love for the Maverick Billionaires! Since Gideon Jones first came on the Maverick scene in *Fearless in Love*, the number one request we get is for his story. Of course, we are just as excited as you are to see him find happiness and love! Especially when it's with a woman as wonderful as Rosie—and her young son, Jorge.

We hope you love Gideon and Rosie's story as much as we do.

Happy reading,
Bella Andre and Jennifer Skully

P.S. More Mavericks are coming soon! Please sign up for our New Release newsletters for more information. BellaAndre.com/Newsletter and bit.ly/SkullyNews

Chapter One

Gideon Jones was so good with Jorge and Noah, two six-year-olds who made enough noise to rival a herd of stampeding cattle. As he handed each boy a cube of bread, Gideon gently encouraged the boys, showing them how to stretch out one hand with the bread in the center of the palm. They were both so attentive, while their bodies quivered with the attempt to stay still long enough for the peacock to feel safe eating from their hands.

Rosie Diaz's heart melted as she watched from the picnic area, where a huge tent provided shade for the tables and dance floor that had been set up for her best friend's wedding. Ariana Jones had first met Matt Tremont when she agreed to be his young son's nanny. Ari showered Noah with love—and it wasn't long before Ari and Matt were in love too. Though Rosie knew their happiness hadn't come without struggles, their relationship was still a fairy tale come true to her. She couldn't be happier that her friend had found love.

It was a gorgeous, sunny Saturday in August as

Rosie's son, Jorge, and Ari's son, Noah, hunkered down before the peacock, his magnificent tail feathers trailing behind him. When Ari and Rosie had been teens together in foster care, this what they'd dreamed of—that their children would end up being best friends.

Rosie and Ari were sisters of the heart—along with their friend Chi, who had also been a part of the foster care system. Rosie had met them when her parents died in her early teens. She loved Ari for her eternal optimism and her loyalty to her brother. She loved Chi for her strength. When her foster family couldn't say her Chinese name—Zhi Ruo—correctly, Chi had adopted their pronunciation as her own, saying it was a powerful name, like Tai Chi.

Rosie believed the three of them would be best friends forever and ever. They'd seen her through the dark days when she was eighteen and pregnant and alone after her baby's father had abandoned her. They'd seen her through Jorge's birth when she was nineteen. Jorge's biological father—DNA being his only contribution—was the one who'd taught her not to trust men. At least until she'd met the Mavericks. In the same way that Ari and Chi had taught her the loyalty and goodness of friends, the Mavericks had taught her the goodness of men.

As much as Rosie wished her parents were still alive, she wouldn't change any of what she'd gone through. She couldn't imagine her life, her world, without Jorge.

Her son was the light of her life, an amazing little human being. Sometimes she couldn't believe he had come from her. She and Ari and Chi had raised Jorge to be the confident, outgoing, loving boy he was.

So how could she regret anything? Especially on such a beautiful day when true love was all that mattered. As a wonderful bonus, she was finally getting to spend time with Ari's brother. Gideon was so patient with the boys, never yelling, never snapping.

With adults, Gideon didn't talk much, didn't smile much. But when he played with Noah and Jorge, it was as if he became the man he would have been if he'd never been scarred by his time in the army, if he'd never lost touch with Ari. When he was with the boys, he became the funny, amazing, big brother Ari had always talked about.

The kind of man to whom Rosie could so easily lose her heart.

Maybe she'd already given him a tiny piece of her heart, especially when she watched him in unguarded moments like this with the boys.

He hadn't yet changed into his tux and was still dressed in jeans and a T-shirt that showcased every rippling muscle. He was a vision of rough, raw, sexy power, accentuated by blue eyes and dark blond hair worn short, as if he'd never completely left the military behind. He could see right into you with those eyes. Or right through you as though you didn't exist. Rosie longed for him to look at her, *really* look at her, to see what was on the inside. He made her warm all over. He made her aware of every beat of her heart. He made her want to trust a man again.

Just then, the peacock stretched out his long neck and pecked the bit of bread from Jorge's hand. Rosie's little boy wriggled with delight, pressing his lips together to suppress the squeal of joy dying to get out. Gideon smiled his approval, ruffling Jorge's hair. Then he urged Noah forward, his nephew all big eyes and wonder as the peacock grabbed the bread out of his hand too.

It didn't matter that Ari wasn't Noah's birth mom; Gideon treated him like he was his own blood. No one ever used the word *stepson*. Ari was simply Noah's mom, Gideon was his uncle, and Matt was his dad. There was so much love among them all, it made Rosie gooey on the inside.

Ari and Matt had decided to have their wedding at the petting zoo and open-air puppet theater in San Jose because it was Noah's favorite spot. They'd rented the whole park for the day, and the wedding itself would take place on the stage. Rosie and Gideon were currently in charge of Noah while Ari was getting ready in the bridal tent.

Rosie, as maid of honor, would need to get herself ready soon, but there had been so many last-minute things to check on. She wanted everything to be absolutely perfect. And she knew that Gideon, who would be giving Ari away, wanted perfection just as much for his sister's big day.

With the docent looking on, Gideon showed Noah and Jorge how to carefully stretch out a hand to pet the peacock's brilliant blue neck. The boys were clearly awed by the bird's magnificence, by his feathers, by the way he ate from their hands and let them touch him.

Though Gideon was ten years older, Ari claimed that when they were kids, he'd never treated her like she was an annoying pest. Instead, he'd played games with her, taken her to the park, made her laugh until her stomach hurt. Rosie supposed that because their mom had been an addict, Gideon had grown up fast, taking care of the two of them.

When he was eighteen, he'd enlisted in the army, wanting to make enough money to help Ari and their mom with living expenses. But he couldn't have predicted their mother would move them around so much that he'd lose track of them—or that he wouldn't get notification of their mom's death until she'd been gone six months. By then, finding Ari while stationed in the Middle East had been impossible. Despite searching for her after he got out, it had taken sixteen years since the day he'd joined up for them to find each other again, after Matt had hired a private investigator to find Ari's long-lost brother.

Rosie would have loved Matt just for that, even if he wasn't such a great guy on top of it. The fact that he was a billionaire—along with his four best friends, the Mavericks—was irrelevant. Although, she thought with a small smile, she wasn't going to lie and say she hadn't enjoyed flying on his private plane last month.

"Sorry I haven't been helping you take care of the final wedding details," Gideon said, his deep voice surprising her. Rosie had been so lost in her thoughts she hadn't realized Gideon had left the boys with the docent, who was explaining about peachicks and peacocks and peahens to her rapt audience. "The boys were so excited about the animals," he added, "I wanted to get them started."

"I'm glad you did." She turned to smile at him. "And I haven't needed any help. Fortunately, the caterers are great. They've got everything set out the way Ari wanted."

Gideon was so tall, broad-shouldered, and powerfully muscled that being this close to him made her shivery inside, her breath catching as her heart beat fast enough for her to feel her pulse in her fingertips. There was that ancient cliché—*he stole my breath*. That's what Gideon did to her.

Not that he seemed to have even the slightest clue what he did to her—or any woman, for that matter. Rosie couldn't remember ever seeing him flirt with anyone, and though he was a devastatingly good-looking man, his hard shell was so intimidating that Rosie had yet to see any woman bold enough to flirt with him either. Even when they played water polo in Ari and Matt's pool or jumped on Noah's trampoline, and she'd catch Gideon looking at her, she wasn't able to read what was in his mind. Did he think she was pretty? Did she make his heart race the way he always sent hers into overdrive?

Gideon hid all his emotions behind a wall no one could scale.

He had been deployed in the Middle East for seven years, and though he hadn't spoken to anyone, not even his sister, about his experiences during those years, it was obvious they'd left their mark on his heart—along with deep, dark shadows in his eyes.

Only with Noah and Jorge did Gideon seem to be his true self. Rosie longed for him to be this way all the time, not just with the boys. She longed for him to relax and laugh with her the way he did with them.

But, just as with every time before, when he caught her eyes on him, his immediate withdrawal was like a physical punch. The smile died on his lips, his blue eyes turned into dark, fathomless pools, even his body seemed to grow rigid. As if he'd turned to stone. As if he couldn't allow himself happiness with anyone but the boys. Even with Ari, whom he clearly loved with everything in him, he held something back.

It broke Rosie's heart. If only they could *all* have

happy endings. Matt, Ari, herself…and especially Gideon.

"What about the parts of the wedding Ari doesn't know about?" Gideon's deep, gravelly voice ran up Rosie's spine as seductively as the brush of his fingertips over her bare skin. *If* he ever touched her. "Not many brides would want to be surprised on their wedding day."

"Ari isn't like any other bride," Rosie reminded him. He'd been wary when Will, Sebastian, Evan, and Daniel had not only suggested a robot theme for the wedding, but also that the details were to be kept secret from the bride and groom until the big day. Though the Mavericks were all massively wealthy and successful men, they were also loads of fun. "Trust me, both Ari and Matt are going to *love* the surprises we have in store for them today."

Since the wedding was at the puppet theater, Ari had decided to have a puppet skit beforehand, while the guests were arriving, and the Mavericks had run with it, going totally wild with their secret plans. Rosie and Chi, and all the Maverick ladies and their family members, including Harper's brother, Jeremy, had worked tirelessly over the last two weeks making themed party favors and table centerpieces. Jorge and Noah, being Lego experts, had been instrumental in directing everyone.

"The fountain is ready to go," Rosie told Gideon.

"And the wedding favors and centerpieces are being set out as we speak." She hooked a thumb over her shoulder at the army of workers stocking the bar and setting the tables. White tablecloths, real silverware, gold-trimmed plates, crystal stemware, no expense spared.

The peacock made a loud *eeeiu*, capturing her attention again. The boys were all agog as the docent explained that it was a mating call.

Gideon gave Rosie a tiny quirk of his mouth, which was as close as he ever came to a smile around her. "Noah and Jorge are fascinated that he's a French peacock named Henri," he told her. "According to the docent, the bird actually came from France—a small town near Toulouse called Le Fousseret. I'm not sure I believe it, but the boys keep saying they want to learn French so that they can talk to him in his own language." He recounted the information dryly, nearly without inflection...yet Rosie could hear his affection for the boys beneath his words.

"You're so good with them," she told him.

Gideon stiffened, the hint of a smile falling away. "They're good kids, really easy." He clearly refused to take any credit. And just as clearly, after speaking only a handful of sentences to her, he was looking for an escape route out of their short conversation.

It wasn't just single women who gave Gideon a wide berth—everyone did. Even the Mavericks had simultaneously welcomed him into the fold and given him all the space he seemed to require.

Maybe it was the magic of the upcoming wedding weaving its spell around her. Maybe it was the warmth of the sun on her skin on this beautiful summer day. Maybe it was the peacock's mating call.

Or maybe it was simply that nine months had been enough time for Rosie to see Gideon for who he really was. Sweet and adoring with his sister. Playful and caring with the boys. Respectful yet protective as he made sure Matt was good enough for Ari.

From the first moment Rosie had set eyes on Gideon last Thanksgiving at Matt's house, he'd captivated her. He was so tall, at least six two, and she'd had to look up, up, up at him. She couldn't breathe, couldn't speak. Even her heart fluttered. His dark blond hair, as short as it was, looked soft enough to run her fingers through. She'd wanted to do it so badly that her hand almost rose on its own. He'd been wearing butt-hugging dress pants at Thanksgiving and a shirt that molded to every single muscle. She'd wanted to touch those magnificent muscles, test whether they were real. Then there was all that bronzed skin from the years working outside as a carpenter, the matching set of tiny lines at the corners of his eyes from being in the sun all the time. He was seasoned to perfection.

Rosie never went gaga over men—she was

immune. But from that very first day, Gideon had made her want things she hadn't thought about in years.

It was his eyes she couldn't forget, however. His gaze shuttered as if he were warning everyone off. Those eyes made her want to make him smile, to give him joy, to bring him happiness. And now, she couldn't help but imagine. Couldn't stop herself from dreaming.

Dreaming of Gideon with Jorge high on his broad shoulders, laughter on Jorge's face.

Dreaming of her hand in Gideon's, feeling his strength, his caring.

Dreaming of him lifting her hand to his mouth, brushing his lips across her knuckles.

Dreaming of love in his eyes and an unselfconscious smile on his mouth. *For her.*

It had been so long since she'd let a man into her life. Not since Jorge's worthless father. She hadn't thought she could ever do it again. And even if she could manage to conquer her own demons for Gideon, she wasn't sure he would ever be able to fully drop his walls for her.

But she was absolutely positive about one thing: She was done tiptoeing around him. Done giving him a wider berth than she would give anyone else. Done worrying that she'd freak him out by treating him the way she treated her other friends.

From here on out, she was going to tease him and joke with him and laugh around him. The way she did with Ari and Chi and all the Mavericks. The same way she'd seen him tease and joke and laugh with the boys.

Never one to let the grass grow under her feet, she said, "Since you're taking care of Noah while Matt and Ari are on their honeymoon, it would be great to get the boys together for a few playdates over the next two weeks. We could take them to the park or for a hike or a trip up to San Francisco. There are so many great ways for us to have fun together."

Taken off guard, he backed up a full step and said, "All four of us, you mean?"

She half expected him to jiggle a finger in his ear as if he couldn't possibly have heard her right. Refusing to take offense at his response, she nodded and said cheerfully, "Yup, all four of us."

When he remained silent—likely trying to think up an unassailable excuse for why the playdates couldn't happen—Rosie decided it was long past time to make yet another big change in their relationship. She'd never touched him before. Gideon's *keep away* sign flashed such a bright neon that even Ari rarely hugged him. But Rosie refused to let nerves stop her from reaching out to put her hand on his arm.

Wow. The barest brush of her hand over his skin left her fingers tingling and set her heart racing.

But Gideon went rigid. And his face turned red.

"You know what a great time the boys have together," she said. "And I've taken off the whole two weeks while Matt and Ari are in Iceland." Before he had a chance to respond, she said, "I've got to run now. They're waiting on me for the hair and makeup session." She ran a hand through her dark curly hair. It badly needed taming. "They've got their work cut out for them," she said with a smile. "Anyway, let me know when you've had a chance to look at your calendar. And can you also make sure the boys get into their tuxes in the groom's tent? Then hand Jorge over to Susan? He's going to sit with her for the ceremony."

"Sure," he said, always a man of few words.

She laid her fingers on his arm one last time, because really, who knew when she'd get another good excuse to touch him and feel those delicious tingles? "Thank you." Then she jogged off to drop kisses on Jorge's and Noah's heads, the heat of Gideon's gaze on her as warm as his skin had been beneath her fingertips.

Just before she turned away, she saw him put his hand right on the spot she'd touched. As if he could still feel her.

Maybe, just maybe, he wasn't quite as immune to her as he always seemed...

Chapter Two

Rosie Diaz was the world's best mom—so sweet, so natural, so full of love. Gideon couldn't help but compare her to his own. Nadine Jones had tried her best, but addiction aside, though he knew she'd loved him and Ari, she'd never been good at showing it.

Whereas, Rosie was always showing Jorge how much she loved him, making him laugh as she chased him down, growling, her hands clenched close to her sides like a T-Rex, grabbing him for one more terrible "Mom kiss." The kid was going to be a heartbreaker, so like his mother with olive skin, deep, soulful brown eyes, and thick, curly, dark hair. One day, the girls would fall all over themselves for him.

The way men must fall all over Rosie.

The way he would fall all over her if he could, if he had a prayer of ever being good enough for her. Which he didn't. Not even close.

The activity hadn't scared off Henri the peacock, and Noah held out a piece of bread to Rosie. Instead of rushing off to get her hair and makeup done, she knelt down beside the boys and fed Henri. Noah leaned into her, Jorge on her other side, resting his head on her shoulder.

Gideon loved Noah with every broken shard of his heart. Noah was Matt's kid by some woman Gideon had met only once. Noah's biological mom had been flighty and talky and flirty, and how Matt had ever hooked up with her, Gideon couldn't figure out. But Matt had been lucky enough to end up with Noah, and they'd both found Ari, so that made it all worthwhile in the end.

Blood didn't matter. In every way except DNA, Noah was Ari's kid. Which meant Noah was now a part of Gideon too. He'd love Noah even if he wasn't Ari's, simply because he was such a great kid. Funny, interested in everything, and so kind. Where other little boys might pluck the wings off a fly, Noah would catch it in a jar to set it free outside.

Wrapping themselves around Rosie, the boys convinced her to feed the peacock one more piece of bread. Of course, she was a softy and gave in, laughing with them.

Gideon didn't know much about Jorge's father except that he'd run out on them, leaving Rosie to raise Jorge on her own. She'd worked hard to earn a degree in accounting from the local college, then found a good job and a nice place to live for her and her son. Not a lot of women could have made it the way Rosie had.

He'd known she was special the very first moment he'd seen her. It was Thanksgiving, and she'd been wearing a dress the color of merlot. His chest clenched as he thought about how perfect, how sweet, she'd looked. How perfect and sweet she *always* looked.

She was petite and curvy and gorgeous, her hair dark and curly. Luscious. He dreamed about burying his face in her beautiful locks, drinking in her scent, one of flowers—orange and lemon blossoms. He dreamed about laying her down on a big bed and exploring her generous curves. He dreamed about making her cry out his name in pleasure.

But simply saying he was attracted to her minimized the strength of his feelings for her. During every Maverick party and barbecue and holiday, he not only felt almost drunk at the sight of her, he was constantly amazed by her intelligence and the sense of peace that radiated from her.

Of course, he could never be with her. Never have her heart. Not after everything he'd done.

Yet his heart couldn't stop longing for her. His heart seemed to have a mind of its own, wanting what it wanted, the impossibility of it all be damned. Even if he could never deserve her. He could never go back and erase his past. He could never scrub out his mistakes. He would never get a do-over to make everything right—not only with Ari, but with his team, the team he'd lost in the Middle East.

"I really need to go now," he heard her say to the boys in a soft voice that did things to him deep inside. Made him want all those things he couldn't have. When she'd touched him so unconsciously just moments ago, the force of his desire—and longing— had nearly dropped him to his knees. "I'll be over in the tent with Ari and Chi getting made up," she said to Jorge, then pointed at Gideon, their eyes meeting. Her coffee-colored eyes were rich enough to fall into. "Gideon is going to watch out for you while I'm gone. So obey everything he says, okay?"

Gideon ached with the realization that Rosie trusted him with her son. He didn't deserve her trust, but he hugged it close as if he were holding her. And when she fluttered her fingers at him to let him know she was finally leaving, his heart fluttered with her.

But he could never let himself touch her. Not when one touch would be his undoing.

If he touched her, he would need to kiss her.

And if he kissed her, he'd never be able to stop.

He'd been to hell while in the service, but though he was back in California, he'd never left that fiery pit behind. And he would never drag someone as extraordinary and wonderful as Rosie into that brutal abyss with him.

As she headed for the bridal tent, he remembered her comment about the stylists having their work cut out for them. Yet Rosie didn't need paint on her face, or a fuss made over her gorgeous hair. Rosie was beautiful exactly the way she was, her petite figure a sexy hourglass that made men drool. She made *him* drool. He couldn't figure out why some great guy hadn't already snapped her up.

If only he could be that guy.

But he couldn't. Not now. Not ever.

He was still amazed that the Mavericks had taken him in. Matt had offered him a home during the weeks when Gideon had been building a new life in California. Daniel Spencer had offered him a job, responsibilities, promotions at his Top Notch chain of DIY stores. First Gideon had been responsible for supplies, then purchasing, and now Daniel had put him in charge of warehousing—*all* the Top Notch warehouses, including the five being built in the Bay Area. Construction of those warehouses was now his baby. He couldn't be sure why Daniel had given him the responsibility—maybe it was because Gideon had been a team leader in the army, or because he'd worked as a contractor after he got out—but whatever the reason, he wasn't going to let Daniel down.

Still, there was a part of Gideon, a huge part, that couldn't figure out why the Mavericks were helping him. Not after he'd left his sister alone for sixteen years—allowed her to be raised in foster care. As far as he could see, he hadn't done a thing to deserve what they'd done for him. Except being Ari's brother. Sure, he worked hard, tried to do the best possible job on everything Daniel threw his way. But he could never repay Daniel. Never repay Matt. Never repay each and every one of the Mavericks for taking in Ari the way they had.

For taking care of her when Gideon hadn't even been able to *find* her.

The boys ran over to him, and Jorge grabbed his hand. "Come on, Gid. The lady's gonna let us feed *bugs* to the peacock." Gideon smiled at the awe in Jorge's voice over the thought of eating bugs.

Noah grabbed his other hand. "Yeah. Real live bugs." His cheeks were flushed with excitement. "The lady said peacocks like bugs even better than bread. They spend all day poking around looking for them in the dirt and plants."

"And we get to touch 'em too!" Jorge said.

"That sounds cool. Let's go check it out." They led Gideon back to Henri the peacock and the soon-to-be-eaten bugs.

Noah would stay with him for the two weeks Ari and Matt were in Iceland. Gideon guessed his sister would have taken her son with them if everyone hadn't stressed that it was a *honeymoon*. That was how much she loved Noah. Gideon loved him with equal fervor—and couldn't bear the thought of anything bad ever happening to the little boy. Especially not on his watch.

"Here you go." The docent opened a plastic bag full of bugs.

They didn't move a whole lot, and Gideon was pretty sure they'd had most of the life refrigerated out of them. Still, Jorge and Noah were clearly thrilled, saying *wow* and *awesome* as they got their handful of bugs.

Gideon got his handful too, and before he could stop the memory from coming, he was over there again, back in the sandbox, his team forced to eat bugs because there'd been nothing else.

But watching the kids go a little nuts with feeding the peacock brought Gideon back to the present, to the sunny California day when his little sister was going to say her *I do*'s.

Finally having had his fill, the bird strutted away, his magnificent plumage trailing on the ground behind him. Jorge made a little face, saying, "I guess we're just chopped liver now."

The docent laughed, her face crinkling with delight. Gideon allowed himself a small smile too, guessing Jorge must have heard that phrase from Rosie.

"You were very good boys," the woman said, and with Gideon's agreement, she handed them each a sucker. "My best kids of the day."

Noah blinked at her. "We've been your only kids today."

"Yes, but you're still the best." She turned with a wave and padded slowly after the peacock.

Jorge tugged on Gideon's hand. "Can we pet the llamas?"

"Sure, kiddo. And the donkeys too."

"They've got donkeys?" Noah was in petting-zoo heaven. "I haven't gotten to feed or pet a donkey before."

As he led them over, a boy hanging on each hand, Gideon let himself relish the joy of being with the kids. Only when he was with them did he feel like he could take a full breath. Somehow, they always managed to tap into the part of him that hadn't been damaged by fiery blasts and guilt and loss.

Daniel had given him two weeks off to take care of Noah, and Gideon had already planned a full schedule of fun things for the two of them to do together. But now Rosie had suggested playdates for the boys. It was a head-smacking moment—of course, he should have realized that the boys would want to do some activities together.

He wanted Noah to have a great vacation while his parents were gone, and Noah never had more fun than when he was with Jorge. They were BFFs, almost like brothers. Only, Gideon wasn't sure he could survive spending hour after hour with Rosie while the boys played...

Somehow, he'd have to find a way to convince her

that it made more sense for them to split up the duties. He could take the boys up to the Exploratorium in San Francisco one day, while she took them to the mummy museum in San Jose another day.

Because he would go stark raving crazy insane if he had to spend too much time with Rosie. She was too beautiful, too tempting, too smart, too good at mothering.

Too damned good for him in every way.

Chapter Three

Rosie peeked out of the bridal tent, opening the flaps only a couple of inches so she could see out but no one could see in. "No peeking, but your guests are arriving," she said to Ari. "And the puppet theater is fabulous. You did such a great job setting it up."

Ari ruffled the skirt of her wedding dress, getting its folds to fall the way they had in the bridal magazines they'd pored over. The dress was amazing, the bodice tightly beaded with seed pearls in shades of silver, cream, and black, and fringed in a scallop of pearls along the empire waist. Ari had chosen to go bare-shouldered, the dress held up only by straps of beads and dipping low in the back. The gossamer skirt flowed down to the floor in creamy waves. The hairdresser just had to attach the wreath of flowers Ari would wear in her hair and the short veil in the back.

She was the most beautiful bride Rosie had ever seen.

When Ari was finally satisfied with the results, she lifted her head and smiled at Rosie and Chi. "I could never have done this without you."

"Take some credit, girl, for your amazing abilities," Chi said. "You're going to make the *best* teacher ever." Ari was working on her master's in education and was aiming to teach elementary school kids like Noah and Jorge.

For so long, it had been just the three of them, Rosie and Ari and Chi—sisters, best friends forever, a team of three. Then came Jorge. And now, in the past year, they'd become a huge family with all the Mavericks.

The tent flaps opened, and Susan Spencer, Matt's foster mother, stepped in. Wearing a flattering dress of aubergine, it was hard to believe Susan was in her mid-fifties, despite her silver cap of hair. It was Susan's smile that made her seem so young—and she was always so full of smiles.

Susan and Bob Spencer were mom and dad to the Mavericks. They'd taken all the boys in as young teenagers and raised them as their own, with no differentiation between the guys and Daniel or Lyssa, their two biological kids. Rosie had always found Susan and Bob to be completely generous and selfless.

Susan's face lit up when she saw Ari. "You are so beautiful, honey."

Ari beamed at her soon-to-be mother-in-law as Susan curled her into a warm embrace, careful not to crease the dress or muss Ari's hair. When she pulled back, her eyes were misty. "We are so happy you're part of our family. Matt loves you so much. And Noah couldn't have asked for a better mom, or loved anyone more than he loves you. They're so lucky to have found you." Susan dabbed at her eyes.

"I'm the lucky one," Ari said. "Thank you for always believing in me."

"Oh, honey, you are exactly the woman I wished for Matt. You are so good for them. You're so good for *all* of us." Then Susan turned to Chi and Rosie. "And you brought us beautiful Chi and Rosie and Jorge too."

Rosie felt the prickle of tears at the way Susan always included her and her son.

"Ari, I'm not done with your hair," called the hairdresser, waving her magic curling wand. "We have to put on your wreath and veil. And it looks like some of your curls are about to droop. We absolutely *cannot* send you out with droopy curls."

Susan ran her fingers lightly over Ari's hair. "Everything about you is perfect just the way it is, honey." She smiled. "But go on, let your stylist do her thing."

While Ari had her hair recurled, Susan touched Rosie's arm. "I'm so pleased that I get to take care of Jorge while you're busy with the ceremony. Thank you for that." Then, with a kiss to Rosie's cheek, Susan slipped away, her subtle perfume lingering in the air.

"This setup is fantastic," Chi said as they once again

peeked through the tent flaps. A red carpet had been rolled out for Ari to make her trip down the aisle, and the usual wooden benches had been replaced by chairs draped in white cloth. A grand piano stood at the edge of the stage, the tuxedoed pianist playing instrumental versions of Ari's favorite music, from *Somewhere Over the Rainbow* to *Evermore* to songs she'd loved as a teenager. "I can't wait for the robots to come to life."

Since this was a puppet theater, Ari and Matt had decided to put on a puppet show while everyone took their seats. Because Matt had conquered the world of robotics, the stage had been transformed into a factory with robots moving product along an assembly line. It was amazing with all the moving parts—levers and gears and robot arms and robot hands.

As the guests filed in to find their places, two puppet robots appeared onstage to take their spots along the assembly line as if they were starting work for the day. The puppets had been inspired by five classic film robots—R2-D2 and C-3PO from *Star Wars*, Wall-E and Eve from *Wall-E*, one of Jorge's favorite movies, and a dash of Lisa from *Weird Science*. Somehow, the mash-up worked, and it was impossible not to smile at the scene.

"Hello, Number Ten," came the deep male robot's voice, a number fifteen stenciled on his vest.

The robot with a ten on her vest said, "Hello, Number Fifteen," as she passed him, her long eyelashes fluttering and a smile on her rosebud-red mouth.

Pink and red hearts fell out of the ceiling to hover over the male robot as he stared longingly after the lady.

Everyone laughed at the loud sound of his wildly beating heart.

Then levers and gears clicked and clacked and the assembly line rolled. The robots patted pieces and parts on the conveyor as if they were manufacturing toys or trucks or toasters.

Rosie glanced at the groom's tent on the other side of the theater, where the boys, already decked out in their mini tuxedoes, were staring at the stage with rapt attention. A man's big hand held the flap aside. Of course, it had to be Gideon. He would make sure they didn't miss a thing.

She would have loved a glimpse of him in his tux, but no such luck.

Onstage, the robots whistled as they worked, like the seven dwarves in *Snow White*. And Fifteen kept shooting hearts at Ten that she failed to notice.

Then a horn blew, announcing it was lunchtime. Ten's hands flew to her cheeks. "Oh no, I've forgotten my lunch box."

With hearts still waving madly over his head, Fifteen held up his lunch box and was clearly about to offer it to her, when a little boy robot with a number one emblazoned on his vest danced onto the stage.

"Mommy, you forgot your lunch." He waved the box in the air.

Ten wrapped him in her arms. "Oh, Little One, you are such a good boy."

Poor Fifteen, stoop-shouldered, picked up his lunch box and began lumbering away.

Little One called, "Number Fifteen, will you come eat with us?"

Looking both surprised and pleased, Fifteen nodded, then hurried back over.

A big yellow sun dropped down over the left side of the stage, and a picnic bench rolled out. All three robots sat down, the sun now dancing over their heads along with the hearts.

With no preamble, Number One turned to Fifteen and asked, "How do new robots get made?"

Everyone in the audience laughed as Fifteen's eyes went wide in horror. "Well, oh, uh," he spluttered.

The guests were still chuckling as Number Ten smiled and patted her son's hand. "Nice try." She leaned toward Fifteen and said, "I've already told him I'll answer that when he's older."

"Okay, then why do flowers bloom in the spring?" the little robot asked.

"Because it's cold in the winter, and they need to sleep," Fifteen said.

"And why do hummingbirds eat all the time?"

"Because their wings beat fifty times a second, and

that takes a lot of energy, which means they need to eat a lot of food to give them energy."

Little One nodded, then asked, "Do you have any little boy robots?"

"No," Fifteen said, shaking his head sadly.

"What about a lady robot?"

"I wish I did," Fifteen said as the hearts above him did a crazy dance.

Little One leaned close to Fifteen. "My mom doesn't have a man robot either."

His implication was clear. The two robots needed each other.

Hearts fell from the ceiling right over Number Ten's head as she reached out for Fifteen. As he took her hand in his, Little One nestling happily between them, the hearts merged over their heads.

The guests applauded as the curtain fell on the puppet factory and the little robot matchmaker with his mom and new dad. Rosie and Ari high-fived in the bride's tent. They'd all put the storyline together during a string of dinners at Matt and Ari's house in the weeks leading up to the wedding. Judging by the laughter and applause from the audience, it had gone over even better than they'd hoped.

Chi pointed to a couple in the audience. The man was tall and broad in a dark suit, and the woman was absolutely beautiful in a yellow silk dress. "I think that's Nicola Sullivan and her husband, Marcus. I've got to get an autograph! Although, I wouldn't want to make her feel she shouldn't have come, if she was hoping to be anonymous for the day."

Nicola was famous around the world as pop star Nico, and Chi, Ari, and Rosie were all huge fans of her music. Rosie grinned, having heard how sweet Nicola was from Harper and Charlie, who'd both spent time with her. "I bet she'd love a little fangirl moment." As Chi dashed off, Rosie called out, "Get an autograph for me t—"

She lost her breath before she could finish her sentence. Gideon had stepped out to escort Jorge to Susan's side.

He was *gorgeous* in a white tux, his hair slightly spiked, his jaw clean-shaven. But what made her heart beat wildly was the way Gideon gazed down at her son in his mini white tuxedo, a joyous smile curving his mouth. That special smile he reserved just for the boys. Jorge held on to one big hand, looking up at Gideon as though he was a hero.

Rosie's heart melted completely.

How could it not?

The rest of the crowd faded away as Gideon bent down to say something to Jorge that made her son smile wide, before he handed him over to Susan and headed back toward the groom's tent, which was on the opposite side of the puppet theater from the bride's. Only as Gideon disappeared from sight did the rest of the wedding come back into focus.

Rosie rested her hand over her heart, stunned by its hammering beneath her fingers. She'd been struck by Ari's brother from the moment they'd met, and her crush had only grown over the past nine months. Grown to the point where she couldn't help but fantasize about the strength of his arms around her and the feel of his mouth on hers.

Jeremy Newman, who was escorting guests to their seats, waved as he spotted Rosie peeking out of the tent. Snapping back to earth and reality, Rosie smiled and waved.

Harper Newman's younger brother was the sweetest kid. He was nineteen now, but he'd been hurt in a car accident when he was a boy and suffered permanent brain damage that had left him with the mind of the boy he'd been. He was just so happy all the time. He adored Jorge and Noah and loved playing their games. And he adored Harper's husband, Will Franconi, who was like a big brother to him.

Looking extremely dapper in his white tux, Jeremy took his sister's arm and walked with her to the Maverick row, where the family would sit during the ceremony while the Mavericks stood up as groomsmen for Matt.

Harper was beautiful in a blue dress the same color as her striking blue eyes, with her soft brown hair in a loose updo. As a corporate recruiter who loved matching people with their perfect new jobs, she was the perfect foil for Will. He had not only built Franconi Imports into a multibillion-dollar company, but he also loved his fast cars—and so did Harper and Jeremy.

With Harper seated, Jeremy made his way back up the aisle to escort Charlie Ballard and her mother. Charlie created the most incredible sculptures out of metal and was engaged to media mogul Sebastian Montgomery. Charlie was stunning in a flame-red dress. Though Rosie had heard it said that redheads should avoid red, especially at a wedding, on Charlie the dress was perfect. Rosie was sure Sebastian, who positively adored the talented artist, would agree.

Charlie's mother, Francine, had severe degenerative osteoarthritis, and Jorge and Noah had helped deck out her walker in daisies earlier that morning. They loved making things pretty for Francine, whom they treated as an honorary grandmother.

Next, Jeremy walked up the aisle with Paige Ryan on his arm, who was radiant in a light pink silk dress, her pretty smile a mile wide. Though Paige had known financier Evan Collins since college, they'd become a couple only at the beginning of the year, after Evan's marriage to Paige's younger sister had broken up. Initially, Rosie had been shocked to hear the news— not because Paige was in a relationship with her sister's ex, but because Paige's sister had done such *horrible* things during the marriage. Rosie shouldn't be surprised by how evil some people could be, not when she'd had to deal with Jorge's father. And yet, she still wanted to believe the best about everyone.

Paige was seated beside Evan's birth mom, with whom he'd only recently been reunited along with the brother and sister he hadn't even known existed until this year. Tony and Kelsey were both smart and fun, and Rosie was enjoying getting to know them better at the various Maverick birthday parties and other celebrations. Kelsey was also one of Ari's bridesmaids.

Jeremy dashed back to escort Tasha Summerfield down the aisle. She was amazing in a gold dress, the sequined bodice glittering in the afternoon sun peeking through the trees. The light caught her long dark hair, turning it into glossy waves. The newest addition to the Mavericks, she'd met Daniel up in Tahoe a few months ago, when they'd bought homes next door to each other. Rosie had spent enough time chatting with Tasha to know that she'd come through some seriously tough times after discovering her father and brother had been running a sophisticated real estate con for years, all behind her back. Daniel, and his unconditional love for her, had been a major support for Tasha as she'd worked not only to rebuild her life, but also to make reparations to the people her family had scammed.

The stage curtain rose again to reveal the robot

assembly line transformed into a wedding scene, complete with an arched trellis trimmed in flowers and vases filled with roses.

Time was ticking down to the big moment, and the makeup artist pulled Rosie away from the tent flap. "It's almost time. Let me make sure you don't need any last-second touches." She dabbed a soft makeup sponge around Rosie's eyes. "You're perfect." Over her shoulder, she said, "We're ready, ladies. Let's get this show on the road."

The wedding was about to begin.

Chapter Four

In the groom's tent, the Mavericks had all put on costumes over their tuxes, as had Noah, who was the ring bearer. Matt and Ari were going to get the surprise of their lives when the Mavericks walked out, followed by Noah.

Matt was backstage with the officiant, plus Bob for moral support. Not that Matt needed it when he obviously loved Ari with every cell in his body. For Matt, there was no last-minute holy-hell-am-I-making-a-mistake questioning, no changing his mind, no worries about the future.

Standing at the tent flap, Gideon watched as Jeremy escorted Susan and Jorge down the aisle, then Bob came down the stage stairs to sit next to her.

A pang nudged Gideon's heart. Their mother would have loved this day, would have shed so many tears of joy watching her daughter walk down the aisle to marry the man she loved. But things hadn't turned out the way their mom had planned. She hadn't planned for her husband to die in a car accident when

Gideon was eleven and Ari was barely one. She hadn't planned to get hooked on drugs. All she'd wanted to do was ease the pain of her loss. In the end, however, she'd not only lost their home, she'd died of a drug overdose…and left Ari all alone.

Gideon had been eighteen when he joined up. Looking back, he should never have left Ari with his mother, despite his good intentions. He should have known better than to trust Nadine Jones to take care of his sister.

If only he could find a way to make it up to Ari for all his mistakes…

He gave himself a hard mental shake. This wasn't the day to think about what might have been, what should have been. It was supposed to be the most wonderful day of Ari's life. For the next few hours, he needed to put everything he'd done wrong on the back burner. Because after all those days when he thought he'd never make it stateside for this moment, after finally escaping hell, after worrying that he'd never find Ari again—they were together now.

And today he would watch her marry a man who would love and respect and honor her. It was exactly the kind of marriage Ari deserved—one where that love, respect, and honor would never falter, no matter what.

With the groom's parents seated, Matt finally took the stage, followed by the officiant.

This was it. Showtime.

Gideon left the groom's tent and crossed to the bride's, his heart beating harder with every step. Rosie was the first woman he saw when he walked in and his heart leaped into his throat at the sight of her.

She was gorgeous in a pale lilac dress, the top crisscrossed in soft pleats, while the straps bared her shoulders, and the neckline followed the curves of her breasts, dipping low. He shouldn't allow himself to even notice, but he couldn't help the way his gaze was drawn right to her. Just as he couldn't help feeling all the forbidden things he shouldn't. Behind Rosie, Chi, Daniel's sister Lyssa, and Evan's sister Kelsey wore dresses identical to Rosie's. But as pretty as they were, Rosie made the dress extraordinary.

She reached for his hand and pulled him inside the tent, her touch like a lightning strike, setting every nerve in his body on fire. All with nothing more than Rosie's palm against his.

"Isn't this amazing? Can you believe Ari is getting married in a few minutes?"

Gideon had thought he was prepared for today. But it wasn't until that moment, when Rosie looked up at him with stars in her eyes, that the magnitude of everything finally hit him. His baby sister was about to be *married*.

He couldn't speak around the emotion clogging his throat.

Rosie must have read his expression. She took both his hands in hers, holding on tightly as she said, "You're going to do great, big brother. You're a huge reason this is one of the happiest days of her life. Ari always prayed you'd return to walk her down the aisle." She paused for a moment, before adding, "I did too." She smiled at him, that glorious, beautiful Rosie smile. "And now here you are, about to see your sister in her wedding dress for the first time." Her smile dazzled him. "Prepare yourself—she looks *amazing*."

But nothing could possibly have prepared him for the glowing vision in front of him. His heart stopped, and his eyes teared up. "You are so beautiful, Ari."

The formfitting top of the dress was patterned with pearls. Thin beaded straps held it up, the material flowing down from the high waist to a long cream-colored skirt so fine he was afraid it might tear if he touched it. Her blond hair was piled up with artfully curling tendrils falling around her face. She wore a wreath of flowers with a short veil in the back. She hadn't covered her face, and her happiness was like a beacon of light. Her makeup was flawless, though his sister, like Rosie, didn't need any of it. Ari was as beautiful on the inside as she was on the outside.

Though their mother and father were both gone, in that moment Gideon could have sworn they were watching over him and his sister with pure joy.

"I'm so happy, Gideon." Her radiant smile matched

her words.

"I know, and I'm glad. Matt and Noah are everything I could ever want for you." But there was so much more he needed to say. He took Ari's hands in his. "I'm so proud of you. You've done so many incredible things without any of the advantages most people have." The life she'd built for herself, the beautiful, smart, funny woman she'd grown up to be—they were all her doing. The same as Rosie. They were both full of so much determination and grit, along with empathy and compassion.

"I'm so proud of you too, Gideon."

But her words only made him think of all the things he *hadn't* done for her. The things he hadn't done for his mom. For his team. And for Karmen.

Thankfully, Ari had found a good man. Matt would never let her down. Matt would always be there for her. Matt would never abandon her to fate.

Without saying another word, Ari went up on her toes and hugged him. Hard. Like she had the day he'd left when she was only eight.

"I love you, big brother," she whispered against his ear.

He said the words back, wishing that his love had been enough to keep her safe all those years.

Outside the tent, "Can't Take My Eyes Off of You" started playing, the number Ari had chosen for her bridesmaids to walk down the aisle before her. Gideon wanted his sister to see the procession—especially the Mavericks and Noah—but even more, he didn't want to ruin her day with all the emotions swirling inside him.

As he walked her to the tent's exit, the makeup artist and the hairdresser swung the flaps wide open. Kelsey gathered up her bouquet, walking slowly to meet Sebastian in the middle between the two tents.

Then Ari gasped.

The arms and legs of Sebastian's white tux were covered with black and silver ducting like the puppets onstage. He held out his arm with a robotic movement, and once Kelsey took it, he walked her down the aisle with stiff-legged mechanical steps, his head moving side to side with ticks and snaps as though he had gears moving his neck. Lyssa went next, meeting a machinelike Daniel. Then Evan took Chi's arm, guiding her, straight-legged like the Tin Man.

"I can't believe they did this!" Ari hung on Gideon's arm, laughing as Rosie straightened the short train of her wedding dress, draping it in perfect folds. "I love it."

When Ari had decided on a robot puppet show in a puppet theater, the guys had decided to go with a complete robot wedding as a surprise. Thank God his sister loved it, her hand over her mouth, laughter bubbling from her lips.

In the grueling hell of a desert sun, Gideon had lost

not only all the years of watching her grow up to become the incredible woman she was today, he'd also forgotten how to laugh.

As he worked to push the grim thoughts away, Rosie passed him with a brush of her hand on his arm. As if she somehow knew—and understood—everything happening inside him.

Of course, she couldn't. He'd never told anyone the full story. Not even Ari. But Rosie seemed to know how desperately he needed a touch, her touch, to snap him back into the here and now on his sister's magical wedding day.

Seconds later, Rosie left the tent to meet Will, taking his robotically extended arm for their walk up the aisle. Gideon should have been concentrating on his sister beside him, but for the moment, all he could see was Rosie.

Her lovely smile.

Her curves beneath the flowing lilac chiffon.

Her bare shoulders.

Her gorgeous skin revealed by the low dip of the dress's back as she walked away.

If it hadn't been for Noah, he might have stood stock-still watching Rosie until she reached the stage. But when Noah marched to the center aisle like a little tin soldier, his legs straight, not one bend to his knees, holding his ring-bearer's pillow like a treasure, he commanded everyone's attention—including Gideon's.

Noah wore a boy-size white tuxedo, with the same black ducting as the Mavericks, his face painted white-gold, his lips in black, his costume topped off by a robot helmet complete with antennas on the top. In white-gloved hands, he clutched the pillow, the rings tied to it.

He was so happy, so proud to have the honor, beaming at Ari as he passed.

Ari put her hand to her mouth, tears of love and joy glistening in her eyes. "He's adorable. I love him so much, I'm going to cry."

Gideon reached for Ari's hand and squeezed it tight. He knew exactly how his sister felt.

Normally, the ring bearer would take a seat in the first row, but Noah marched right on by, following Will and Rosie. When it was his turn, he would stand between Matt and his best man, Will. It was exactly right; Ari was taking them *both* into her heart forever.

Then the pianist changed songs, signaling that it was Ari's turn. With his heart in his throat, Gideon led his sister to the top of the aisle and waited for their signal from the wedding planner. In moments, he would give her away to her future husband. It was an awesome responsibility. One that meant more to him than Ari or Matt would ever know.

At last, Rosie and Will reached the front and separated to walk up the steps to the stage on either side of the groom and officiant. As Rosie turned to take her position, across the seemingly vast distance, their eyes met…and even though he knew it was crazy, he let himself imagine he was walking down that aisle to meet her. As if she were his future. His forever.

Of course, she wasn't. She never could be.

But even Gideon, a man with a past that felt far too huge to overcome, had his secret dreams.

Chapter Five

Ari was radiant in her elegant gown, her hand looped through Gideon's muscular arm as he walked her down the aisle. They were brother and sister through and through, his hair a darker blond, his face tanned from years spent working outdoors, but their eyes were the same blue.

When Gideon's eyes had met Rosie's just moments ago, she could have sworn she felt a thread of deep connection. Maybe it was simply their mutual love for Ari...but it had felt like more. Like something special was taking place between the two of them. Special enough that his walls were starting to drop, whether he intended that or not.

Seated in the first row with Susan and Bob Spencer, Jorge gave Rosie a thumbs-up for making it down the aisle without tripping in her heels. She'd been afraid she might. Oh, how she loved her kid with all her heart and soul. Though he could sometimes be a handful, especially around bath time, at least he still let her give him butterfly kisses on his cheeks—and when he was really tired at night, he still liked to curl up on her lap.

Matt's expression as he watched his bride come down the aisle—as though Ari was nothing short of a *miracle* and he was the luckiest man alive—brought fresh tears to Rosie's eyes.

Everything about the wedding was absolutely perfect, from Ari's dress, to the flowers, to the song she'd chosen for her walk down the aisle. Her bouquet cascaded with pink peonies, peach orchids, white magnolias, and red roses. The bridesmaids carried mini versions. The garland of flowers in Ari's hair matched the colors of her bouquet. The piano version of "The Rose" by Bette Midler was the ideal metaphor for the way Ari had blossomed to life with Matt and Noah.

Rosie would never forget their days in foster care, the hard times when they'd turned eighteen and were sent out into a world they weren't prepared for. Then meeting Jorge's father—and falling for his lies. Jorge's birth. All three of them—Ari, Chi, and Rosie—had come so far. In the moments before she would reach out to take Ari's bouquet, Rosie touched Chi's fingers, curling their pinkies together the way they had when they were girls. She felt Chi's smile straight through to her heart and smiled just as wide.

This was Ari's fairy tale come true. And it was absolutely *perfect*.

Of course, thinking about fairy tales and Prince Charming shot her gaze straight to Gideon, standing so tall, so handsome, so proud beside his sister.

Rosie was surprised—and instantly breathless—when he turned his intense blue gaze on her again. Was it an artist or a writer who'd said the eyes were the windows to the soul? She was pretty sure they had been talking about the *Mona Lisa*'s eyes. Someday Rosie would take Jorge to see the famous painting. For years, she'd saved every extra dime so that they could walk through the Louvre in Paris and stand mere feet away from Leonardo da Vinci's masterpiece.

For now, however, she could dream about painting Gideon's eyes. Eyes that were faded blue when he was buried deep in the past, pale blue when he was standing on the edge of a party he wasn't sure he should join, dark and stormy blue when someone he loved was threatened, a beautiful ocean blue when he was with the boys. And right now, sky blue with happiness, with joy.

Yes, someday she would take Jorge to the Louvre. And maybe someday she could also help Gideon to be ocean blue or sky blue all the time, every day.

She'd always been a wishful thinker. Even in the worst of times.

Rosie snapped out of her daydreams as Ari turned to give Gideon a hug, then let go of him and lifted her skirts to run up the stairs to Matt.

Matt met his bride halfway, capturing her tightly in his arms and kissing her as he swung her around, to the delight of every wedding guest. Finally, he let her back down, and together they walked to the center of the stage, with Gideon still standing at the base of the stairs.

The music faded, and the officiant turned a page of his book. "Who gives this woman to be married to this man?"

Rosie was sure she saw Gideon's eyes change to a soft baby blue. She had never seen him cry, but in this moment, she knew he was close.

"I do," he said as he climbed the stairs, his deep voice hoarse, as if the words were almost too much. "For my parents who can't be here. And for myself." He kissed Ari gently on the cheek, whispering something that made her tear up.

Then Matt briefly let go of Ari's hand to give Gideon a one-armed hug. "Thank you," he said softly enough that only the attendants on stage could hear. "I'll take care of her, I swear."

"I know you will," Gideon said, his voice solid again, but no less full of emotion. "I trust you to take care of my sister. To love her. And to stand by her side forever."

For Rosie, the two men's softly spoken words to each other and their mutual love for Ari made one of the most poignant moments she'd ever witnessed.

Then Gideon left the stage to take the empty seat reserved for him on the end of the first row, next to

Jorge.

The officiant smiled down at Noah. "Who gives this man to be married to this woman?"

Noah stepped forward, taking his father's hand tight in his. "I do." His little boy's voice rang out true and clear. "I give him to my mommy forever and ever."

As Noah raised his hands to join Matt's and Ari's together, the makeup artist's reminders not to ruin her hard work were forgotten by one and all. When Ari handed her bouquet to Rosie, she had to pull her friend into a hug, and Chi immediately joined. Tears were streaming down both Rosie's and Chi's faces as they whispered, "I'm so happy for you," just as Ari said, "I love you both."

Other than the night Jorge was born, this was the best day of their lives.

Rosie brushed her tears from her cheeks as the officiant began. "We are gathered here today to witness the marriage of Matt Tremont and Ariana Jones. Matt, would you like to begin by saying the vows you have written?"

Matt held tight to Ari's hands as he looked deep into her eyes. "I love you," he said, the three words resonating out to everyone at the wedding. "Until I met you, I was little more than a hollowed-out shell, faking my way through life. But you not only saw the real man inside me, you also made me believe I could shed the dark shadows from my past to truly become a better man. A good man. A trustworthy man. The kind of friend and father and partner I always longed to be. A man who will love you, just as Noah so perfectly put it—" Matt smiled at his son before turning his gaze back to Ari. "—forever and ever."

Though Ari's eyes were gleaming with tears from Matt's beautiful vows, her voice was steady and strong. "The first time I met you, I lost my breath. Not just because you were so handsome, but because I could see in your eyes what a wonderful man you are. And when I met Noah…" She let go of one of Matt's hands to take Noah's, with Matt doing the same, demonstrating to one and all that they were a tight-knit family circle. "I knew I would always love both of you, no matter what. With you, the dark shadows of my past can't scare me anymore. With you, I finally know the kind of happiness I hadn't dared to dream of. For richer or poorer, in sickness and health, wherever life takes the three of us—" She bent down to give Noah a kiss on the cheek, getting a fairy dusting of his gold paint on her lips. "—I'm yours, Matt and Noah Tremont. Forever and ever."

The officiant had to clear his throat before saying, "By the power vested in me by the State of California, I now pronounce you husband and wife. Matt, you may now kiss your bride."

Matt put his hand to Ari's cheek, his gaze soft, his

touch loving. At another wedding, they might have given each other a hot, sexy kiss, a bend-her-over-his-arm-and-ravish-her kiss, but with Noah looking on, Matt and Ari's kiss was gentle, binding them into a family.

Rosie smiled, certain that the ravish-her kiss would come later…and go on and on and on, if Ari's blushes whenever she dropped a tidbit about their love life were anything to go by.

At last, the officiant called, "I give you the Tremont family."

Matt, Ari, and Noah descended the stairs together to the "Feather Theme" from *Forrest Gump*. It was so sweet, so beautiful, so simple. And Noah was adorable in his robot helmet and gold-and-black makeup.

Rosie took Will's proffered arm when it was her turn to descend the steps. As they passed Gideon and her darling kid, she heard Jorge whisper, "Isn't she the prettiest mom ever, Gid?"

Though she didn't turn to see his reaction, she felt Gideon's eyes on her like a physical touch. "Yeah, kiddo," he said in that low voice that sent thrill bumps running up her spine. "She sure is."

Chapter Six

"I swear," Chi said with a happy sigh as she clinked her champagne glass with Rosie's an hour later, "that was the *most* beautiful wedding in the world. Especially when Noah gave Matt away. Did you know he was going to do that?"

Rosie shook her head. "I asked Jorge if Noah said anything to him about it, but he just zipped his lips like it was a big secret."

"Adorable," Chi said.

Rosie agreed, looking over at the boys, who were once again fascinated by Henri the peacock. The bird had wandered onto the dance floor, his tail feathers swishing behind him, and the docent was helping Jorge, Noah, and Jeremy place a trail of breadcrumbs to tempt Henri back to the grass. By now, Noah had taken off the robot helmet, the paint on his face, and the black ducting on his arms and legs.

They'd finished the wedding-party photos—with and then without the robot costumes—and now Ari and Matt were posing for the bride-and-groom shots while the rest of the guests enjoyed refreshments and appetizers. The drinks were prepared with antenna-shaped swizzle sticks, which Jorge and Noah ran to collect whenever a glass was emptied, and the appetizers were served on gear-tipped toothpicks.

Though Gideon stood at the opposite end of the bar nursing a beer, he didn't join Rosie and Chi. Instead, he remained alone, all of his thick walls back in place in the wake of the emotions that had obviously been roiling through him during the ceremony.

Rosie's chest ached with longing to reach for him, to make him smile with gentle teasing. Not simply because she wanted to help heal him…but because she liked him. Liked him enough to want him to be happy. Truly happy.

Just as Matt and Ari had said to each other during their vows, sometimes the dark shadows from your past could be so thick that you got lost inside them. Chi and Ari had helped pull Rosie from that darkness.

But would Gideon ever allow anyone to help him?

Now that his photographs were done, he'd loosened his bow tie. To Rosie, he had never looked sexier. The man was positively mouthwatering.

Chi homed in on Rosie's gaze. "He's so sweet to have paid for the whole wedding, even splurging for the pianist from the San Jose Symphony." Chi spoke in a voice low enough that Gideon couldn't hear.

Gideon wouldn't let the Mavericks pay for a thing,

even though they were all as rich as Croesus. Gideon had lived on the cheap for years, moving from place to place so he could follow construction work, and he'd arrived in the Bay Area with nothing more than a duffel bag. And still, he had granted Ari's every wish as though he were a genie.

"Ari said the guys finally stopped trying to give him money to help out when he refused to take even a penny." Rosie tugged on a strap of her dress that had started to fall off her shoulder. She thought she saw Gideon's gaze land on her bare skin, before skittering away as Daniel and the other Mavericks came up beside him.

Daniel clapped Gideon on the back. "You did a great job up there." His voice was loud enough to carry to Rosie and Chi.

"Ari's happy. That's the only thing that matters." Yet again, Gideon refused to take any credit.

Daniel had loosened his tie along with removing the black ducting from his arms and legs, as had all the Mavericks. His white tux jacket was undone, revealing his cummerbund. "I predict that in no time, you're going to have your own construction empire." He turned to Evan, Sebastian, and Will. "Another billionaire, I guarantee it."

Gideon was a master of the impassive expression, likely something he'd learned in the military. But Rosie thought she could see something flicker through him as Daniel heaped him with praise—a combination of surprised pride, swiftly followed by disbelief that the praise was anything more than Daniel blowing smoke.

"Ready to break ground on the first warehouse?" Daniel asked.

Gideon nodded, a spark finally coming into his eyes, his excitement over the warehousing project getting the better of his natural reticence—especially when the other guys started asking technical questions.

Chi moved to block Rosie's view of Gideon. "You've got it bad, girl." Again, she spoke in a low voice no one else would overhear.

Rosie blinked in surprise at her friend. For all that they usually shared everything with each other, she had never admitted to either Chi or Ari just how much Gideon affected her. Not only how attractive she found him, but also how deeply he tugged at her heart. "Is it that obvious?"

"Only to anyone within singeing distance," Chi replied with a playful smile. "The sparks the two of you have been shooting off today with all your secret glances have been totally hot."

Hope lit in Rosie's heart. "I wasn't sure if I'd imagined the way he looked at me."

"You aren't imagining a thing," Chi confirmed. "However much he might be trying to fight it, Ari's brother has it just as bad for you as you have for him. The question is, what are you going to do about it?"

The billion-dollar question. "Gideon is a tough nut to crack."

"Maybe I should buy you a huge nutcracker?" Chi suggested. She had a flair for the dramatic.

Though Rosie smiled at Chi's teasing suggestion, she knew that was just the problem—Gideon was *already* cracked. Her heart ached with how badly she wanted to help mend his fractured soul by showing him that he was amazing, loving, caring, strong, and wonderful.

Before Chi could push her more on the subject, the DJ started the music, the "Feather Theme" again, and Ari and Matt entered their reception.

Ari clapped her hands to her mouth first when she saw all the robot-themed decorations and then again when Sebastian, looking like he would burst with pride, whipped the cover off another big surprise— Charlie's champagne fountain. It was a cross between the *Wizard of Oz*'s Tin Man and the *Lost in Space* robot, and Charlie had added additional arms sticking out all around the fountain.

"You guys are amazing!" Ari said, laughing and crying at the same time.

Matt was grinning like a crazy person. Or like the happiest man in the entire world now that he had his friends, his son, and his wife to complete him.

Ari was clearly awestruck as she picked up a crystal flute and tipped it under one of the fountain's hands, marveling when the robot's face plate lit up, swirling with reds and greens and yellows and blues like one of those old mood rings, and then the champagne flowed into her glass.

Noah wrapped an arm around Ari's leg. "Can I try?"

Charlie bent down to his level. "I made a special arm for you and all the kids here today." She gave him a glass and told him to hold it under an arm that stretched out from the robot's hip, until his glass filled with lemonade.

"Me too, please!" Jorge was practically shaking with excitement as he filled his glass. "Wow," he said with such wonder he might have been looking at the paintings in the Sistine Chapel. "This is so cool."

Ari pulled Charlie into a hug. "It's amazing, Charlie. Thank you so much."

"You're awesome, as always, Charlie." Matt toasted her. "Thank you."

"It was a labor of love," Charlie replied, her cheeks beginning to turn as red as her dress. She grinned as she added, "I thought you could put it to good use at the barbecues at your house."

"You mean the margarita parties," Sebastian quipped, his arm tight around Charlie's waist as he held her close.

Noah tugged at Ari's dress to get her attention. "Me and Jorge helped with all the Legos on the tables."

Ari stroked his hair. "They're amazing. And you're awesome, sweetie. Thank you." Then she tapped Jorge's nose fondly. "And you too. You guys are the best."

"So tell me how it all works." Of course, as the robot guy, Matt needed to know all the particulars.

While Charlie described her magnificent machine, the rest of the guests lined up to fill their glasses from the fountain. Gideon backed away, slowly, as if he didn't want anyone to notice him.

But Rosie noticed.

Her heart fluttered with emotion—and desire. The desire to bring him back, to help him be a part of things, to show him how wanted and needed he was.

Especially by her.

Chi was right. She had it *bad*.

* * *

Gideon didn't recognize the song Ari had picked for her first dance, but as he hung back, watching from the sidelines by the bar, he noted that its sweet melody was perfect for the newly married couple's waltz.

He wondered if they'd practiced, or if Matt Tremont was simply proficient at everything. Despite the Mavericks' humble beginnings in a grimy neighborhood of Chicago, each man seemed to be a master of anything he touched. Ari had told Gideon their story—how the Spencers, with little money of their own, had taken in each of the Mavericks as teenagers to live with them and their children, Daniel, who was the same age as the Mavericks, and Lyssa, only a baby at the time. No question about it, they were an impressive lot, Susan and Bob Spencer especially, for their incredible generosity.

Bob slid his arm around Susan's shoulders as they watched Matt and Ari's first dance, Susan misty-eyed, Bob rubbing her shoulder. When the DJ announced that it was time for Mom and Dad to join in, Bob escorted Susan to the dance floor, then handed her into Matt's arms while he took Ari into his with tenderness.

Matt's fellow Mavericks watched, all smiles. Noah slipped his hand into Chi's while Rosie held Jorge's. She was so happy, so comfortable in her skin, such a great mother.

So *great*, period.

"And now," the DJ called, "it's time for the wedding party to get on the dance floor to help usher our bride and groom into their new life together!"

Gideon watched as Rosie paired again with Will, her partner on her walk down the aisle. She was so full of life and laughter as they twirled around the dance floor, her skirt swirling around Will's legs.

What, Gideon was desperate to know, would it be like to hold her in his arms? To make her laugh that way? To feel the warmth of her body against his?

But he already knew. It would feel like *heaven*.

A small hand curled around his. "We gotta dance, Uncle Gideon. 'Cause we're part of the wedding party, right?"

Of course Gideon couldn't resist Noah's request—and wherever Noah went, Jorge went too.

As Gideon led the two boys onto the dance floor, Sebastian rolled Francine out, twirling around her walker as she bounced her knees and swayed in time with the music. It was the signal for all the Mavericks to join in. Kelsey and Lyssa and Chi swung the boys and Gideon into a big circle, stopping only to drag Jeremy in with them when Will whirled Harper away from her brother.

Through the crowd on the dance floor, Gideon could no longer see Rosie, but his whole body ached to swing her into his arms.

Then at last, Ari and Bob were close enough that he could cut in and dance with his sister.

"I know I've already said it, but you look so beautiful, Ari." She led them into a perfect turn. He'd never been a dancer, but she was so graceful that she more than made up for his two left feet. "Seeing you this happy…" The words caught in his throat. "It's everything I ever wanted for you."

"First, you're too handsome for words." She kissed his cheek without losing a beat. Then she said, "I am happy, Gideon." She paused for a moment before adding, "Everything has worked out just the way it should."

She'd told him so many times during the past nine months that he didn't need to beat himself up for anything in the past, but he knew she was just being kind. Yet even now, on her wedding day, she went out of her way to let him off the hook.

"Thank you," she said softly. "For everything."

"You don't have to thank me. You know I'd do anything for you. And I wanted your wedding to be everything you'd ever dreamed of."

Not that he thought it could make up for the years he was gone, for the years he'd left Ari alone to fend for herself. Nothing could make up for his mistakes. But with all the money he'd been saving over the past ten years, paying for her wedding was the least he could do.

Beside them on the dance floor, Paige clung to Evan, a glow about her so bright it was like a spotlight. Charlie had joined Francine and Sebastian. Daniel and Tasha swayed together. Then Rosie floated past, this time in Matt's arms.

Gideon's chest clenched. What he wouldn't give to hold her. To whirl her around the floor. To breathe in the sweetness of her hair, the lightness of her perfume, to feel her body against his.

Then Matt was reaching for Ari. "You don't mind if I take my wife back, do you?"

A moment later, his sister was swept from Gideon's

arms…and Rosie was twirling straight into his embrace.

* * *

Being held by Gideon was all Rosie had imagined—and more. The strength in his hands, the hardness of his body against hers, his delicious scent in her head. Though he held her as stiffly as the Tin Man, her skin tingled head to toe with the thrill of finally being in his arms.

She'd been aware of his well-defined muscles when he'd played Marco Polo in the pool with Noah and Jorge. But there was nothing like her body pressed to his, his arm around her waist, his heart beating against hers.

Maybe his obvious reticence about dancing with her should have tempted her to let him disappear into the shadows again. But now that Rosie had decided to take off the kid gloves, she wasn't about to miss this made-in-heaven opportunity. From here on out, she was going to treat him the same way she treated all her friends—with total openness and honesty. Which, in this moment, meant expressing just how much the wedding had meant to her.

"I have to tell you how touching it was when you walked Ari up the aisle. The makeup artist had warned us not to mess up her work by crying, but I couldn't help it. And when Matt hugged you like you were already his brother?" She smiled into Gideon's dark blue eyes. "It was such a great moment. When Noah gave him away, I was a total mess. And then again when they said their vows while holding Noah's hands." She couldn't remember the last time she'd felt so happy that she was floating on air. It wasn't just the wedding—it was this moment with Gideon, his arms around her, his maleness intoxicating her, and finally, after what seemed like forever, the chance of getting to know each other. "It was all so beautiful, wasn't it?"

Where she'd been extremely loquacious, he barely managed a nod. But she was still in his arms, and right now, the feel of him against her was all that counted. Other couples floated past them, Evan with a beaming Paige in his arms, Will and Harper, Tasha and Daniel, Charlie in her flame-red dress, Sebastian's arms tight around her.

"And the boys?" she continued as though they were having a perfectly normal, two-way conversation. "They're having *such* a good time today. And," she said as she pointed across the dance floor, "I'm pretty sure Kelsey and Lyssa are in love with those two kids." Chi was out there with the boys too, playing ring-around-the-rosy.

"What's not to love?" he agreed. Though his voice was a little croaky, at least she got a verbal response this time. Probably because they were talking about the boys, the two people who were always able to break through the walls around Gideon's heart.

Well, Rosie could absolutely work with that. At least for now, when she was so enjoying their dance, the heat and strength of his body against hers, the sense of aliveness that made her want to stretch her arms around his neck and lay her lips on his. If only the song could go on forever, surely he'd realize it would be so much easier to let himself relax when they were together.

"Doesn't this song seem like it's been playing forever?" he asked.

She laughed, because it was so close to what she'd been thinking—from the completely opposite point of view. "Are you trying to say you're not having a good time dancing with me?"

"No." He shook his head, hard, even stiffer against her now. "Of course I didn't mean that."

"I was just teasing," she said with a little smile, hoping against hope that he'd smile back. God, she wanted so badly to show him that he could dance, he could laugh, he could be playful with more than just the boys. If only she could show him that he didn't need an excuse to be happy, that he was allowed to feel joy. Barring those choices, she opted for saying, "I am *really* loving this dance with you."

In an instant, his eyes turned a smoky blue. It was a new look for him, one she'd never seen before. Maybe the smoke was *her* special look. She *hoped* it was about her, that he was thinking about how good she felt, how lovely she smelled, how sexy it was to have his arms around her, their bodies pressed tightly together. Because those were all the things *she* was feeling.

She wound her arms around his neck, holding him closer, letting him feel everything she thought, everything she wanted, everything she needed to give him.

Naturally, that was when the song ended.

Gideon stopped so fast, she almost tripped. Then he flew from the dance floor like a jet plane taking off into the wild blue yonder, leaving her standing alone in the middle of all the dancers, her arms raised as if they were still around him.

A beat later, the boys rushed her, squealing and laughing, but she could still feel the imprint of Gideon's body against hers, could still smell his aftershave, could still feel his muscles under her fingertips.

And she knew she would wake up in the night longing to feel every moment with him all over again.

Chapter Seven

Gideon was still recovering from the world-rocking shock of having Rosie in his arms—and the shock of her saying how much she enjoyed dancing with him—when it dawned on him that she would be seated next to him at dinner.

Matt, Ari, Noah, Bob, and Susan were seated at the head table, which was decked out with three Lego robots and a trimming of flowers. Jorge, of course, begged to sit with Noah, so they pulled up an extra chair for him. And somehow, whether by design or coincidence or divine intervention, Rosie was now mere inches away from Gideon. Again.

After their dance, he simply couldn't breathe. Not without smelling her sweet, luscious scent. It was enough to bring him to his knees...or worse, to tempt him to kiss her the way he'd wanted to for so damned long.

Thankfully, Rosie seemed oblivious to his careening thoughts as she pointed to the abundance of forks in front of them. "If I hadn't waitressed when I was in school, I'd have no idea which one of these to use for what." It didn't matter what she said—her voice was like music, like stardust falling on him. "It always seemed like a crazy waste of dishwashing when people were perfectly happy to use one fork for everything."

He was saved from a response by Bob Spencer, who stood to give the welcome speech. In his mid-fifties, Bob had lost most of his hair, but he was fit. During his working years, he'd been a baggage handler at O'Hare International Airport, and despite injuring his back, he still had the muscles he'd earned lifting heavy luggage day in and day out.

The Mavericks had seen to it that Susan and Bob had a good life now, trying to pay the Spencers back for all they'd done, even though it was obvious that Susan and Bob had no need for payback. They were good people. The kind of people Gideon wished he and his mother could have been for Ari all those years ago.

"Friends, robots, countrymen," Bob began, and everyone laughed at his play on Shakespeare. "Thank you for coming to celebrate the marriage of our son Matt to Ariana, whom we already consider to be our daughter."

Gideon not only appreciated that Susan and Bob had welcomed Ari with open hearts and arms, but also that Bob referred to Matt as his son, rather than as his foster kid or his adopted son. It had been the same in that hot desert terrain—bonds were made in the sandbox, made by the tears no one ever shed, made by the blood spilled to save your buddies, not simply by the blood running through a man's veins.

"I had a whole bunch of really bad jokes I was going to tell, but my lovely wife—" Bob winked at Susan. "—told me to keep it short and sweet. I promised I'd do my best." He grinned at the crowd. "Though my sons and daughter would be happy to tell you that short and sweet has never been in their dad's wheelhouse."

"Isn't he wonderful?" Rosie leaned in close to whisper…and Gideon barely managed to keep from pulling her straight into his arms.

How the heck was he going to make it through this meal without giving in to his baser urges?

"We couldn't have been more fortunate than the day Ari agreed to be Noah's nanny," Bob continued. "Not only did she give Noah all the love in the world, she also loved our Matt with her whole heart. Just as we love her with all of ours."

Ari was wiping the tears from her eyes as Bob held out his arms and said, "Come here, my precious girl, give me a hug." Ari stood to throw herself into his arms, exchanging words the microphone didn't pick up.

With his arm still around Ari, Bob picked up his glass. "I would like to toast this fabulous new family. Susan and I couldn't be happier. To love everlasting."

Everyone raised their glasses, echoing, "To love everlasting!"

Gideon turned to Paige on his right, who clinked with her water glass. Then Rosie held her glass up to his, and as the crystal chimed, she smiled. "That was the perfect toast, wasn't it?"

"Perfect," he agreed. But he wasn't merely talking about the toast, he was talking about *her*. Rosie was perfectly beautiful, perfectly sweet, perfectly kind and compassionate.

Only the waitress, who leaned between them to whisk away the salad plates and replace them with their entrees, stopped him from pulling Rosie close to taste the champagne on her lips.

He got the steak, Rosie got the salmon. She gave a soft moan of pleasure at her first bite. "You've got to taste this." She held out a forkful of salmon.

She couldn't possibly know how much restraint it took not to gobble *her* up when she was so near, when she smelled so good, when he was sure she would taste so much better. If she knew how she affected him, if she knew how little willpower he had, she'd be running a mile a minute to get away. And she surely wouldn't be so generous with her affection, the same affection she gave to her closest friends.

Steeling himself, he leaned close, shut his eyes, breathed her in, and let her feed him the bite of salmon. He savored it as he would savor her, if he could.

"Good?" she asked.

"Good." He was afraid his voice would crack if he said more than one word.

"Steak," she said, that beautiful sparkle in her eyes.

"What?" He was too mesmerized to understand.

She pointed to his plate. "Let me try yours. Just to compare."

He cut a chunk off his steak, and when he would have handed her the fork, she wrapped her hand around his wrist and pulled him closer. Close enough to put her mouth on his utensil. Close enough to drive him mad when the sound she made as she relished the food reached straight into the heart of him.

"That was good," she said. Then she looked into his eyes and smiled again. "I'm really glad we're sitting together. I was hoping you would end up being my dinner date."

Wait…

Was she *flirting* with him?

He couldn't wrap his head around the idea. Not only because Rosie could have *any* single guy at the wedding. But also because he'd gone out of his way to make sure she couldn't see the depth of his attraction to her.

Thrown off his game more than he could ever remember, he was damned glad that Will Franconi chose that moment to rise to his feet for the best man's toast.

"I've known that big lug up there—" Will pointed at Matt. "—since we were beating each other up on the playground."

As the Mavericks *huzzah*ed, Rosie leaned over to whisper, "The way I heard it, Matt was the runt who got picked on, and the Mavericks protected him. But look at him now."

"We have to thank Ari for being willing to take on Matt and all his robots," Will continued in a teasing tone. "Fortunately," he said with a wink in Noah's direction, "she has Noah to help Matt keep one foot in the human world too." Then Will's expression turned sincere, heartfelt emotions written on his face as he looked at his lifelong friend. "I love you, man. And I know you've picked the perfect woman to love, and be loved by, for the rest of your life." Will held up his glass, and when the guests had followed suit, he said, "To true love."

As everyone echoed the toast—apart from Gideon, who simply held up his glass without actually saying the words—he was amazed by how easily Will threw the word *love* around.

But he didn't have long to mull it over before Rosie was being handed the microphone. She smoothed out her dress before standing up to give her toast, gorgeous in lilac, her shoulders bare, her skin infinitely kissable. Gideon momentarily wondered if she was nervous…

Before remembering that Rosie wasn't afraid of anything.

"Dear Matt and Ari." As she smiled, her eyes were shiny with tears. "I love you both so much. And I'm so happy for you and for Noah." The little boy wriggled in his seat when his name was mentioned. "Ari, you and Chi are the sisters of my heart. We made it through a long, hard haul, and we did it together. I couldn't have made it to this point in my life without you. And I definitely wouldn't have wanted to go through any of it without you either."

Gideon knew most of what Ari's long, hard haul had been. But he didn't know about Rosie's difficult road, not beyond the basics that she'd lost her parents young and had ended up in foster care. Despite the care he'd taken over the past nine months to make sure she never guessed his feelings for her, he couldn't help but want to know every single thing about her. What made her laugh. What she dreamed about. What she most longed for. What her perfect day looked like. And, in the dark of night, how sweet her sounds of pleasure would be if she ever let him make love to her the way he secretly fantasized about.

"The four of us—you, me, Chi, and Jorge—we were a family for so long," Rosie continued. "And now we are so lucky to have Matt and Noah in our family too. I love the way our family just keeps growing. How we keep getting stronger every day."

Gideon saw the first tear fall down her cheek before she wiped it away. Unable to control the uncontrollable, he gave in to instinct, the need to be there for her, and beneath the table where no one could see, he gently touched Rosie's knee, just enough to let her know he was right there, right beside her whenever she needed him.

There was an almost imperceptible movement, her knee against his hand, just the slightest brush, but one that felt as deliberate as his touch had been. Then she said, "I'll always be here for you, my sweet sister. I will always love you. And I am so happy that you, Matt, and Noah have found each other." She raised her glass. "Here's to Ari, Matt and Noah...to happiness, to a wonderfully bright future...and to love!"

As the wedding guests cheered, applauded, and downed champagne, Ari blew Rosie a kiss. And when Rosie sat, with everyone at the table congratulating her on her great speech, Gideon's greatest wish, his greatest desire, was that he could kiss her too.

Chapter Eight

As the rest of the Mavericks roasted Matt with humor and love, Rosie swore she could still feel the light pressure of Gideon's hand against her knee beneath the table. While she'd poured her heart out to Ari and Matt, she'd felt as if Gideon understood absolutely everything she was feeling…and that he could see right inside her heart.

For a few wonderful moments, between her toast and sitting down, something had flared between them. He'd looked like he wanted to drag her against him and kiss her breathless.

Of course, it hadn't lasted. As soon as the DJ announced the end to all the toasts, Gideon scooted back from the table and practically sprinted away.

"You look like you need a drink." Chi handed her a full champagne flute.

"I might have had too much already," she confessed as they tapped glasses.

The music and dancing started up, but instead of heading for the dance floor, Kelsey Collins dragged

Lyssa Spencer over. A waiter passed their little group, and the two women grabbed glasses.

"What a great party." Lyssa was the only Maverick sister, ten years younger than her brothers. Rosie could see the resemblance between her and her brother Daniel, with the same chocolate-brown eyes, the same wavy dark hair, though hers curled past her shoulders. "And Jorge and Noah are just adorable out there."

They were tearing up the dance floor, getting down to boogie with whoever would take them on. Adorable was right.

"They're going to be a couple of little heartbreakers one day. Speaking of which…" Kelsey glanced over the assembled guests. "Please tell me I'm not the only one who's noticed just how many gorgeous men there are here."

"There are," Chi agreed, "although all the gorgeous Mavericks are already taken."

Lyssa made a face. "Ick. They're my brothers. I can't think of them that way."

"Well, there must be *someone* here you've got your eye on," Kelsey said.

Like Lyssa, Kelsey was ten years younger than her oldest brother, Evan. Kelsey's twin, Tony, was out on the dance floor with an older woman who was holding him way too close. Or maybe she just needed him to prop her up after too many champagne toasts. Kelsey and Tony weren't identical, but they shared similar features and the same light brown hair, though Kelsey's was long and streaked with blond. It was Tony and Evan who could have been the twins, despite their age difference.

When Lyssa didn't answer quickly enough, Kelsey pointed out an exceptionally good-looking, broad-shouldered man with closely cropped hair. "How about him?"

Lyssa snorted. "That's Gabe Sullivan. He's a firefighter in the city. And he's most definitely taken. But that's okay, because I've actually got my eye on *him*." She pointed out a man halfway around the dance floor. He was tall, handsome, and definitely in shape—and considerably older than she. "I like older men," she said, obviously anticipating their responses. Lyssa sighed, a little bit dreamy, a little bit playful. "Oh yes, Cal Danniger *definitely* has my name written all over him. In lipstick."

"What the hell?"

Lyssa whirled around. Her brother Daniel was standing right behind them.

Glowering as protectively as Rosie had ever seen him, Daniel said, "Cal Danniger is *not* for you."

Lyssa put her hands on her hips and held her brother's gaze, her eyes equally full of challenge. Almost as though she was daring him to say the wrong thing. "Excuse me?"

Daniel breathed deeply, obviously restraining

himself from saying something harsh in response. He was usually so easygoing. Clearly, Lyssa had found his trigger point and pressed down hard on the red detonation button. "Not only does Cal work for me," Daniel growled, "he's also twenty years older than you. He's *off-limits*."

Lyssa narrowed her eyes as she took a step toward her brother, coming toe-to-toe with him. "He's for me if *I* say he's for me."

Whoa. The Mavericks were usually one big, happy family. The guys adored Lyssa, and she adored them. Then again, Lyssa was twenty-six, she had a great job in Chicago, she supported herself—and Daniel was being downright overprotective.

Especially when he said, "You're not listening, little sister. I won't allow you to date him."

"Uh-oh, major explosion time," Chi whispered as Lyssa tipped up her chin defiantly and opened her mouth to blast him with a fiery reply.

Fortunately, before any volcanic eruptions could ensue, Tasha Summerfield appeared at Daniel's side. Clearly, she'd seen the moment brewing from afar. "There you are," Tasha said as she looped her arm through Daniel's. "This is my favorite song. Come dance with me."

Rosie very much doubted that "Achy Breaky Heart" was Tasha's favorite tune, but right now it was far more important to pull brother and sister apart before things got ugly.

Still, Daniel managed to slash his sister with one last look, again saying, "He's not for you," before Tasha whisked him away.

Eyes narrowed on her brother's back, her lips in a tight pucker, Lyssa was utterly infuriated. "Could he be any more overbearing?"

"He's just looking out for you," Chi said, always diplomatic.

Rosie agreed. She would have given anything to have a big brother looking out for her when she'd met Jorge's dad.

"I know," Lyssa said. "But it won't just be him. All *five* of them are going to think they need to protect me. Six, when you add Gideon into the mix." She grimaced. "You'd think I was still fifteen and one of Daniel's friends was hitting on me."

"Doesn't he realize that now you're going to absolutely want Cal?" Kelsey shook her head. "It's like waving the red flag at a bull. Or rather, the matador— since you're way too pretty to be a bull."

Lyssa mimed waving a red flag from side to side, then lowered her voice dramatically. "He's the bull—" She gave a quick nod in the handsome Cal Danniger's direction. "—and he won't know what's hit him."

Chi curled her arm around Rosie's neck and pulled her close to say in a low voice, "Maybe *you* should shake your flag at the object of your desire."

"My flag or my booty?" Though he'd fled the table at lightspeed, Rosie was still relishing the ecstasy she'd found in Gideon's arms while they danced, as they'd fed each other morsels off their plates, when he'd touched her during her speech.

"How about both?" Chi suggested with the naughtiest of giggles.

"What are you two whispering about?" Kelsey bumped hips with Chi, knocking her lightly into Rosie.

"We're choosing our own bulls." Chi smiled with a gleam.

"Ooh…do tell." Kelsey leaned in toward Rosie. "Is there a guy here that you would consider bringing home to meet the adorable Jorge?"

As the DJ changed the music and announced the bouquet toss, Rosie was saved from admitting that the guy already knew Jorge, and Jorge already adored him.

★ ★ ★

Gideon stood on the fringes, just beyond the circle of people surrounding the dance floor where Ari held up her bouquet. Rosie mingled with the crowd of brightly dressed ladies, Jorge dancing around her excitedly, probably telling her she had to jump high to catch it, since she was shorter than the other women.

She'd let down her gorgeous hair, her curls caressing her shoulders, and Gideon ached to run his fingers through the silkiness.

He ached for a lot of things he would never have. And he needed to be okay with that. After all, he had so much now—his sister back in his life, a fabulous nephew, a good job, a great boss and company to work for.

If only that meant he could stop thinking about the past, could stop constantly reliving the hell it had been, and get closer to Rosie than merely the fringes of her life.

"Okay, ladies," Ari called out. "Get ready!"

"Come on, Mom, you can grab it." Jorge's voice carried from amid the flock of women.

What a great kid. He wasn't shy, he wasn't frightened of life. He was fun and proud and wonderful. Just like Noah.

Ari threw the bouquet high and wild, petals falling as it arced through the air. There was a hue and cry as the women jumped for it in their heels.

Gideon's gut clenched for a long moment as he thought of Rosie catching it. As he thought of the tradition, that whomever caught it would be the next to marry. That she'd finally find her perfect hero…and it wouldn't be him. He should want a great guy for her, someone who would be a good father to Jorge, but his chest hurt even *thinking* of Rosie with another guy. Strangely, for all her beauty and brains, he'd never seen her with a man—never heard even a whisper of a date. The same went for him. But his reasons were surely different from hers.

Simply put, since he'd met her last year, all other women had lost their allure.

In the end, however, Rosie didn't catch the bouquet. "I can't believe I caught it." Lyssa Spencer held the colorful flowers away from her, looking slightly horrified.

She wasn't the only one who looked horrified, Gideon noted, as all five of the Mavericks instantly assumed protective stances, lest any hapless man at the party dared to approach their precious little sister. Gideon didn't envy the guy who tried to date Lyssa Spencer. No man in his right mind would want to face down that firing squad.

Gideon faced one every day—a firing squad of brutally dark memories he would never be able to outrun.

Pushing his way out of the gathering of women, Jorge raced to him. "I really wanted Mom to catch it, but she didn't jump high enough. Did you see, Gid?"

Rosie joined them before he could reply. "I could have caught the bouquet if I'd felt I needed it. But I've always thought that if true love is meant to be, it doesn't need divine intervention." Her eyes twinkled as she ruffled her son's hair.

Gideon had to look away from the brightness of her smile. It offered too many things he couldn't have. Not only her beauty and innate sensuality, but also her faith in true love. It was still alive inside her heart, even after the hell Ari hinted Rosie had been through with Jorge's father.

On the dance floor, Ari gave Lyssa a huge hug while the photographer snapped pictures. Then the wedding organizer pulled up a chair while the DJ announced that it was time to take off the garter.

Rosie explained to Jorge, "It's a piece of fabric that traditionally held up the stocking on a bride's leg. Nowadays the groom throws it to the single men in the same way that the bride throws the bouquet to the single women."

Ari sat in the chair while her new husband bent down in front of her and lifted her skirt. "Nice tennis shoes," Matt said in front of their rapt audience.

"Thanks." She lifted one foot so everyone could see her bedazzled Nikes. "I wanted to make sure I could run up the aisle to be in your arms."

As they kissed, the women sighed, the men clapped, and Jorge exclaimed, "Ewww," screwing up his face. Gideon agreed—he wasn't sure he could handle watching his sister being kissed senseless, even by her husband.

And when Matt began to trail his hand up her leg toward the garter, Gideon knew he should restrain his protective urges, at least for today. But this was his sister, for God's sake.

"Get on with it, man," he called out, his voice gruff.

Rosie grabbed his hand without so much as a pause—yet again crossing the barriers he'd put up between them. He'd be lying if he said he didn't love the feel of her palm against his, her softness caressing his callused skin.

"You're doing great, big brother," she said gently. "Not much longer now."

Ari's dress rode high enough to reveal the garter settled a couple of inches above her knee. Matt started to laugh when he saw it. "It's got robots on it."

Ari nodded. "I had to sew on each one individually."

Of course, Matt started kissing her again amid their laughter.

Rosie squeezed Gideon's hand before he could rush the stage to pull them apart. "They're so good together," she said. "I love the way they're always laughing."

She was right. Matt would go to the ends of the earth to make sure Ari never saw another sad day in her life. "All I ever thought about when I was deployed was making it back to see my sister laugh again." He spoke without thinking, from deep down in his heart.

There had been so many dark days and nights when he thought he'd never see home again, never leave the endless heat and sand and gnawing hunger, never find Ari.

Thank God he'd made it back to her. And thank

God she'd found a man, a family, a group of friends who made her so happy.

As all the emotions rioted through him, Rosie held his hand, giving him so much sweetness, so much comfort. Though he knew he should let her go, he couldn't help but drink her in. Just for a few precious, stolen moments.

Matt whipped the garter off, holding it up in a victory salute. This was Gideon's cue to drop Rosie's hand—after all, now that Matt was done touching Ari's leg, Gideon didn't need Rosie to keep him from rushing the guy. But it was a hell of a fight within himself to actually let go.

"Okay," the DJ said, "all you single guys, get out there and catch that garter."

There were murmurs through the crowd as men were pushed forward. Daniel entered the fray, soon joined by Sebastian and Evan.

"I hope you have a wedding dress ready if I catch it," Evan called to Paige, who laughed and blew him a kiss.

Rosie turned to look at Gideon. "You're single. Shouldn't you be out there with everyone else?"

"I'm fine here."

"Come on, Gid." Jorge grabbed Gideon's newly freed hand. "I'll go if you go."

"Don't be a fuddy-duddy, Gideon," Rosie teased. "I did it."

Gideon might have protested again, but in addition to Jorge's pleas, Noah was tugging on his other hand. He had to do it for them.

"If I jump high enough," Noah said, "I hope I can catch it. Those robots are cool. I want 'em bad."

"If I catch it, we'll share," Jorge offered.

"If I catch it," Gideon told them, "I'll give it to both of you to share."

Jeremy joined them. "I want to help catch it for you guys." Jeremy was always so great with the boys.

"And if I catch it, I'll turn it over to you." A newcomer grinned at the boys.

"Uncle Cal!" Noah high-fived him.

Gideon had met Cal Danniger a couple of times in Daniel's office. He was the business manager for the Maverick Group. From what Gideon could tell, he was a solid guy—not to mention brilliant. Which made it more than a little strange that Daniel was currently glaring at him. What the heck could Cal have done to get on Daniel's bad side?

With a drumroll from the DJ, Matt started his windup, and Gideon braced himself to catch the garter for Noah and Jorge. It sailed wide and to the left, just out of his reach, but fortunately, Cal Danniger was able to grab it out of the air before it flew past him and into Daniel Spencer's open palm.

"You're the winners, boys," Cal called out as they jumped up, down, and around in a circle, hooting with glee.

Cal was about to hand over the garter when Lyssa stepped into the fray, the bridal bouquet in her hand. "Not so fast." She looped her arm through Cal's. "We've got to have pictures taken first." She grinned at Noah and Jorge. "Then it's all yours, I promise."

There was a lot of laughter and good-natured ribbing as Lyssa sat in the chair Ari had just vacated, then raised her skirt and stuck out her leg for Cal to do the honors, cameras flashing all around them. Only the five Mavericks—especially Daniel—didn't look happy. Not in the least. Clearly, deeply protective urges were something Gideon shared in common with them.

Once Cal had slid the garter up Lyssa's leg, the crowd cheered again.

Noah's loud voice cut through the applause. "But now that it's on her leg, how do we get it back?"

Jorge shrugged and held up his hands in a ya-got-me gesture.

There was laughter all around. Only Daniel's face remained impassive, his gaze glued to Cal Danniger's hand on the garter as he helped Lyssa take it off and toss it to the kids.

A few seconds later, Noah and Jorge were holding the garter between them. "Are they going to cut the cake soon?" Jorge asked.

Gideon appreciated how quickly, and happily, kids jumped from one thing to the next. They didn't stew, didn't wallow, didn't hold grudges, didn't wither with regret.

He'd been like that once.

"There's more dancing first," Rosie told them.

"Dancing?" Noah moaned. "But we're ready for cake *now*."

"Me too," she said with a laugh. "But maybe if we dance hard enough, we'll forget about dessert for a little while."

She was so close, so sweet, her warmth overwhelmed Gideon's senses. Before he lost every shred of self-control, he managed to step away without anyone noticing.

"Okay," he heard Jorge say, "but only if Gid dances with us too." And then a beat later, "Where's Gid?"

But Gideon was melting into the shadows.

He'd already let himself touch—and be touched by—Rosie too many times today. He couldn't dance with her, even if it was with the boys.

If he pulled her into his arms again, if he held her close, if he closed his eyes and imagined, he would never be able to let her go.

* * *

Rosie saw Gideon fade away when he thought no one was watching. He'd come back out for the boys if they went after him, but she understood that today had been huge for him—walking Ari down the aisle, giving her away, having to smile and chat with so many strangers.

So she took the boys' hands and said, "Let's dance with Ari and Matt and Chi. I bet Lyssa and Kelsey will join in too."

Once they were out on the dance floor, she spotted Gideon on the fringes. He nursed a beer he never seemed to finish. Watching. Hiding out. As though he didn't realize he was as much a part of the family as Sebastian or Will or Daniel—when it was so very obvious to Rosie that he was.

Chapter Nine

At last, the cake had been cut—Ari and Matt loved the robot cake toppers Rosie had found—the last dance had been danced, the limo was waiting to take the newly married couple to the airport, and Rosie and Chi had helped Ari pack up her wedding dress. Doreen, Matt's driver, would take everything, including the presents, back to their house for when the couple returned from their honeymoon.

Ari was alone in the bride's tent, changed into traveling clothes—comfy jeans and a top—when Gideon found her wiping tears from her eyes.

His heart seized. "What's wrong?" Everything was supposed to be perfect. He *needed* everything to be perfect for his sister, couldn't bear for anything to mar her special day.

She gave him a wobbly smile. "Oh, nothing. It's just silly."

"Did someone say something to you?" He'd find whoever had hurt her and—

She put her hand on his arm. "It's nothing like that.

Matt has never left Noah for two whole weeks. He's really nervous about it."

Ah, now he understood. Gently, he asked, "Are you sure Matt's the only one who can't bear to leave Noah behind?"

Another tear rolled down her cheek. "I don't know if I can go," she admitted. "Two *weeks*." She made it sound like two *years*. "We're supposed to be a family. He should be coming with us."

"Oh, honey." He folded her into his arms, hugged her tight. Gideon rarely felt like he had the right words. Right now, however, he knew exactly what his sister needed. "You *are* a family. But sometimes you need alone time too, just you and Matt. Especially when you're celebrating your marriage. There will be so many other times that Noah will be with you, so many trips to Disney World and anywhere else you guys want to take him. You can even take him back to Iceland on a later trip."

"I know you're right," she said, her voice muffled against his tux, "but I keep thinking we should have scheduled just a week, rather than two."

"It's your honeymoon."

She tipped her head up, blinking tears away. "But—"

"I'll look after Noah as if he's my own. I've got his back. I've got your back. Nothing bad will ever happen to Noah when he's with me, I promise." He'd once made similar promises to Ari when she was eight years old, that he'd take care of her no matter what. And he'd failed. But he'd never fail her—or Noah—ever again. "I will protect Noah with my life."

Ari put her hand to his cheek. "I know you will. Thank you for loving him as much as I do."

"How could I not?"

Finally, she gave him a real smile. The smile of a very happy bride—and the best sister a guy could ever ask for. One who hadn't given up on him…even after he'd given up on himself. "I love you, Gideon."

"I love you too, Ari. More than you'll ever know."

"I've always known," she said softly.

After they hugged again, and she used his handkerchief to dry her eyes, he wrapped his arm around her and walked her outside the tent to where Matt stood by the limo with Noah in his arms.

"Have a great time." Gideon shook hands with his new brother-in-law—*whoa*, it was a helluva thing to realize his little sister was married now—then there was a tearful hug between Dad, Mom, and child.

Finally, Matt put Noah down, and Gideon took his nephew's hand. "I'll take good care of him." He repeated the promise to Matt.

"I know you will."

"And I'll take good care of Uncle Gideon," Noah said with equal solemnity.

"That's right, kiddo. You've got my back." He held Noah's hand tight while they all hid their smiles.

After everyone else got in their good-byes and hugs—Susan, Bob, the Mavericks, Jeremy, which took nearly as long as the wedding ceremony had—Gideon stepped back, picking up Noah and hugging him close for the final good-bye waves as the limo pulled away.

Once Ari and Matt were out of sight, Noah slid to the ground and said to Jeremy, "You'll take good care of my puppy, won't you?" Gideon's apartment couldn't take dogs, so Jeremy, Harper, and Will were going to keep the puppy for the two weeks.

Jeremy nodded so fast and hard that his hair flopped up and down on his forehead. "I sure will. Harper's going to help me do training and everything. Our puppies are going to be so happy together." Tasha had given puppies to both Jeremy and Noah from the litter she and Daniel had found abandoned in the mountains.

"Come on, Jeremy." Harper waved, her other hand held firmly in Will's. "Time to go."

"See ya later, alligator," Jeremy called over his shoulder as he raced off.

"In a while, crocodile," Noah shouted back. Then he turned to Gideon. "I was thinking, you and me are gonna have so much fun together while I'm staying with you, but I don't want Jorge to feel left out."

The kid was good. He knew exactly how to yank Gideon's heartstrings. "I wouldn't want that either." He had no idea how he'd get through seeing Rosie again so soon—especially when all he wanted to do was hold her in his arms and kiss her breathless. "Should we set up some playdates?"

"Yes!" Noah raced to Jorge. "Uncle Gideon says we get to play together while I'm staying with him."

"I hope that's okay," Gideon said to Rosie. She'd mentioned playdates earlier, but they hadn't actually agreed on anything.

"Of course it is," she replied. "In fact, Jorge already told me they want to spend every single day together. I didn't make any promises, but I figure we can play it by ear and see what works for everyone."

Jorge cut in to ask, "Mom, can we go say good-bye to Henri the peacock? He's right over there."

"Okay, but stay where I can see you."

Gideon was still rolling with shockwaves as Noah and Jorge ran off to see the peacock. He'd thought they'd set up a couple of playdates and he'd be done with it. But seeing Rosie every single day for the next two weeks? He'd go completely mad.

Or worse, he'd kiss her.

But he couldn't ignore the sad look that had been on Noah's face as he'd watched Matt and Ari drive away. The image was burned on Gideon's retinas. So how could he say no when nothing would make Noah happier than to spend the next two weeks with his best friend?

Two weeks in which Gideon would have to chain

down his base urges. Yeah, right, that would take a gargantuan effort, considering how close he was to the edge while doing nothing more than standing beside Rosie. She was in his head, mesmerizing him with the scent of her skin, the feel of her body, the softness of her curves.

"I was thinking we could take them some fun places," she said cheerily, without a clue about all the feelings raging inside him. "Maybe the San Francisco Zoo or some of the museums. What do you think?"

How could he possibly say no when Jorge was doing such a great job of erasing any fear or sadness Noah had been feeling over Matt and Ari's two-week trip?

"Sounds good to me." He was committed to two weeks with Rosie. Two weeks where they would be together for the boys. Two weeks of no looking, no touching, no X-rated thoughts about Rosie.

He could do this. He had to do it. For Noah.

Even if he went crazy in the process.

★ ★ ★

Matt curled his fingers around Ari's as the limo pulled onto the freeway, and raised her hand to kiss her knuckles. Reading her mind, he said, "Noah will be fine. He loves spending time with his uncle. And I'm sure there will be plenty of playdates with Jorge and Rosie too."

They were married. Ari almost couldn't believe it. Just as she'd told Gideon, it was a dream come true.

"I know Gideon will take good care of him," she replied. "It's just…" She loved Noah so much. And she wanted to include him in everything.

"I'll miss him too. But I'm also really looking forward to fourteen days and nights of wedded bliss with my wife." Matt pulled her in for a long, luscious kiss, the kind of kiss she'd never get enough of. When he finally released her, he said, "Plus, I think it's going to be really good for your brother to spend a couple of weeks hanging with Noah."

She agreed wholeheartedly. "Just before he walked me down the aisle, he told me how proud he was of me. But when I tried to tell him the same thing, he cut me off." She sighed. "It's like he can't hear anything about what a great guy he is."

"He's still working through the past," Matt noted. "Going to war, leaving you behind, not being able to find you. All those things would scar any man, especially one as devoted to family as Gideon is."

"I just wish I could find a way to make him see that he didn't fail me, especially when he was only trying to do his best." Frustration edged her voice. "I mean, what eighteen-year-old kid joins the army to send money home to his family? That alone should prove to him that he has nothing to be sorry for, regardless of what happened after he left. That wasn't his fault."

"You're right. Gideon is a great brother. A great son. A great man, period." Matt held her tight. "Which is why I completely trust him with Noah."

Ari had fallen in love with Matt and Noah. But she had fallen for his family just as hard. And she hoped Gideon would one day realize that he was worthy of being part of a family again. Part of *her* family.

"I love you," she said to her handsome, sexy, wonderful, insightful husband.

"Forever and ever," Matt said as his lips touched hers.

Chapter Ten

Gideon brought Noah over to Rosie's place bright and early on Sunday morning, the day after the wedding. She and Jorge lived in the cottage at the back of a property owned by a nice woman in her early seventies. Once a carriage house in the late 1800s, the cottage was quaint, with a small backyard. Two bedrooms, one bathroom, a family room, and a kitchen with a breakfast nook were all she and Jorge needed.

She'd thought long and hard about what to do and where to go on their first outing. The safer choice would be to go somewhere loud and busy enough that Gideon wouldn't have to interact with her too much. There were plenty of places that fit the bill—the trampoline gym would be wall-to-wall kids and parents, and the local public swimming pool was always overrun in the final days of summer. But then Jorge had suggested they take Noah and Gideon to one of their favorite places, somewhere most parents wouldn't even consider for a playdate. Chi was right— playing it safe wasn't the right move. If she wanted to make headway over Gideon's walls, taking big risks would be the only way to get there. Besides, spending some time working with paints and brushes always made Rosie feel better. If they were lucky, maybe it would do the same for Gideon.

Jorge and Rosie had agreed to keep the location a secret for as long as possible. Partly for the fun of surprising Noah and Gideon—but also, at least as far as Rosie was concerned, making sure that Gideon couldn't find a way to back out.

Which was why she'd sent Jorge, Noah, and Gideon straight out to the backyard while she gathered up the many supplies the four of them would need for the day. She even packed the car. Actually, it was Gideon's SUV, because her tiny hatchback was too small for everything they'd need.

Standing at the kitchen window, drying her hands on a dish towel, she watched Gideon with the kids. His jeans were snug in all the right places, sending her heart rate bouncing into the stratosphere. Beneath his T-shirt, his muscles flexed and rippled as he played ball with the boys. She had to fan herself, especially when he bent low to catch a wild throw, and his jeans stretched tight across his behind. He hadn't shaved since yesterday, and she liked him with that hint of stubble. Liked it so much that she could practically feel the phantom brush of his whiskers against her skin. Her hand trembled as she hung up the dish towel, and her breathing was just the tiniest bit shaky.

After the boys tired of that game, he pushed them on a tire swing her elderly landlady had allowed her to hang on the big tree. Their voices carried through the closed window. "Higher, Gid, higher."

At the moment, his eyes were ocean blue, and he was smiling that smile only the boys ever saw. Yet again, he looked like she imagined he'd been as a teenager, before he'd gone to Iraq.

Although he'd never truly been a carefree teenager, had he? Not with the weight of a drug-addicted mother and a little sister to care for on his shoulders.

No one's life was simple, Rosie mused as she packed their lunch into an insulated bag. She'd grown up as an only child in a run-down neighborhood in a raggedy house her mother had always kept spotlessly clean—but she'd been so happy. So carefree. So utterly unaware that she was missing anything at all. How could she have known when she had her parents' love and attention? As much as any child could ask for. When her mother and father saw how much she loved to draw on the sidewalk with her bits of chalk, they'd found the money to buy her brushes and paint. And they'd spent hours in the library with her, poring over coffee-table art books, as excited about learning from the works of the old masters as she was, despite neither of them having a passionate interest in art. They'd taken her to museums on the free days, even when their feet must have hurt from their long days out. They'd encouraged her to spend as much time as she wanted studying her favorite paintings.

After her parents died in a car accident, and with no other family in the state, eleven-year-old Rosie had nowhere to go but foster care. Her life had changed in ways she could never have imagined. She'd had no terrible foster home experiences, although she'd never fully bonded with any of the families either. Still, she always had her memories of her loving parents, the life lessons they'd taught her about being kind to others and true to herself, along with the love of art they'd nurtured in her.

Once lunch was packed, Rosie wiped down the kitchen counter. Her home was also spotless, a trait inherited from her mother. And the lunch she'd made—shredded beef empanadas—was delicious, a recipe she'd learned at her father's side. He'd always loved to cook.

Ready to go, she paused at the French doors leading to the backyard. Just one more minute to watch Gideon's smile, one more glimpse of the real Gideon Jones.

No matter how gruff or closed off he could be with everyone else—including her—the way he smiled with the boys revealed the man he was on the inside. A man she very much wanted to know. If only he would let her…

With his back to her, Gideon shouldn't have been able to hear the door open over the boys' shouts and laughter. Yet his shoulders stiffened, and even before he'd turned to face her, his smile was gone, and shadows filled his eyes. Clearly, he was back to being on guard with her, just as he had been for the past nine months.

Only, yesterday at Ari's wedding, she had changed. Rosie was no longer satisfied with Gideon's one-word responses and expressionless glances. She wanted the smiles he gave the boys. She wanted the happiness that glowed in his eyes when he looked at them. She wanted Gideon to share all that with her too.

At the very least, she wanted to know that she was his friend, no matter what.

"Everything's ready," she called. "We can head out now."

Gideon helped Jorge and Noah scramble down from the tire swing, then the boys raced across the small lawn to her.

"What's the surprise, Rosie?" Noah asked. "Jorge says you have something awesome planned for today. He wouldn't tell us, but you could if you wanted to."

She smiled at him. "It's not a surprise if I tell you."

"Do you know, Uncle Gideon?" Noah asked.

"All I know is that Rosie knows how to have fun. So I'm sure the surprise will be great."

It was one of the nicest things he'd said about her.

Rosie was practically glowing as they drove toward her surprise destination. Okay, so maybe they weren't officially in the friend zone yet—and they certainly weren't *beyond* the friend zone, not by any stretch of the imagination—but it was a step in the right direction.

In the backseat, the boys chattered, talking about Noah's video call that morning with Ari and Matt in Iceland, asking what they were going to eat for lunch, pointing out landmarks, plastering themselves to the passenger side window when they passed the Flintstone House along Highway 280. The home, made of free-form domes, had been a landmark as long as Rosie could remember. Previously adobe-colored, it was now painted deep purple and burnt orange and rusty red.

"It's got dinosaurs," Jorge exclaimed from the backseat as he gazed at the huge metal sculptures filling the backyard.

"Look!" Rosie exclaimed. "That's Charlie's T-Rex." She'd almost forgotten Charlie had sold it to the owners of the iconic house. "Doesn't it look amazing?" Everyone agreed that it most certainly did.

Once they were in the city, she told Gideon where to turn, and as soon as they entered Lincoln Park, Jorge started to bounce in the back. "Mom, can I tell them now?"

She grinned at him in the rearview mirror. "Yup,

now would be good."

They crested the hill, and a gorgeous classical structure appeared. "The Legion of Honor. It's a museum," Jorge explained, "with all these really cool paintings. Mom and I come here all the time, just like she used to come here with her parents. And we go to the de Young Museum too."

"Why don't you tell Noah and Gideon about the special activity we do at the museum?" Rosie suggested.

"We paint!" So excited, he sat on the edge of his seat, straining against his seat belt. "There's this one room where they let us set up easels and copy the paintings. Then Mom and I compare our pictures. It's so much fun," he told Noah and Gideon. "You're going to love it just like we do!"

"Are you really allowed to copy famous paintings?" Noah asked.

"Yeah. But it's not like stealing or anything. It's just to mess around and pretend to be a famous painter. Although Mommy doesn't need to pretend, because her paintings are so awesome that she really could be famous if she wanted to."

As Gideon parked in the last vacant spot in the roundabout, he finally spoke. "I didn't know you liked to paint."

"It's just a hobby." Once, long ago, she'd dreamed of her paintings hanging in galleries. Back when painting was all she thought about, all she yearned to do. Until she got pregnant, and everything changed. Still, Jorge's faith in her artistic ability was touching.

"While I was doing my accounting courses in college—" Accounting was what paid the bills. "—I also took as many painting technique and art history classes as I could squeeze into my schedule." She was ecstatic that Jorge loved art as much as she did. "Jorge's drawings are amazing. Next time you're over at the cottage, I'll show them to you." She would have done so today, but she hadn't wanted to accidentally give away their secret destination or the fact that she planned for them all to paint today.

"Are me and Gideon just going to watch you guys paint?" Noah asked, his mouth drooping, clearly not liking that idea.

"No way," she told Noah. "We're *all* going to." She smiled at Gideon, trying not to betray her nerves about his reaction. There was more than a fifty-fifty chance he'd totally regret agreeing to their playdate, especially when she added, "Even you, Gideon."

As expected, he looked more than a little shell-shocked. Despite her jangling nerves, she acted cool and calm as she climbed out of the SUV and opened the back. Gideon's needle was definitely leaning toward *regret*.

"Our easels. Yay!" Jorge jumped in the air, and Noah naturally jumped with him. They were true pals;

whatever excited one excited the other.

Only Gideon remained silent as he helped her pull out the sketch pads and easels, which folded down to the size of backpacks.

Once they'd gathered up everything, including paint palettes and brushes, they crossed the road and climbed the long, wide path through the central columns and on to Rodin's famous sculpture, *The Thinker*. Rosie took a dozen pictures of the boys mimicking the pose and then in front of the mini Louvre pyramid in the middle of the courtyard. Throughout, Gideon hung back a couple of feet, his needle edging ever higher in the *regret* direction.

As they walked through the ticket booth, her favorite docent waved. "Hey, Cherise," Rosie called.

"Good to see you, honey." Cherise was in her sixties and had been a museum docent back when Rosie used to come here with her parents. "You've got friends." She ran her eyes up and down Gideon's impressive frame, not in the least abashed to show how much she appreciated his form. "How lovely. You know how much our patrons love to see artists at work."

After they'd passed, Gideon finally spoke again. "People are going to see our paintings?" His voice might actually be tinged with terror.

Before Rosie could respond, Jorge said, "I like it when people look at our paintings. They always say nice things about them, about how talented me and Mom are. I'll bet you guys get lots of compliments too."

Gideon didn't look convinced, even by Jorge's enthusiastic response. Rosie could have smoothed things over by telling him the playdate was just for the boys, that all he had to do was dab his paintbrush on the paper and pretend. But she'd already decided not to pussyfoot around him anymore—even if he clearly wasn't at all thrilled about painting. Plus, a part of her still hoped that he might let himself get into it, rather than holding back like he usually did.

Crazier things had happened.

As she led them back to the last room that housed the Impressionists, with every painting they passed, she felt as though she'd come home to good friends. "I love *The Russian Bride's Attire*. And the Renoir and Anthony van Dyck too. These paintings, they feel so…" She breathed deeply, as if she could drag in their essence from the air in the room. "So wondrous. Even after all the times I've been here, I still can hardly believe this museum has Van Gogh and Manet and Monet and Salvador Dali and Degas. That I don't need to travel to France or Spain to see them." She turned to Gideon. "Do you know Van Gogh destroyed most of his initial paintings because he thought they weren't good enough?" She shook her head. "Just imagine if those paintings were still around. Not for how much they'd be worth, but for how beautiful they'd surely be."

Jorge pulled on the hem of her shirt. "I want to do the Salvador Dali, Mom."

"The Dali sounds great, honey." She turned to Gideon. "What do you think about doing Monet's *Water Lilies* with Noah? They're one of my favorites—almost everyone's, really."

"Monet was my mom's favorite painter," Gideon said. "She had a book about *Water Lilies* when I was growing up."

It was Rosie's turn to be stunned. After getting his back up over painting in public, the last thing she expected was for him to open up to her in any way.

Finally, she found her voice. "There's a reason his paintings of the lilies in his backyard in France are popular around the world—they're undeniably beautiful, in all seasons." When he didn't say anything more about his mother, she offered, "I'll help you two set up."

Though he thanked her, she knew that painting in a gallery was the last thing he would choose to do with his free time. If not for the boys, she suspected he would have sprinted out of the museum and back to the SUV.

After she set up Noah's and Gideon's easels, along with sketch pads and palettes, she got Jorge going. Her son liked to work in colored pencil, sometimes charcoal. He often started out at the easel, then moved to a bench and worked with his sketch pad on his lap.

She positioned her easel so she could see Noah and Gideon without being obvious that she was watching them.

Jorge raced over to whisper in Noah's ear as his friend made great swipes of color across his pad.

When Jorge ran back, she reminded him, "Walk, sweetheart. Be respectful."

"Sorry, Mom."

But his excitement was catching. She wanted to race to Gideon, whisper in his ear as he picked up his brush, looked at the paper, then at the paints. He stood unmoving for so long, she thought he wouldn't do it, after all. That he might just walk away.

Until, suddenly, he grabbed a brush and began splashing color on the pad.

The museum was surprisingly empty for a Sunday, though that could have been due to the gorgeous day outside. Patrons occasionally stopped to watch them paint for a few seconds before walking on. But the person getting the most attention was Gideon. And Rosie knew exactly why.

Though he clearly had no artistic training, from the first brush of paint across the paper, both Gideon and his painting seemed to vibrate with energy.

At first, he used the same colors as the *Water Lilies*—blues and greens, dabs of purple, a little red. But as he continued to paint, the colors grew darker, covering the brighter tones he'd started with, until it bore no resemblance at all to the original Monet.

Yet, in every drop of paint, there was something so visceral, so gut-wrenching, as if the very flowers he was trying to paint were dying right before him. He swirled pain and grief and anger and regret across the paper, his hand flashing, slashing, dashing, the colors mixing, bleeding, running.

He moved as though he was in a trance, as though everything was coming out of him without conscious effort. He anointed the painting with pure, raw emotion.

And what he created was *amazing*.

★ ★ ★

Slashes of color flew across Gideon's vision, flaming reds and burning oranges and intense yellows over dark, bruised blues and guilt-ridden browns and howling blacks. And rising up out of the swirl of color were the faces of Hank Garrett... Jonny Danzi... Ralph Esterhausen... Ralph's wife and kids... And Karmen. Loyal, dedicated Karmen, who never should have been there in the first place.

Gideon's team.

Gideon's responsibility.

Gideon's failure.

"Uncle Gideon." Noah grabbed his free hand. "Come and look at what I made!"

Gideon blinked. Once, then again. Until the faces, the fire, were gone, leaving nothing more than blobs of paint—red and orange and yellow streaks across a background of blue and brown and black.

Yet he still felt the horror. And he could still hear the screaming.

"Uncle Gideon!" Noah yanked harder on his hand.

The insistence in his nephew's voice helped him pull his broken strings back together, at least long enough to focus on what Noah was saying. "Hey, kiddo, what's up?"

"Come see my painting. You're really going to like it." Paint streaked Noah's face, his hands, his clothes. "Your painting is super cool too!" he said, a huge smile on his face.

Gideon moved, his limbs rubbery and jerky, as though they had to learn how to work again. Slowly, he came back to the here and now—to the well-lit museum, to the cool, smooth floor beneath his feet, to the cream-colored walls filled with masterworks. And especially to Noah waiting expectantly for a response to his painting.

"Way cool, kiddo." Though his nephew's work was really good, clearly depicting lilies floating in the water, Gideon's voice was barely more than a rasp, harsh in his throat. He put his hand on Noah's shoulder, squeezing it. "You're doing a great job, just like I knew you would. Do you want to paint something else?"

Though he'd spent much of the past ten years mostly silent, usually speaking only when spoken to, today he needed to keep talking to drown out the explosions in his head. "We could do that Van Gogh or the Manet if you want."

Noah shook his head. "Nah, I'm going to help Jorge with his instead. See ya!"

His nephew raced off, leaving Gideon alone with Rosie. And with the horror that he'd painted. The atrocity, the blood and guts and guilt and fear and pain he'd spilled all over the page.

She stood in front of his easel, studying his painting with intense focus. "It's amazing, Gideon."

That's when he knew—she saw it all. Everything he worked so hard to keep hidden inside. All the things he'd never shown to anyone else, not even Ari.

Only Rosie had ever been able to clearly see the hell he'd returned from. Only Rosie had ever truly seen the darkness that festered inside him. The darkness that would always be there, made up of guilt and regret and sorrow and a desperate wish to rewind the calendar to get everything right this time. A desperate wish that could never come true.

Rosie called his painting *amazing*, but she was only being kind. Because that's who Rosie was, one of the kindest, sweetest women he'd ever known.

He didn't deserve her kindness. Not after all the pain he'd caused so many people.

Ashamed by all he'd let go on the easel—the depth of the darkness inside that was now splattered in thick paint on paper stunned even him—he reached around her and tore off the sheet. He wanted to rip it into a million little pieces. Before the boys could gaze at it too long and know true terror. Before Rosie took a closer look and saw how truly dark Gideon's memories were.

But Rosie stopped him. "No." She put her hands over his. "I never let Jorge rip up his paintings. I've told him a dozen times that everything he creates is good, whether it's technically perfect or not, whether it's simple or complicated, whether it stays on the surface or goes deep. Especially then. So that's what I'm saying to you now, Gideon. What you've created is good. I won't let you destroy it."

Years of raising a strong-willed little boy gave her a grip firm enough to take the painting from him before he could stop her. Though it was still wet, she rolled it up and slid it into one of the cardboard tubes they'd brought with them.

His insides screamed to get it back. But he didn't move.

Jorge ran up to them. "Mom, I'm *starved.*"

As though she hadn't needed to damn near tear the painting from Gideon's hands a moment before, she smiled at her son and said, "Me too. Let's pack up now and have our picnic on the lawn out front."

Chapter Eleven

Noah and Jorge chattered while they ate their empanadas out on the lawn. They threw the stale bread Rosie had packed for the birds, then ran around like pirates on the burning deck of a ship.

But Gideon didn't engage. He didn't look at her, didn't even look at the kids. His eyes were dark, still full of the pain she'd seen in his painting. So much for her hope that he'd feel better after spending time with paints and brushes…

Maybe she shouldn't have studied his painting so closely. Maybe she shouldn't have told him how amazing she thought it was. Maybe she should simply have helped the boys gather up their stuff and pretended she hadn't seen everything Gideon obviously didn't want anyone to know. Heck, maybe she should never have taken the risk of bringing them to paint in the museum. They could have jumped on trampolines instead, never needing to say a word to each other, never needing to examine their feelings, never going deep on any level.

But Rosie didn't believe in holding back her feelings. Even if she did, she couldn't possibly have held back her visceral reaction to his revealing painting—and the deep emotions roiling within its dark, wild colors.

For a few incredible minutes, he'd let it all out. And though he obviously regretted it, something told her just how important that release had been. It was one of the many reasons why she found art so magical. Even when someone tried to close themselves off, art had a way of pushing past boundaries...and of giving hope. Even when all hope seemed lost.

She hadn't let him destroy the painting. If only it was as easy to stop him from destroying himself.

Still, she had to give him some space now. Anyone who had painted something so powerful needed time for recovery and reflection.

While Jorge and Noah chowed down on the empanadas, then played on the grass, Rosie and Gideon ate their lunches in silence. When they were done, Gideon collected the picnic remains and carried them over to the trash.

"Mom, can we go back to look at the paintings before going home?" Jorge asked. "I want to show Noah the one where they're all looking at the monk, except the lady who's looking straight out of the painting and right into you."

It was one of her favorite paintings too. "It's called

Holy Day in Monterrey, 1759 by Miguel Fernando Correa. And yes, we can go back inside for a bit." She glanced at a stone-faced Gideon. "Unless Gideon and Noah need to head home now?"

"Uncle Gideon, please say we can stay longer," Noah urged.

Once Gideon nodded, Jorge turned to Noah. "The painting I want to show you is like the *Mona Lisa*'s eyes following you."

"Who's the Mona Lisa?" Noah asked.

Jorge told him about the painting in the Louvre and the glass pyramid that was like the pyramid in the Legion of Honor's courtyard, but way bigger.

"Someday Mom's gonna take me there," he boasted.

And she swore she would. Someday soon.

"I want to go too," Noah exclaimed as they raced back up the concrete walkway to the courtyard.

They followed the boys back into the museum, and she explained everything she knew about the paintings, relishing their interest even if Gideon was in shutdown mode.

As Jorge ran back, pointing to a new painting that hadn't been there the last time they'd visited, she decided to have a normal conversation with Gideon, even if it was only one-sided. "They're little sponges, soaking it all up. Jorge is getting better at remembering the names of artists and paintings too."

"I saw his drawing. It was very good."

She almost tripped, the sound of his voice shocking in its unexpectedness. It was a little rough, as though he hadn't used it for a while. Which, to be fair, he hadn't.

"Yes," she said, trying to appear as if nothing special had happened. She was almost afraid to say more, in case it set him off like the painting had. But now that he'd had some time to process what he'd painted, she didn't want to start walking on eggshells with him all over again. Not when it seemed that doing exactly the opposite might be a far better way to reach him. "I'd like to get him art lessons." She was saving. Rosie was always saving. Her accounting job was good, but with a cottage in Willow Glen and a little boy who grew like a weed, the money leaked out as though it were sitting in a colander instead of a bank.

"Art lessons would be good," he agreed as he watched the boys crowd up to the new painting. "What is it they're looking at?"

"I'm not sure. The Legion of Honor rotates its collection regularly, especially if any restoration work needs to be done. Sometimes, the paintings are sent out for other exhibitions, like *Water Lilies*, which was included in a Paris show. Plus, they switch artwork back and forth with the de Young Museum in Golden Gate Park. They also store a bunch of stuff down in the basement. Once—" In her excitement, she reached out to put her hand on his arm. "Cherise took us down there. If you think it's fabulous up here, the basement is a treasure trove. Everything's packed up to keep it from deteriorating, but still, to be in the presence of all that magnificence…"

Suddenly, she realized she was touching him. But though it was likely the last thing she should have done when he was only just starting to thaw again, she couldn't bring herself to pull away.

And despite everything—or maybe because of it all—heat flared between them. A blaze even hotter than the one that had ignited at the wedding. At last, she drew back her hand.

The boys speed-walked—it was the closest they could get to not running—to the Correa painting. "See, she's watching *you.*" Jorge pointed at the beautiful woman, dressed in black, a black lace mantilla on her head. "While all the other people are listening to the monk."

"Cool," Noah said, his voice soft with the awe of a child who was seeing something extraordinary even if he didn't know why it was so.

As for Gideon, Rosie was surprised by how closely he examined the painting. It wasn't that he seemed to be a philistine when it came to art—he had definitely appreciated Van Gogh and Degas and Rubens. It was more that this particular painting was connecting with him on a deeper level than anything else in the museum had, even the incredible Monet.

"Every time I look at this painting," she said, "I swear I see something new. The detail in the faces, the clothes, even the trees around the square—it's phenomenal."

He took a step closer, his brow furrowed. "I haven't seen this painting before. I would have remembered if I had." It was almost as though he was speaking to himself. "But I swear, it's familiar to me."

"Maybe," she guessed, "you've seen other Miguel Fernando Correa paintings? He's widely collected throughout the world."

Gideon continued to stare at the painting. "Maybe. Although I've never heard his name before today." At last, he took a step back, gave the painting one final glance, then looked at Noah and Jorge as they admired a Cellini bust of Cosimo I de' Medici. "There's so much wonder. So much amazement. In absolutely everything around them." He said it as though remembering his own long-ago past.

Then he amazed her by giving the smallest of smiles, the corner of his mouth lifting slightly, pulling her heart up with it.

With the boys filled with astonishing images, and Gideon only half stone instead of full stone, they finally made their way back down the Peninsula toward home.

"Uncle Gideon, can we go back to Rosie's house?

She's gonna have a barbecue with hot dogs and sweet potato fries."

"Yeah," Jorge agreed, "Mom makes the *best* sweet potato fries." He put his hands together dreamily.

It was overkill. Her son liked her fries, but he wasn't *dreamy* about them. He obviously wanted Noah to stay and play.

"We can't just invite ourselves," Gideon said to his nephew.

"Of course you're invited." She'd bought enough for all of them, hoping that they'd go from the museum to dinner.

"Plus, you have to show us how to play that game, Gid." Jorge added inducement.

"What game?" Rosie asked.

"Hopscotch." He glanced at her. "You draw a grid on the sidewalk with chalk."

"We used to play that." She thought of all the games she used to play as a kid. Freeze tag and kick the can and hopscotch. Things that didn't cost money. You didn't need a video game console, you didn't need a TV. All you needed to keep yourself entertained was a little ingenuity. "I can get dinner ready while you show them," she offered. "There's room for hopscotch out on the patio." Though tiny, it could still handle a hopscotch grid.

"We have chalk," Jorge said. "So can you show us, Gid?"

★ ★ ★

How was he supposed to say no?

He'd promised Ari he'd take care of Noah. And take care of him Gideon would, by making sure he had the most fun possible for the next two weeks.

"Sure," he said, forcing his lips into a smile. "Bring out the chalk, Jorge, and we'll lay some down."

He hadn't forgotten his horrifying painting. Nor had he forgotten that Rosie had seen his raw and bleeding insides splatted all over the paper—or that she'd had to take the painting away from him before he could destroy it. But with two little boys to play with, there wasn't room to ruminate. Not *much* room, anyway.

On the back patio, he showed them how to draw the hopscotch grid, how to toss the rocks and make the jumps. They teetered and sometimes fell over and always laughed, whether they were standing upright or not. And eventually, Gideon was able to laugh with them.

A while later, they ate grilled hot dogs and sweet potato fries—and yeah, they really were the best—then they hopped the scotch again. Kids were tireless.

Rosie watched them through the kitchen window as she cleaned up and did the dishes. Gideon had offered to help, but she'd told him to play with the boys.

Gideon had worried that after his post-painting

outburst, she might think he was too much of a nut job to be around her kid. But she wouldn't have invited him to dinner if that was the case. Right?

"This is super fun, Gid," Noah said. "Were you as old as us when you learned?"

"I was. And then I taught your mom how to play when she was six. We didn't have a lot of money growing up, so we needed games that didn't cost anything."

"Not even Legos?"

"We had those, but they weren't like the Legos you have now. They were just simple blocks in a few colors, and since we got them from the thrift store, lots of pieces were missing. But we had fun with them anyway."

He'd always taken care of Ari because their mom wasn't capable. After his dad died when Ari was just a baby, their mother had lost all sense of herself. She'd turned to drugs to manage her grief. Only ten years older than Ari, he'd had no choice but to take care of her since their mom couldn't. And yet, for as much as he'd been a lifeline for Ari, she'd done the same for him, a shining light with her big smile and quick mind. He'd loved spending time with her. It never felt like babysitting.

"My mom buys stuff at thrift stores too," Jorge told him. "We like looking through everything for the best deals."

"Can I come with you sometime?" Noah asked, clearly not realizing his father was so wealthy that he could have bought an entire chain of secondhand stores.

"Sure," Jorge said, then called out to Rosie. "Are you gonna come play with us, Mom? Otherwise, Gid is probably gonna be too tired to keep playing for much longer."

She laughed, that sweet musical laugh that reached right up under his ribs. "Perfect timing. I'm all done in here," she said, then came out to join them.

He should have taken Noah home already. But there was something so comforting, so easy and normal, about playing hopscotch with Rosie and Jorge and Noah until the sun went down and they had to turn on the porch light so they could make out the chalk lines.

Even in the aftermath of what had gone down at the museum this afternoon, Rosie's easygoing demeanor allowed him to move through the rest of the afternoon and evening without making a big deal of anything, without beating himself up *ad nauseum*, the way he normally would. And now, his jaw actually ached from so much smiling. Probably because his face wasn't used to it.

"Okay, you guys," Rosie finally said, looking pointedly at her watch, "it's past Jorge's bedtime."

"Can Noah sleep over since it's already so late?"

Jorge was ever hopeful.

"Please, Uncle Gideon, can we do a sleepover?" Noah was just as optimistic.

"You don't have any pajamas," Gideon pointed out.

Of course, Jorge was quick to offer, "Noah can borrow some of mine."

Gideon looked at Rosie to see what she thought of an impromptu sleepover.

She gave a one-shouldered shrug. "It's okay with me if it's okay with you."

He smiled at Noah. "Okay, you can stay."

The boys whooped, then raced inside.

"Don't forget to brush your teeth," Rosie called, then turned to him. "Noah's actually got clothes and a few other things here—and since they're always wanting to spend the night, Jorge's got stuff at Noah's house too. I've even got twin beds in Jorge's room." She barely paused for breath before adding, "I'm sure they'd love it if you tucked them both in. And after that, why don't you stay for a glass of wine? You know, to rehydrate after all that hopscotch."

He should say no. He should go. He should do whatever he could to blast clear of Rosie's sunny, sexy orbit. But what came out of his mouth was, "Okay, thanks. A glass of wine after story time sounds good."

Chapter Twelve

She left him to tumble the boys into the twin beds in Jorge's room while she opened the wine. Jorge's walls were lined with bookshelves housing an astonishing library for a six-year-old. Like Noah, he was a voracious reader. Reading, Legos, and building cities in Noah's huge sandbox were obviously Jorge's passions. But especially art.

Just like his beautiful, talented mother.

"Are these all your drawings?" Gideon asked Jorge. The walls were papered with them.

"Yeah," Jorge said proudly.

"They're good." Really good, like something an adult would do.

"Thank you." The boy beamed with pride.

"You're both such talented guys," he said. "You with your amazing Lego creations and sandbox buildings, Noah, and Jorge, with your paintings."

"Didn't you like my painting?" Noah asked.

"'Course I did, kiddo. I'm going to hang it on the wall in my office." Though Gideon was out and about most of the day, he also had an office at Top Notch headquarters, which was peppered with pictures of Ari and Noah. If he happened to stare a little too long and often at the pictures Rosie was in—as one of Ari's best friends, it was inevitable there should be plenty of Rosie photos—well, no one needed to know about that. Least of all the woman wanting to share a glass of wine with him in the living room. "In fact, I'll put your painting right next to the Lego spaceship you built me," he told Noah.

"You can have one of my drawings too, Gideon," Jorge said, his voice hopeful.

"Wow, thanks. Everyone is going to want to work in my office." He lowered his voice. "But now let's get you both to bed."

He gave them each kisses, pulled the covers up to their chins, then started the what-to-read negotiation.

They considered one of the *Horrid Henry* books by Francesca Simon, or one of the *Boxcar Children* books, but in the end Jorge and Noah agreed that the story they most wanted to read was one of the *Magic Tree House* books by Mary Pope Osborne.

Revolutionary War on Wednesday was set in Colonial times, just as General George Washington was about to lead his army in a sneak attack.

Gideon sat on the edge of Noah's bed, opened the book, and began to read aloud.

Noah leaned against his side, looking at the

pictures. "Look at those funny clothes they're wearing."

"That's how they dressed back then, during the Revolutionary War," Gideon said.

Of course, Jorge had to scramble out of bed to see so that both boys were huddled on either side of Gideon.

"You were in a war, weren't you, Uncle Gideon?" Noah gazed up at him with his innocent child's eyes.

"Yes, I was. In Iraq, in the Middle East."

"I know where that is," Jorge said. "We had a really big map in our classroom last year when we were learning all about the continents and stuff."

As Gideon continued to read aloud, the characters jumped from the magic tree house into the biting cold of a Pennsylvania December.

"Was it cold like that where you were?" Noah wanted to know.

"Nope. It was hot," he said. "Really hot. And sandy. Dusty. The dirt seemed to get into everything." He leaned close to say, "Even in your underpants."

They giggled in unison.

"You get used to it." He shrugged. "You can get used to anything." In the end, he'd barely noticed the dust and the dirt. It was only when he came home, when he no longer had to wash the sand out of his clothes and his pores, that he noticed the difference again.

They got back to Annie and Jack in the story as the characters came upon a regiment of patriot soldiers in raggedy clothes, some even without boots on their feet, just rags.

"Did they give you boots, Gid, when you were over there?" Worry laced Jorge's voice, as if he were afraid Gideon had been marching through hot sand in bare feet.

Gideon suppressed a smile. "Yeah, kiddo, we had boots. We had everything we needed to survive. You'd be amazed what you can fit in a pack. It was heavy, but your pack was your life preserver." His gear had saved his life more than once.

"Can we see your pack?" Noah asked, excitement in his voice.

"I'd show it to you." He shook his head. "But I don't have it anymore."

"Bummer," they both said.

He moved them along in the story, to the troops on the banks of the Delaware.

"Did you have to push cannons like they did?" Jorge leaned back to look up at him.

Gideon laughed outright this time. "We had trucks to move artillery. And we had rifles instead of muskets. But we didn't have to use them a whole lot. Mostly, we were on patrol or tower duty or helping out the villagers. And we had some good times back at base."

It wasn't until the words came out of his mouth

that he realized what he'd said. Whenever he'd looked back, it had seemed as if every day had been a firefight, every day your life was on the line, every day another IED went off. But maybe his memory had played tricks. Because while he had always been on the edge, and his senses had been heightened—because, hell, everyone over there was armed—the reality was that a lot of the time, nothing had happened.

In fact, for the first time in a really long time, he remembered the pranks he and his buddy Zach had pulled on some of the other guys. He remembered card games and razzing his buddies in the little downtime they were actually given.

The boys and their questions made him think, for the first time in forever, about the good stuff, not just the bad.

He kissed the top of Noah's head, then Jorge's, then read about Jack and Annie getting stuck in George Washington's boat about to cross the Delaware. At last, when their questions stopped, he realized the boys' eyelids were drooping.

He helped Jorge back into his own bed, kissed him one last time, then leaned over to cover up Noah. It wasn't until he put the book back on the bookshelf that he noticed Rosie standing in the doorway, a wineglass in each hand.

"You're a very compelling reader," she said softly. And then, "You can take these out to the living room while I bestow a few kisses of my own."

He had to work hard to push away his desperate longing for her to bestow kisses on *him* as he took both glasses, his fingers grazing hers, their bodies close in the confines of the short hallway, her scent making his knees weak.

The soft murmur of their voices drifted out to the small living room as he set the glasses on the coffee table. He decided to buy the book for his Kindle so he and Noah could keep reading, and it would be available for sleepovers. The story had been good for the boys. And honestly, it had been good for him. He'd never talked about what the war had been like. But answering the boys' questions had made him rethink his experiences. Maybe that wasn't so bad.

This morning, before their museum outing, he'd gone straight into the backyard and hadn't had a chance to see much of the cottage. Now, he noted that the living room walls were covered with Jorge's drawings, some of them framed, some of them tacked to the plaster.

But Jorge's paintings weren't the only ones hanging. Rosie's were here too.

From what he'd seen on her easel at the museum today, he knew she had artistic ability. But now he realized just how deep her talent truly ran.

She worked in paint, acrylics, oils, a few watercolors. She favored faces and landscapes. There was a series done at a harbor he thought might be near Santa Cruz. There were paintings of Jorge and Noah, Ari and Matt, and their friend Chi. Rosie had also pushed her imagination with renderings of Jorge as a young man and Ari as an old woman. But it was a painting of a man watching a group of people laughing that really caught Gideon's eye. Though the viewer couldn't clearly see the man's expression, he looked like a man on an island, one who had forgotten how to laugh, how to have fun.

It was almost as though she'd painted *him*.

Regardless of who Rosie's subjects were, with every single painting, he could see the way *she* viewed life. The picture of old Ari wasn't a depiction of decrepitude, but a woman who'd lived a long, interesting life and who had enjoyed every second of it. Her rendition of Jorge in manhood showed a young man with hope in his heart.

At last, the door to the boys' room closed, and her footsteps fell in the hall. "I give them ten minutes of whispering and giggling, then they'll both zonk out." She plucked a wineglass off the coffee table, the one with the soft wisp of lipstick on the rim, then handed him the other, tapping her glass to his. She nodded toward the living room gallery. "Jorge's paintings are great, aren't they?"

"They are." He was always so careful with his words around her, lest he say more than he intended.

Like how much he wanted her. Or how he couldn't stop thinking about her. But he needed her to know something. "You've got a tremendous amount of talent. Why are you an accountant instead of a full-time artist?"

She curled into the end of the sofa. "First, thank you. And second, I like numbers. Working as an accountant is how I can afford the things that Jorge and I both need to live in the Bay Area."

He had great respect for everything Rosie had achieved—not only was she doing a great job of raising her son, she was also saving for Jorge's art lessons and a trip to the Louvre. But Gideon already had plenty of money he would be more than happy to use in helping her out. He'd saved his re-up bonuses, he'd invested well, and he hadn't spent much of anything while he drifted around the country working on jobsites. He'd been saving for Ari, hoping he'd find her one day. Only, by the time he'd found his sister, she hadn't needed his money anymore. Even the wedding hadn't put much of a dent in his savings.

He had way more than enough to pay for art lessons. And he could buy them plane tickets to Paris too. If only he could think of a way to offer without it coming across as charity, which it definitely wasn't.

But his brain was so scrambled from a day spent looking at her, longing for her, breathing in her enticing scent, watching her laugh, that the best he could come up with was, "Seems to me that if you quit the accounting gig and painted, you've got a fortune here." He gestured to her living room walls.

She shook her head. "Do you have any idea how many struggling artists are out there? Jorge needs the stability I can give him through a good, steady job. He's my number one priority."

Everything was about Jorge, and he saw all over again what an amazing mom she was. If the boys ran when they should have walked, or were about to make a bad decision, she didn't scold, she corrected. She built up their fragile little-boy egos, never tore them down.

Exactly the way she hadn't torn him down despite what she'd seen in his painting…and his complete loss of control when he'd been about to rip it up.

He'd always seen Rosie as invincible. But now he realized that she needed someone to build *her* up.

"You really don't know how good you are, do you?" He sat beside her, because he didn't want to stand over her as though he were lecturing. Except that sitting close beside her on the love seat, the scent of her hair was a million times more intoxicating than the wine. It made things happen inside him. It made need rise up. The desire to touch, to kiss, to hold. Impossible things. He had to concentrate on her art, nothing else. "Have you asked Ari to show your work to Charlie and Sebastian?" They were both artists. They'd know which galleries to point her toward.

Rosie moved restlessly on the couch, uncurling her legs, turning, tucking them beneath her again. "No. Ari's as practical as I am. She knows that accounting is the way to pay the bills."

Rosie never made excuses. But this sure sounded like one. He wondered how he could get hold of one of her paintings. He could take it to Daniel, who could show it to Charlie and Sebastian. Surely, they would make her understand how amazing she was.

But even as he thought it, he knew he couldn't go behind her back like that. Just as he couldn't give her the money to pay for Jorge's art lessons. Rosie had done a great job leading her own life—she didn't need a screw-up like him stepping in with advice and handouts.

"Speaking of being amazing," she said softly, "the painting you did today was so emotional, so heartrending. It really moved me."

Every muscle in his body went rigid. Every bone felt like it might crack.

In an instant, he was right back there in the museum, slashing paint on the paper like a madman. Then he was back further still—in Iraq. Caught in the fire and pain. He saw the faces of his men. He saw death.

He saw Karmen one last time.

And that strange sense of ease he'd felt talking to the boys and answering their questions while they read a book? It collapsed under the weight of that haunting memory.

"I've got to go." He almost spilled the wine trying to get the glass onto the table.

She leaned forward, reaching out. "But—"

He didn't give her a chance to finish. Or to touch him. "It's late."

Too late for him to be with someone as sweet and wonderful as Rosie. Not after everything he'd seen. After everything he'd done.

He was almost out the door when she spoke again. "Are we still on for trampolines tomorrow?"

He'd almost forgotten they'd promised the boys another outing. He couldn't bail on Noah or Jorge. "We're still on."

* * *

Rosie hated the way Gideon had gone, so abruptly, his expression so dark and tormented. And yet...

He'd taught the boys how to play hopscotch. He'd relaxed at dinner. He'd played for hours. He'd smiled. He'd laughed. He'd come out of his shell. He'd kissed the boys good night. He'd read to them. He'd complimented her artwork.

Then Rosie had become complacent, thinking this meant that the incident at the museum had blown over, that they could talk about it now. Thinking that since the boys could get through to him with their simple questions over a story, maybe she could get through to him too. Thinking about how close they'd become yesterday at the wedding when they'd danced, when they'd shared dinner, when they'd twirled around the dance floor with the boys, when she thought she'd no longer have to tiptoe around him like everyone else, even the Mavericks.

So she'd stopped giving him room…and pushed.

He hadn't clammed up with the boys as he told them a bit about what life in a war zone had been like. And maybe that's exactly what Gideon needed, just simple questions from curious boys. Where he didn't feel he was being forced to confront his past.

The only good thing about his leaving was that he'd been gone by the time the phone rang. At least then she didn't have to explain about the two previous calls. Or how frightened she was by this third one tonight.

The calls came from a blocked number, a breather on the other end of the line. That was all, then she'd hung up. They could be nothing. There wasn't a single thing that pointed to it being Jorge's birth father. Not after all this time, when she hadn't heard from him since the day he told her that having a kid wasn't in his life plan.

But she couldn't shake that feeling. Couldn't pretend she didn't hear the soft whisper of her name in all that breathing. Couldn't help being afraid that if

Jorge's father had resurfaced, it couldn't be for anything good. She would *much* prefer an obscene phone call.

Rosie hadn't even told Ari and Chi about the calls, not with the wedding so close. Ruining Ari's perfect day and honeymoon with worry was out of the question.

And if Gideon found out, she could only imagine how he'd react. Gideon was a protector. Like all the Mavericks. He would have freaked.

Just the way she was freaking.

She'd been keeping tabs on Archibald Findley, of course. Just a few searches on the Internet every couple of months. So she knew where he was.

When he got married, she was actually relieved at the proof that he had completely moved on with his life and would now be creating a family with someone else. But that relief had evaporated a month ago when she'd found that TV interview, the one where Archie and his perfect trophy wife had told the interviewer about their heart-wrenching experience with infertility.

Rosie hugged her knees to her chest, sipped her wine. Told herself, yet again, that she and Jorge were safe here. That Archie wouldn't find them. That he wouldn't even *try* to find them. That he wouldn't bother, not after he'd kicked her out of his life when she told him she was pregnant.

But she couldn't ignore the phone calls. Just as she

couldn't ignore the fact that his wife couldn't give him a child.

While Rosie could.

And had.

Chapter Thirteen

They went to the House of Air trampoline park in San Francisco. The boys took trampoline lessons, learning how to maintain their balance and perform a couple of simple aerial tricks like cartwheels and somersaults. Then they'd done air dunks and played dodgeball and even tried rock-climbing. Noah declared he wanted to have his next birthday party there.

"Ari's going to kill me," Rosie said when she and Gideon were alone for a moment. "I've created a monster."

"No way, she'll love it," he assured her. "She always wants to find new and different things for him to do. Plus, now that he's had lessons, he can practice on his own trampoline without Matt being so nervous."

As soon as Gideon had woken this morning, he'd vowed to do whatever it took to maintain his equilibrium, while being as friendly and relaxed as possible with Rosie. She'd already put up with more than enough crap—she didn't need his long face or a dark cloud of gloom hovering over them for the next two weeks. It was long past time to pull it together. Not just for Ari or Noah this time, but for Rosie and Jorge too.

Fortunately, there was nothing like hours of jumping and dodging and climbing to make you stop thinking about anything at all. Except Rosie.

Because no matter how hard he tried—or how many vows he made to himself—he couldn't ignore Rosie. The way she moved, the way she laughed, the way her tank top hugged her beautiful curves, the way she pulled her hair up off her neck. A neck he wanted to kiss so badly that his insides literally ached with the need.

"You don't have to make dinner again," he told Rosie back at her place as they stood side by side at her kitchen window, watching the boys play. "I can pick up pizza."

Gideon had shown them a string game called cat's cradle, and now, seated cross-legged on the grass facing each other, Noah and Jorge were blissfully unaware they were being observed.

Rosie was right, they were like sponges. All he'd done was mention the game he'd taught Ari as a little girl, and they simply *had* to know how to play it too. After today's activity, he'd have thought they'd be falling asleep, but they just kept going. Kids were amazing—energetic, vigorous, resilient sponges.

Their voices were audible through the glass. "I think it's like this." Jorge leaned forward to touch the string linked between Noah's fingers.

"Isn't this the coolest thing?" Noah replied when they nailed the string's pattern.

"You were a teenager when you showed Ari all these games, weren't you?" Rosie asked Gideon.

"I was, but I liked spending time with her." He grunted a laugh. "Even if my friends in high school thought I was weird for wanting to hang out with my little sister."

"I think it's wonderful how much you cared about her. How much you *still* care about her." Rosie touched his arm, then just as quickly withdrew. He wished the touch had lasted longer. Wished it had been more than just a touch.

When Ari was tiny, he'd already been afraid to leave her home alone with their mom. Even without the drugs, his mother had never quite known how to be the kind of mom Rosie was with Jorge. Though Nadine had done her best, she never knew the right thing to say or do or when to give hugs. Which was all the more reason why he shouldn't have joined the army and left Ari alone when she was eight. But they'd needed the money, and he figured signing up was the best way to get it. Working at a fast-food joint certainly wasn't going to cut it.

But with time, his memory had worn down some

of the hard edges and smoothed out the bad parts. "We didn't have cable," he told Rosie. "Just this old black-and-white TV with rabbit ears. So we watched old movies and TV shows and reruns like *Leave It to Beaver* and *Father Knows Best*, even *The Little Rascals*."

"And your mom loved old Westerns, didn't she?"

"I take it that means Ari told you where my middle name came from?"

Rosie's eyes twinkled as she confirmed his assumption. "I like your middle name. Gideon Randolph Jones. I love that it was inspired by the old Western star Randolph Scott. Those old shows were different, weren't they? The kids played jump rope and used hula hoops and pogo sticks instead of iPad and PlayStation devices."

He nodded. "It was a simpler time."

Was that really true? There'd been nothing simple about carrying his mom to bed when she was on the nod from junk. But he didn't want to think about that, not here with Rosie and the boys playing outside.

"Ari was an inquisitive little girl," he told Rosie. "As she got older and I realized I didn't know the answers to her questions, we would go to the library to figure out whatever we wanted to know. That's how we learned about history and science, and so many games. If she heard about one at school, we'd learn it on the weekend."

"I love that you did that for her."

He shrugged. "It wasn't hard."

She touched his cheek then, made him look at her. When he finally let his eyes meet hers, she said, "It might not have been hard, but most sixteen-year-old boys wouldn't have bothered. You were very sweet to Ari. And she knows that."

He swallowed. He'd done so many things wrong when it came to his sister, it was nearly impossible to acknowledge the things he'd done right.

"When we were in foster care, she used to talk about you all the time," Rosie told him. "I always wished I had a brother like you."

But he didn't want to be her brother. Not in the least. "Do you have any sisters?"

She shook her head. "I was an only child. I was born here, but my parents' family were in Mexico. My dad was a tree trimmer, and my mom was a cleaning lady, so we didn't have a lot of money. But they always sent home what they could."

"How'd you lose them?"

"A car accident when I was eleven."

"I'm sorry." His heart broke for the eleven-year-old girl she'd been. "Why didn't you go to your family in Mexico?"

"I knew how badly my parents wanted me to be an American. That's why they came here, to make sure I was born here. That's why they sacrificed so much. So I never told anyone about my relatives in Mexico, in case the authorities wanted to send me back. Besides, I didn't know them. California was my home." She was matter of fact about her story, but he knew how much it must have hurt. That it likely still did. "I missed my parents so much. But I found Ari and Chi. And then I had Jorge." She smiled. "And now with the Mavericks, I have a huge family."

He couldn't keep his gaze from her gorgeous mouth, her lush lips. He could feel his breath rising and falling in his chest, he could feel his heart beat. And he could feel the warmth of her skin. Her scent was sweet and heady, like the champagne they'd toasted with at the wedding.

"Gideon," she whispered with those kissable lips.

He wanted to touch her, wanted to brush his fingertips over the smoothness of her skin. And then her lips parted, and she was so close, so very, very close. It would be so easy. God, he wanted to kiss her. Wanted just one taste.

A taste to last a lifetime.

"Mom, Gideon!" Jorge called. "Look at the cool things we're doing with the string!"

Gideon started and stepped back. He hadn't simply been about to *kiss* Rosie.

He'd been about to *devour* her.

"Gideon." Her eyes were the deepest chocolate, melting him.

He was breathing hard, as though he'd been

running around the block. "I'll ask the boys what kind of pizza they want. They can go with me to pick it up."

He backed toward the door, because if he didn't, he'd give in to that look in her eyes, the temptation of her lips, of her kiss.

And if he kissed her, he'd be completely lost.

* * *

Gideon and the boys went to pick up the pizzas, leaving Rosie alone for a little while.

Alone and *buzzing* from that almost-kiss.

At last, he'd been about to give in to the sizzle between them. She'd almost been able to taste his lips. Feel the heat of his body against hers. And if Jorge hadn't called them, she couldn't have made herself pull back. Not when she wanted Gideon so badly.

Of course, when they came back with the pizzas, Gideon acted like the moment had never happened. She wasn't surprised by his reaction. Nor was she hurt. How could she be, when she was still floating on a cloud of hope that he'd let himself get that close to her in the first place? She was still his friend first and foremost, but she wasn't planning to lie to either of them by denying her longing for him.

They played card games after pizza. Gideon was a fountain of old games from bygone eras—snap and spoons and spit—and the boys were fascinated with every new one he taught them. Who needed an iPad or a video game or even a TV when you had Gideon?

He was so good with Jorge and Noah, exactly the way she imagined he'd been with Ari when she was six. And even if he sat as far away from her as possible and directed nearly all his comments to the kids, she had a great time.

Then Noah yawned. Caught by the contagion, Jorge yawned too.

"I believe it's bedtime," she said.

Gideon nodded, gathering the cards together into a pile. "We'll get out of your hair."

"Can I come with you guys, Gid?" Jorge begged.

"Yeah, Uncle Gideon, can we have another sleepover?"

Thankfully, Gideon read her face and said, "Not tonight, guys."

"But, Gid," Jorge started, until Rosie shot him a look, which made him immediately clamp his lips.

Last night's phone call had unsettled her, and though she knew Gideon would take special care with the boys, she wanted Jorge with her. She wanted to be able to walk into his bedroom after he'd fallen asleep, pull the covers up, though he would inevitably kick them off, and know without a shadow of a doubt that he was safe.

"We're going to meet up for a hike tomorrow morning," she told the kids. She and Gideon had already planned it. "So you'll see each other again very soon." Which meant she'd get to see Gideon again. Very soon. Though somehow it didn't feel like soon enough.

Jorge knew when not to push. "Okay." He couldn't help the tiny pout. Neither could Noah, as he and Gideon packed his Lego pieces into his backpack.

"Thanks for the pizza," she said. She tapped Jorge on the back, and he repeated, "Yeah, thanks, Gid, it was yummy."

The boys did a complicated handshake good-bye, then she kissed Noah's cheek, finishing off with a hug while Gideon scooped Jorge up for a big squeeze. Then the boys were racing for the door, following the beep of Gideon's key fob as he unlocked the car door.

For a moment, Rosie and Gideon were alone. She felt the heat of the night around them, the scent of lavender in the air and the lingering sweetness of their almost-kiss.

She could feel him battling with himself as he considered whether or not to say something. Finally, he said, "My complex has a pool. You and Jorge could come for a swim after the hike, if you'd like."

She beamed. She would move at whatever speed he was comfortable with—but she wouldn't hide her pleasure at being with him. "Sounds great. I'll pack our bathing suits." For a moment, she swore heat flared in his eyes, turning them smoky.

When he and Noah drove away a few minutes

later, she could only hope that if just the *thought* of her in a bathing suit could heat him up, then the reality of it would finally spark him into full-on flames.

★ ★ ★

Gideon knew he was playing with fire. He shouldn't have come so close to kissing Rosie. But he didn't know how to stop. Not when every self-control trick in his arsenal was failing.

Back at his apartment, he sent Noah to get ready for bed. The kid needed a little independence, rather than having his uncle hanging over him while he brushed his teeth. Besides, Noah wanted to arrange all his Lego creations and toys and books that he'd brought with him. He'd been so tired after all the excitement of the wedding that there hadn't been a chance, and last night, he'd stayed with Jorge.

For years, Gideon had lived in junky apartments. It hadn't mattered to him where he lived—not when his sister, and Karmen, were both lost to him. But when Ari had asked him to watch Noah while she and Matt were on their honeymoon, he'd realized he couldn't bring Noah to a dive in a sketchy neighborhood.

So he'd found this complex with a pool and a second-floor apartment with two bedrooms, two bathrooms, a vaulted living room, and a workable kitchen. The complex wouldn't take Noah's new puppy, but in all other ways, he'd tried to make it great for his nephew. He'd bought cookware and metal utensils and porcelain crockery because paper plates and plastic forks wouldn't cut it anymore. Fortunately, he already knew how to cook—he'd had to learn as a kid when their mom no longer had the capacity.

He'd bought a big-screen smart TV so he and Noah could watch movies and play video games and furnished the second bedroom with twin beds in anticipation of eventual sleepovers with Jorge. He also got a love seat that pulled out into a bed and some bean-bag chairs because, heck, what kid didn't love a bean bag? Plus, he had a waffle maker, a blender for smoothies, and a grill for toasted cheese sandwiches.

Unfortunately, the mental inventory of his kitchen wasn't pushing away thoughts of Rosie. Of how he'd almost kissed her. Of how he wanted her with raw need. A desire he had no business feeling.

Not after what he'd let happen to his team. Not after what happened to Karmen.

As always when he thought of Karmen, it was with a mixture of guilt and grief. And just like always, he reached for the last thing she'd given him. The only piece of her he had.

He kept the painting locked away in the bottom cupboard of the bookshelf, locked away as if he could lock away all the emotions that went with it. When she'd given it to him, Karmen had explained it belonged to her grandmother. He could hear her now, telling him the story.

"*Abuela* said it was very special, magical, and that because of its powerful magic, I would one day be compelled to give it away. She said the power in it must be passed on and that I would know the right moment to let it go." She'd held it out to him. "And now you are the one who needs it most."

He remembered laughing off her story, wondering what the hell he was supposed to do with a painting out in the damned sandbox anyway. Especially when he'd never kissed Karmen, never touched her, never told her he had feelings for her. Feelings that seemed inappropriate for a woman he worked with. But because they were friends, and she'd been so insistent, he'd taken the little painting and tucked it in with his small stash of personal items.

Two days later, his entire team and Karmen were dead.

And all he had left of her was the painting.

He wished she'd told him more, explained what he needed to do instead of reeling off a bunch of magical mumbo-jumbo. He would have done whatever she wanted, fulfilled the legacy, but he didn't have a clue what to do with it. Since it had come from Karmen's grandmother, Gideon guessed the artist might be Mexican, but it was signed only with initials.

What exactly could the painting mean? What was its power, its magic? On the surface, it was a religious depiction of two angels, one with dark skin and hair, the other light-skinned and light-haired, their arms outstretched to each other, their index fingertips touching.

All he knew was that the angels hadn't saved Karmen. The painting hadn't saved her. And Gideon sure as hell hadn't saved her.

The artwork in his hands made his heart hurt, made his eyes ache, made every bone in his body feel like it was breaking. Karmen had said it should stay with him until he felt the moment was right to pass it on. But what if he was never able to let go? Not only of the painting, but of Karmen and his guilt over the deaths of his team members? All his fault, all his responsibility.

Warm fingers touched his neck, and Gideon belatedly realized Noah was slipping his arm around his shoulder. He hadn't even realized his nephew was there. He'd been buried in his memories, his guilt.

"It's okay, Uncle Gideon, I get sad sometimes too."

Awe passed through him, that this amazing, beautiful, wonderful child knew exactly the words Gideon needed to hear.

So many times, he'd held Karmen's painting. So many times, he'd held back tears, never letting himself cry despite the shame, the guilt, the unworthiness. But in this moment, with Noah's gentle words ringing in his head, he laid the painting aside and wrapped the child in his arms.

Then he finally let out the tears he'd denied for so long.

He didn't know how hard he squeezed Noah or how long Noah held him. Until his nephew said, "I'm ready for bed. Will you tuck me in, Uncle Gideon?"

"Yeah, sure thing, kiddo." Gideon picked him up.

And as he carried the boy to his room, Noah reached up to wipe the tears from Gideon's cheeks.

Chapter Fourteen

"This is a great hike, Gideon. How'd you find this place?" Rosie asked.

He had picked up Rosie and Jorge at nine to beat the heat, then taken them to a rarely used trail in the Santa Cruz Mountains. "Some locals told me about it."

The redwood trees were immense, bathing the trail in cool shade. Squirrels darted between the branches, and a couple of minutes ago, two deer had bounded across the path in front of them. There were no car engines, no gas fumes, just an earthy peace that settled into Gideon's bones.

The boys were racing ahead, then running back, probably getting twice as much exercise as he and Rosie were. "Watch out for poison oak, you two," Rosie called after them. She'd had them all put on a protective lotion too.

He felt strangely light after last night, when Noah's little-boy hug had broken some sort of dam inside him. And following Rosie up the trail added to his sense of lightness. He shouldn't be looking at the gorgeous sway of her hips, but it was impossible *not* to notice everything about her. Not just how sexy she was, but that she was a good mom to Jorge, and Noah too. A good friend to Ari. Not to mention smart and talented and dedicated.

"Last night Jorge wanted me to read more of *Revolutionary War on Wednesday*," she said, "but I told him we needed to wait for you and Noah. You did such a great job answering their questions the other night." She turned around and walked backward a moment. "I hope it wasn't hard for you to read it. I know it's not about your war, but it could still be disturbing for you."

"Maybe a bit," he admitted. "War is war. No matter what the time period is." He shrugged, trying to make it look offhand. "But I don't mind telling them."

She cupped a hand around her mouth conspiratorially. "What was that about sand in your underwear?"

He laughed. And damn if it didn't feel good. He didn't want to be grilled, but talking to Rosie was different. "You obviously heard every detail," he said with a smile. One that felt a heck of a lot easier today.

"I was shamelessly eavesdropping," she said, then turned forward again to call to the boys, "Don't get too far ahead of us old folks back here." Then she spoke to him over her shoulder. "You said some days it was boring over there. Really? Boring?"

"Yeah." He half snorted the word. "Tower duty could suck. Six hours of watching for anything suspicious. But we did good works too, trying to build trust with the locals. We constructed schools. Even dug a well for a small village whose well had become contaminated." It had felt good at the time. Worthwhile.

"Did you ever get time off?"

"Not a lot. Idle hands and all that. They wanted to keep us busy. But we figured out how to have fun. Me and my buddy Zach, Zach Smith—they called us Alias Smith and Jones—he was a huge prankster. We both were, to be honest. One time we switched the gear for Shrimp—he was the tallest guy in our unit—with Dozer."

"Don't tell me. Dozer was the shortest." The laughter in her voice filtered back to him, doing things to his insides.

"You got it. So Shrimp tries to pull on his pants and starts cussing up a storm that the locals he'd paid to do his laundry had shrunk all his stuff. And Dozer says, 'Give me twenty bucks and I'll let you use mine 'cause they seem to have stretched.' Swear to God, Shrimp gave him the twenty bucks."

He hadn't thought about all that in years. They'd played a whole lot of harmless pranks, and it kept the guys laughing. Over there, laughter had been like medicine.

Talking to Rosie was like medicine now.

"Why did Shrimp have to pay someone to do his laundry?" she asked, holding a low-hanging branch out of the way so it didn't slap his face. "Didn't you guys have some sort of unit that did all that stuff?"

"Nope. You did your own. If the base was big enough, you might have a couple of machines or even a real laundromat. But small bases without any running water, you'd have to handwash it all in a bucket." Or you stank, he mentally added.

"Now I'm feeling all high maintenance for needing running water for my washing machine and my dishwasher and my garbage disposal."

He thought of Karmen. Before she'd joined up, she'd been a real girly girl, according to Mrs. Sanchez, her mother. But Karmen had lived like the rest of them with never a complaint.

"You'd have done fine," he told her. Rosie was the furthest thing from high maintenance. "You get used to the food and the routines and the job and the people." He'd gotten used to it, even the guard tower, though, thank God, he'd eventually been promoted out of that duty. He'd reenlisted a few times and might even have re-upped again.

If he hadn't lost his team.

In all the time he'd been back, he'd never thought of any of this. Not until now. He'd only thought about that day, the IED, his team, Karmen. But he'd realized when he was answering the boys' questions the other night that every day hadn't been a firefight. Sure, there'd been bad times. But there'd been a lot of good days too.

And talking to Rosie about it was as much a release as letting it out with Noah last night had been.

"Thanks," he said softly.

She stopped a second, looked back at him. "For what?"

"For listening." And for not asking the hard questions, he thought to himself. He had the sense, though, that when the time was right, he could tell Rosie. She would listen like a friend.

Because, he suddenly realized, she *was* his friend. She always had been, since the day Ari had introduced her.

* * *

When they returned to Gideon's apartment complex for an afternoon of swimming, the boys rushed off to Noah's room to change into their swim trunks. Rosie had her bathing suit in her carryall.

As Gideon went into his bedroom to put on his trunks and she used the hall bathroom to change into a one-piece and a semi-sheer cover-up, Rosie marveled at how differently today had turned out to be. Far from what she'd expected.

After last night's almost-kiss, she'd assumed he'd

tell himself he'd been crazy and resume efforts to block her out. But if anything, he'd seemed more easy and open with her on the hiking trail than he'd ever been before. He'd talked about the war, what it was like in the Middle East, about daily life. He'd even laughed— with her, not just the kids. There hadn't been dark clouds hanging over him. Twice in two days, he'd opened up about his life over there.

He was letting down his walls, not just with the boys, but with her.

He was starting to see things differently, that it hadn't been only darkness. There'd been good things too. And he'd shared all that with her. He'd let her help him, taken what she had to offer. Just the memory of it made her heart feel fluttery.

Gideon's apartment was surprisingly kid-friendly, with bean-bag chairs, a big-screen TV, an Xbox, lots of children's books, and a toy box full of Lego pieces and robots and dump trucks and cranes and diggers. Noah was a great one for building. Ari said he wanted to be a structural engineer when he grew up. Trust the son of a robotics billionaire to decide at such a young age that he wanted to be something so specific.

Rosie was about to plop down on the love seat to wait for Gideon and the boys when she saw the painting. Right before she almost crushed it.

She tipped her head, looking at it sideways. Then looked at it the other way. The painting was small, a twelve-by-twelve square in a plain frame. But the detail was phenomenal, the two angels rendered precisely. It wasn't a print—she could tell by the fine lines in the paint that it was old. Well used, well handled, and well loved.

She wondered why such a precious piece of art wasn't hanging on Gideon's wall.

It wasn't until she bent over and examined it more closely that she saw the initials.

Oh my God. It couldn't be. Could it?

"What are you doing?"

She jumped away from the painting so fast, she almost fell backward. Gideon hadn't yelled, his voice hadn't even been harsh, yet she still felt like she'd been caught snooping.

"The painting. I almost sat on it. But thankfully, I didn't. And when I looked closer at it, I—"

Her words fell away as he grabbed the painting, holding it close to his chest. Agitation had turned his eyes stormy.

"Where did you get it?" she asked softly. How long had he owned it? Did he even know what it was? Maybe it wasn't real. But what if it was? She had so many questions, it was hard to sound casual.

"A friend gave it to me," he said, a hint of caution in his voice.

It must have been some friend. "Can I look at it? Please?"

For a moment, she thought he might not let the painting go. Finally, he turned it around for her to see.

Good Lord. "It's amazing," she whispered. "Do you…" She had to take a breath before asking, "Do you know the artist?"

He shook his head. "It's just initials. *MFC.* I have no idea who painted it."

She wasn't an expert, by any means. But she had not only studied art history, she *loved* art history. And she loved the work of *this* artist most of all.

"Do you remember Jorge's favorite painting at the Legion of Honor?"

He nodded. "The scene in the square with the lady. I liked that one too."

"Did you notice the signature on it?" When he shook his head, she said, "It's by Miguel Fernando Correa. He always signed with his initials." She pointed to the corner of the painting, barely able to contain the excitement rippling through her body. "*MFC.* Just like that."

★ ★ ★

Rosie would never lie to him.

But he still couldn't believe it was true.

They were all outside at the pool, the boys splashing around with the inflatable rafts Gideon had bought them, while beside him on a lounge chair, Rosie was typing into her iPad.

"I'd never seen your painting before," she said. "It's a very different style from his other work that I'm familiar with, but even when I first saw it, there was something about it that grabbed me in the same way *Holy Day in Monterrey* does."

"When we were in the museum..." He spoke slowly, as though he was only just beginning to put several disparate puzzle pieces together. "I felt the same way. Like there was something familiar about that painting. Something I couldn't put my finger on, but couldn't ignore."

Gideon had always been careful to put away the painting in the bottom cupboard of the bookshelf. Until Noah's kindness and empathy last night had made him forget the very thing he never forgot. No one had ever seen Karmen's painting. Not until Rosie.

She looked at her shoulder, which was turning a little red in the sun. "I think I'm burning." Setting her iPad aside, she reached into the bag by the side of her chair and pulled out a big tube of sunscreen.

He told himself not to look as she slathered her legs. But his eyes refused to listen to his brain, hungrily tracking every move.

Gideon could feel his breath in his chest and hear his pulse beating in his ears as she smoothed lotion over her arms, her shoulders, the nape of her neck. Then dipped low into her cleavage, making sure she covered the line of the suit.

"Do you need some?" She held up the tube.

Unable to speak, he simply held out his hand. She was still rubbing her lotion in when he was done.

"Can you get my back for me?" she asked.

Touch her? The thought thrilled and terrified him.

She smiled over her shoulder, and he could have sworn there was a challenge in her eyes as she nonchalantly slid her legs to the other side of her chair and presented him with her back.

He glanced briefly at the boys. If they called his name, if they asked him to play with them, he wouldn't have to find out if his self-control was up to the task of touching Rosie without dragging her into his arms and kissing her breathless. But Noah and Jorge were having so much fun on their own that, for the moment at least, Gideon and Rosie were forgotten.

He squeezed the lotion onto his hand, spread it out between his palms, taking his time, steeling his nerves.

Then he touched her.

Sweet Lord.

Her skin was so warm. So smooth. With a delicious golden glow. As he glided down, down, down, she was fire beneath his fingertips.

And he was burning up all over.

She made a noise, a hum, almost a moan—but that had to be his lust-filled brain playing tricks on him.

"I think you missed right here." She reached back to point to the base of her shoulder blades, then held her ponytail out of the way.

His hands were actually shaking as he glided up, rubbed the lotion in circles over smooth skin, then up to her nape, massaging her.

"Oh my gosh." She made another of those sweet little sounds. "I always get knotted up right there." This time it was definitely a moan. He felt it deep inside his own chest. "Mmm, that's *perfect*."

As he used his thumb on the knot he could barely feel, could she hear his labored breathing? Could she feel the drumming pulse in his fingertips? Did she have any idea at all how much he wanted her? With every last fiber of his being.

Finally, she turned her head to look at him again. "Thank you, Gideon. I feel so much better. Do you want me to get your back?"

"No, I'm fine," he said so quickly it was almost one word. He was anything but *fine*. His blood was still rushing like Niagara Falls as he leaned back in his chair.

"Did you ever try to research the painting?" She went back to her iPad as if nothing had happened.

While he was a mess of ragged nerve endings.

"No." As he watched the boys splashing and laughing, he wondered how he was supposed to explain about Karmen. "My friend—it belonged to her grandmother." He'd held so much back from everyone for so long, but in the span of these past few days, his carefully constructed barriers seemed to be crumbling one after the other. His throat constricted. He'd heard boa constrictors could swallow their weight in prey—but he felt like he'd swallowed an elephant. "She said the painting was magical."

He'd never told anyone about the painting, not even Ari. Though his sister knew he'd met with Karmen's mother, they'd never discussed what happened over there—the sandbox, the hellhole.

But now that Rosie had not only seen Karmen's painting—but had also seen his painting that was of everything *except* Monet's *Water Lilies*—he knew he needed to tell Rosie.

And it would be as much a release as talking to the boys about the war, as much as telling Rosie about daily life in the sandbox, as much as letting go last night with Noah. Each word out of his mouth was like a revelation, not only to Rosie or the kids, but to himself.

"Her name was Karmen Sanchez. She was a combat medic working with my unit."

* * *

Rosie had never felt anything as good as Gideon's hands on her. His touch had been hotter than lying in the sun, sweeter than feasting on vine-ripened grapes. She never wanted him to stop, and for a few blissful moments, she'd focused on nothing but his touch. And yet, though his fingers no longer glided over her skin, this moment, when he was actually trusting her with his story, with his past, with his pain—this moment was monumental.

"She was a great soldier," he said in a low voice made raw with emotion. "She wanted to join up right after her cousin died in the Twin Towers, but her parents made her finish college. After that, she was in all the way. She wanted to make a difference."

"She sounds heroic." Just like Gideon.

"Too heroic," he said softly. "I tried to get her to stay inside the wire."

"Inside the wire?" She didn't want to interrupt his flow, but she needed to understand.

"Back at the base. Where it was safe. She could have taken care of the wounded back there. But she wanted to follow us outside the wire."

"Couldn't you have ordered her to stay inside?"

"She wasn't in my command, not directly. Medics go on patrol with whatever team needs them. But she was with my team a lot—enough that she was one of us. And she was good. Calm under fire. Everyone respected her. She did whatever she had to do, took whatever risk was necessary to save others."

Karmen sounded like the kind of woman Rosie strove to be for Jorge, even if she often fell short. "She sounds amazing."

"She was." He swallowed hard. "She gave me the painting a couple of days before she died. Like she thought I'd need its magic." He ran a hand over his face. "There was an IED."

He was so silent, so still, she didn't know whether it was better to be quiet, or to try to draw him out with a question. Especially when she was almost positive this was the first time he'd opened up to anyone about it.

Yet he continued on his own. "My guys. They got taken out." He held his breath a long moment, as if absorbing the blows all over again. "And Karmen, she rushed in like she always did. Because that's what she did, she helped whoever needed her. Regardless of the risk to her own life." Regret was etched into the lines of his face. "A sniper shot her."

"I'm so sorry, Gideon." Rosie wanted to gather him close, hold him the way she would hold Jorge, soothe his pain. "You must have loved her very much." A woman as brave, as fierce, as fearless as he.

"She was a close friend."

Though she didn't believe that was all there'd been to their relationship, she didn't push. Instead, she said, "I'm so sorry about your friends, your team."

He stared at the boys splashing their way across the pool, his eyes hidden behind his sunglasses, his features immobile. Until he finally spoke again. "It's almost like she had a premonition, and that's why she gave me the painting. She said I was supposed to pass it on when the time was right. All this time, I've been waiting for some sort of sign." Frustration rose in his voice as he said, "I just wish I knew what the *magic* is that she was talking about."

Rosie didn't want to utter some meaningless platitude like, *You'll know it when it happens.* Instead, she said, "If it's truly magical, then wouldn't it be the painting's job to tell you when the time is right?"

He thought about that for a long moment. "I'd have to believe in magic," he said. "But I suppose if I did, that would make sense."

Surprised, and pleased, that he didn't fight the idea of *magic* for too long—even if he wasn't completely sure he believed in it—she said, "Whatever happens with the painting, I have faith in you, Gideon. Just as Karmen did."

He sat in silence as if absorbing her words. After long seconds, maybe even minutes, he turned to her. "I don't know what I could have done to earn your faith in me. But I'm not going to lie and say I don't appreciate it. Because I do."

"Thank you for having faith in me too, and for sharing your story." She flashed him a smile, trying not to make a big deal of the *massively* big deal of a conversation they'd just had. "What do you say we join the boys in the pool?"

They jumped into the pool, where they spent the rest of the afternoon playing Marco Polo and doing cannonballs off the diving board. And though neither of them said another thing about the painting, or

Karmen, for the rest of the day, Rosie knew in her heart that they'd chipped away great big pieces of the wall that Gideon had built around himself. What he'd experienced had been the worst life could throw at him. But today, during their hike, he'd acknowledged that some good things had happened over there.

It meant so much that he'd been able to share both the worst and the best with her. It meant so much that he'd unburdened himself. It meant so much that he'd let her in. She could already feel the healing begin for him. And she was glad his walls were dropping.

So damned glad.

Because Gideon deserved every good thing life could bring him.

Even magic.

Chapter Fifteen

Gideon had admitted to Rosie that he'd failed both his team and Karmen. Yet Rosie hadn't hated him for it. He'd been right: Sharing his story with her had been a release, easing more of the tension twisting his insides. The ache would never go away—but his body felt looser now. For the first time in a very long while, he didn't feel like a coiled snake ready to strike.

After the boys finally agreed to get out of the pool and dry off, Gideon made spaghetti for dinner, with homemade sauce, not bottled. Rosie prepared the salad, while the boys slathered garlic butter on the bread and watched it toast under the broiler.

After the four of them ate, they played Monopoly. For just a little while, he thought about nothing but games and the boys. And about Rosie, of course, which was a given since he couldn't get her out of his head, no matter how hard he tried.

At eight o'clock, Rosie told Jorge, "Time to go. Let's clean up the board, guys."

"Can Jorge sleep over?" Noah had perfected that

please-please-please pout, his hands together in pleading. Jorge imitated him.

Gideon was sure she'd give in, but she shook her head.

"No, honey, you need to come home with me."

"I won't let anything happen to them." Had she reacted more to his story than he'd thought? Didn't she realize that he would never make the mistakes of his past, not with the boys?

"It's not that," she said, meeting his eyes. "I would never doubt you."

His heart felt at least two sizes bigger with her sweet words. "Then what is it?" The boys were carrying the Monopoly box to Noah's room, letting the adults battle it out. Smart kids. "I thought we'd promised the boys sleepovers for these two weeks." Hah. Three days ago, he'd been the one fighting the idea.

She gathered up her stuff, tossed her iPad in her bag. "It's nothing. We just can't do it tonight."

Nothing meant it was *something*. If anyone knew that, he did. "Tell me about nothing, then."

She pulled the elastic band out of her ponytail, running her fingers through her silky hair. Just that quickly, he was back by the pool with lotion on his palms and her smooth skin beneath his fingers.

"Rosie...talk to me." He'd shared with her, now he hoped she'd do the same with him. "Please."

She crossed her arms over her breasts, hunched in on herself in a way he'd never seen her do before. "I've gotten a couple of hang-up calls."

"You mean like obscene phone calls?" His skin crawled, and his fingers curled into fists.

She shook her head. "There's just someone breathing on the other end of the line. And I..." She paused, her face going pale. "I think I know who it is." She looked down the hallway toward Noah's room. The door was closed. "I think it's Jorge's father."

He'd wondered more than once about Jorge's father, but he'd never felt he could ask either Rosie or Ari for information about Rosie's past. Not when he hadn't been willing to share *his* past beyond the imperative details.

She lowered her voice, even with the closed door. "We broke up before Jorge was born. Even though I was only nineteen, Jorge and I were way better off without him."

"Was he abusive?" Again, Gideon's hands clenched into fists at his sides.

Her lips flatlined. "No, he just didn't want to be a father."

"And you haven't seen the guy since?"

She sniffed, part disgust, part anger, part *I don't care*. "Like I said, he wasn't interested in having a kid. He left when I told him I was pregnant."

What an asshole. But there had to be something

more to make her so worried today, something he wasn't getting. "So what makes you think it's him calling now?"

"It's just a feeling."

Until now, he'd always been the reticent one. But the tables had turned, and he was fishing for information. Enough, at least, to know if he needed to tear the guy apart with his bare hands. Or worse. "But he doesn't say anything when he calls?"

She grimaced. "I might have heard my name."

"Your *name*?"

"Yeah, just a whisper." Her lips twisted. "Sort of like he's taunting me. *Ro-o-o-o-sie…*"

This was not good, really not good. "Why do you think he's come back after all this time?" he asked. Although he could guess.

She breathed in, huffed out, then confirmed his suspicions. "I think he wants Jorge."

No. Gideon's heart seized as though someone had squeezed it in a vise. "But you said he didn't want to be a father."

For the next few minutes, she gave him the whole story about seeing her ex in a TV interview with his wife, talking about babies and infertility. Rosie was nearly certain that meant the wife was infertile.

"And you think that after seven years," he said, "this guy gets married and suddenly decides he wants to have kids?"

"Yes. Or maybe his wife decided for him."

"So he dumped you when it suited him, and now, because it suits him, he's barging back into your life because he covets your son."

"Yes." She closed her eyes, dipped her head. "I know my ex. Because his wife can't have a child of her own, he thinks it would be a great idea to take mine. He would only think of himself—it's the way he's wired. Which I didn't figure out until too late."

Gideon wanted to wrap Rosie in his arms and make it all better. He wanted to snap his fingers and wipe all her pain, and her fears, away. He wanted to smash her ex down. But most of all, he wanted to keep Jorge safe forever.

"When I met him," she said in a low voice, "I thought he was smart and charming. He was older, and I let him beguile me into thinking that he could help my art career. I believed everything he said. I thought he was something special. But he wasn't. He didn't care about my art. He didn't care about me. And he sure as hell didn't care about Jorge." Her voice rose slightly, with frustration and anger.

His fists bunched tight with the need to crush the guy. And his heart ached with the need to pull Rosie close, to hold her, to feel her lean on him, to give her whatever she needed.

For now, however, all he could do was gather as many details as possible. "Was he some sort of art professor?"

"Archie was a gallery owner." She laughed, but there was no humor in it. "He hated it when I called him that. He always insisted on Archibald. Archibald Findley."

Archibald Findley. Gideon hated the man, hated the pompous name, hated anyone who could treat Rosie and Jorge the way he had, as though they were disposable.

"He owned a prestigious art gallery in San Francisco called Impressions," she continued. "Everyone wanted their work to be shown there. If you got into his gallery, you had made it."

As she spoke, Gideon could see how it had been for her all those years ago. A girl only months out of high school, needing affirmation from some big, important person that she could be great.

"He told me my paintings were amazing. He told me I was talented. He told me I was going to be such a huge success. And I believed him. He was going to do this big show just for me. But there was always one more little thing that needed to be tweaked on a painting." She sighed. "Then I found out I was pregnant. And there was no more Archie, and there was no more show, and I was alone. If he had been a good man, I would have wanted him in Jorge's life. I would never have kept my son away from his father, unless it was absolutely necessary." Her expression hardened. "Archie made it clear to me that it was absolutely necessary that both I, and the baby, went away, lest we ruin the fancy life he'd worked so hard to build." She swallowed hard. "He told me never to make the mistake of contacting him again. Or to try to get child support. He said the best thing I could do was—" It was obvious that she could barely say the words. "He wanted me to get rid of Jorge."

Gideon couldn't stop himself from laying his hand on her cheek. "I'm so sorry, Rosie."

She covered his hand with her own, as though to take strength from him before saying, "I wasn't alone, fortunately. Because I had Ari and Chi. They helped me through school. They helped me with Jorge. Anything I needed, they were always there. Jorge and I, we would never have made it without them."

Her skin was warm beneath his palm—and her hand over his was sizzling. "I see now why you love my sister so much."

She smiled with memory. "I loved her before that. Chi and Ari and me, it was like we were sisters who were separated until we were thirteen."

He'd always thought of Ari as being alone, out there by herself against the big bad world. But she'd never truly been alone. Not when she'd had Rosie and Chi. It eased a small piece of his soul to know the three of them had been so close and supportive of each other while he was gone.

Unfortunately, none of that changed the situation with Rosie's ex. He was still the worst kind of man, and he still needed to be shut down. "I say we take a trip up to *Impressions*—" He didn't hold back the snide note in his voice at the stupid name. "—in San Francisco and put the fear of God into the guy."

She pulled away as she shook her head. "No. No way. That would be like spraying a hose into a hornets' nest. We should just leave this whole thing alone. As long as I keep Jorge near me, I feel so much better."

He didn't want to upset her any more than she already was, but he had to make her face reality. "What are you going to do when Jorge goes back to school and you return to work? Because if it really is your ex, and he really is after Jorge, then he's probably waiting for you both to be in two different locations, leaving Jorge vulnerable." Too much was at stake to pretend otherwise.

Her face turned pale and stricken.

"I'm sorry," he said. "I don't mean to scare you. But we've got to be prepared for anything." Especially since Gideon knew firsthand that sometimes the worst really did happen. "Let me take care of this for you, Rosie."

He would do anything to keep her and Jorge safe.

And this time he absolutely would not fail.

★ ★ ★

What had she done?

Gideon was a big protector, all muscle-bound, military style. She should have known he wouldn't let this go. She trusted him and respected his opinion—of course she did. Only, if Gideon went poking around, then Archie could very well retaliate, not just against her, but against Jorge *and* Gideon. She would never forgive herself if anything happened to her son or the man she was coming to care for so deeply.

"Archie doesn't live in San Francisco anymore," she told him. "When he left, he shut down the gallery in the city. He's somewhere out in Vegas now."

Gideon's eyes took on that dark, stormy cast. "Las Vegas doesn't mean you're safe."

For a guy who didn't talk much, he sure as heck was doing a lot of talking now. "Look, really, I can handle it."

"Rosie—"

"I'm just going to get Jorge and take him home. We'll be fine." She sidestepped Gideon and headed to the bedroom door.

But when she opened it, the boys were already fast asleep in the twin beds, their faces angelic.

Foiled at every turn. She sighed as she closed the door on them. "All right, you win. He can stay." In fact, now that she had calmed down a bit, she could see that Jorge might even be more protected here. Because if Archie was planning something, then the safest place her son could be was with big, strong Gideon. "I'll head out now and be back early, before they wake up."

But Gideon was shaking his head. "I don't think you should go home by yourself. Not when you'll be safer here too."

"I really can't." Her mind worked to find a valid excuse. "I mean, I don't have a change of clothes. Or even a toothbrush."

Even as she spoke, her heart was urging, *Stay*.

"I've got an extra toothbrush," he countered. "Brand new. And I can lend you a clean T-shirt until we get back to your place tomorrow morning."

"You have all the answers, don't you?"

He grinned. Gideon Jones actually grinned. With her. And without the boys nearby. It was amazing.

It might even be a miracle.

Plus, he was right that she would be safer here. She shuddered at the thought of Archie prowling around outside her cottage. What if he showed up tonight and she was alone? What would she do? What *could* she do?

The truth was she didn't know exactly what Archie was capable of, or to what lengths he'd go to get what he wanted from her. All she knew was that he had a lot more money than she did. If it came to a fight in court, he might win. No matter what, she needed to keep her son out of a potentially ugly court case.

Then Gideon added one more inducement. "I'll worry about both of you all night long if you go. Please stay."

The wind went out of her remaining protests. Yes, she wanted to be independent, but she wasn't stupid. And her heart squeezed tight at the thought of Gideon worrying about her.

"Okay," she finally said. "I'll stay the night. Thank you." She held out her hand to shake his, as if they were making some sort of deal. As if they were business associates instead of—

She didn't know *what* they were. Even *friends* didn't seem quite right anymore.

When he took her hand in his, there was nothing even remotely businesslike in his touch. She felt the earth move, felt it shake, felt her world tilt. The way it had when she was dancing with him. And when he'd cupped her cheek only minutes before.

"You can have my bedroom," he said in a low voice, "and I'll sleep out here on the couch."

"I can't let you do that." She fluttered a hand at the love seat, then raked her eyes over his long, tall, gorgeous frame. "There's no way you'll fit."

"It's a pull-out sofa. I'll be fine."

"I don't mind taking the sofa."

"Nope. Ari would read me the riot act if I didn't treat you right." He followed up his words with another smile.

She'd already been a goner before this. But when he was charming? And smiling? And touching her every five minutes?

No woman alive would stand a chance.

She held up her hands in surrender. "All right, I'm sold. I'll take your bed. But I'm going to make you a really nice breakfast tomorrow in return."

"Deal."

Who would have guessed that tonight she'd be sleeping in Gideon's bed?

The only thing better would be if he were sleeping in it with her.

Chapter Sixteen

Gideon handed Rosie a new toothbrush, then showed her where the extra pillows and blankets were. "If you need anything else, just tell me."

"Thank you," she said softly. "Not just for your bed tonight, but for listening. And not getting all judgy about any bad choices I might have made."

"You heard my story, so you know I can't make judgments." Not that he would have anyway. Rosie was the world's best mom to Jorge and the world's best friend to Ari. Nothing in her past could change that. "I'm glad you're staying, Rosie."

It was the most he'd ever allowed himself to say about his feelings for her. Considering everything they'd shared tonight, shutting down again no longer seemed the only—or the best—option. Actually, it was kind of impossible now. They'd come too far.

"I am too," she said. "Thank you for everything."

She stunned the hell out of him by going up on her toes and kissing him, her mouth pressing against his.

Then her lips were gone, she was on her own two

feet again…

And his heart was full to bursting.

He wanted to pull her into his arms and kiss her senseless. But it hadn't been that kind of kiss. It had been something better, something more important. Sweet and rich with gratitude and friendship.

And trust.

He backed out of the room, waving his hand stupidly. "Good night." He closed the door. Ten seconds later, he had to knock again. "Sorry. I need to get some sweats to sleep in." He also grabbed his toothbrush, his shaving kit, and a T-shirt.

She was smiling when he closed the door behind him again.

"She must think I'm an idiot," he muttered as he grabbed his laptop, unable to stop reliving the moment her lips had touched his.

No one would ever be as enticing to him as Rosie. He'd known it almost from the first time he set eyes on her. And now that he knew how it felt to kiss her, even if the kiss was barely more than a breath of air over his lips, he couldn't imagine ever feeling for anyone else what he felt for her.

He wanted to slay her dragons, but to do that he needed to find out more about Archibald Findley. He'd make sure Findley didn't dare to even *try* taking Jorge from Rosie.

He was typing *Archibald Findley Impressions Gallery*

Las Vegas when it hit him why Rosie painted only for herself: She was afraid Jorge's father would find her if she put her artwork out there.

All the more determined to help her, Gideon silently vowed to do whatever it took to make sure Jorge and Rosie were safe.

* * *

Gideon had been floored when she'd kissed him, his eyes dazed for long moments afterward.

Truthfully, Rosie had surprised herself. She hadn't planned the kiss—but she hadn't been able to ignore her instincts either. Not anymore. Not after everything they'd shared today, from his humorous memories about life in the army, to his heartrending story about the death of his comrades, to her complicated confession about her mistakes with Archie.

What would he have done if she'd asked him to share the bed with her? She had been *so* tempted, when her lips were on his and his muscles were hard and enticing beneath her fingertips. She'd ached for it.

But she hadn't acted on it. Gideon wasn't ready for that. And in all honesty, neither was she.

For Gideon's part, he'd only just begun to trust her. It meant so much to her that he did, but she couldn't make the mistake of moving too fast with their bodies while their hearts still needed to catch up. Especially when he wasn't the only one wrestling with his choices from the past.

Since learning she was pregnant with Jorge seven years ago, Rosie had steered clear of dating. After all, she'd made a truly crap decision in letting herself fall for Jorge's father, and with a son to raise, she couldn't afford to trust another man unless she truly knew him and his intentions. Gideon was different. Despite his silences and stony expressions, he'd interested her from the start. With all the glowing things Ari said about her brother, with every moment Rosie had watched him with her kid, with Noah, she'd learned to see past Gideon's walls to the man he really was.

A good man. An honorable man. A caring, loyal man.

Even if he no longer seemed to believe those things himself.

Post-kiss, with her lips and her body still tingling, she wasn't tired. With her iPad in her lap, she knew exactly what she had to do for Gideon: find more info on the painting. Over the years, she'd learned a lot about Miguel Fernando Correa, since she and Jorge both loved the painting in the Legion of Honor museum. Tonight she would research Gideon's painting specifically, since it was so different from Correa's other work.

Fortunately, one of her electives in college had been art research—what resources to mine, what clues to search for, how to dive into the rabbit hole of a piece's origins.

At last, she could put all that knowledge to use. For Gideon.

⁂

The boys had yet to come out of Noah's room the following morning when Gideon heard his bedroom door open. His heart stopped at the sweet sight of Rosie, her gorgeous curly hair wild around her beautiful face, her tempting mouth beckoning him over for another kiss.

As he'd tried to fall asleep last night, he kept thinking about her smiles, her laughter, about her lying in his bed...and sleep became a distant memory, knowing she was only a wall away.

She stopped in the middle of the living room when she saw the sleeping bag wadded up on the bean bags he'd pushed together. She pointed in horror. "You didn't sleep on those, did you?"

He'd jumped into the shower in the hall bathroom before everyone got up and hadn't put the living room to rights yet. Grabbing the sleeping bag, he started stuffing it into its carrier bag. "It's not a big deal. I've slept in worse places."

"Right." Her pretty smile was nowhere in sight as she hugged her iPad to her chest. "Of course."

She must be imagining what it had been like in the Middle East, with the dust and the sand and the wind and the death. But he didn't want her to go there, just as he didn't want to go there himself anymore. He wanted them both to remember only the good things he'd told her yesterday, about him and Zach, about building schools, about helping villagers.

"The boys are playing in Noah's room," he said. He smiled thinking of them. Being with Rosie and the kids made him smile more than he was used to. A lot more, considering *zero smiles* was his default expression. "They said no parents allowed."

Thank God the mention of the boys brought back Rosie's good humor. "They're probably building an amazing Lego structure ten feet tall to show off to us."

"Probably." He found himself smiling again, just from the look on her face when she talked about her son.

"Well, I promised you a nice breakfast." She clapped her hands lightly. "Time to get started."

"I already made coffee."

"Man of my dreams." Her lips curved up, and his heart beat faster with how badly he wanted that to be true.

In the kitchen, she poured coffee into the mug he'd left on the counter for her. She must have had more than just a swimsuit in that bag she'd brought with her, because she was wearing a different shirt from yesterday, and not one of his. Colorful and slightly sheer, the flowery cover-up was spiced up with a bright tank top underneath, leaving her bare shoulders a mouthwatering sight through the filmy material.

He needed to control himself. Especially the need to truly be the man of her dreams. In her bed, in her life, in every way possible…

When she turned, leaning back against the counter, her eyes sparkling from the hit of caffeine, he had to confess what he'd done last night. Her trust meant everything to him. He wouldn't break it now, or ever.

"Look, I have to tell you—" he began.

She said, "I think you should know—" at exactly the same moment.

As they both stopped speaking, he lost himself in her coffee-colored gaze, in the scent of her in his kitchen, in the vision of her asleep—and naked—in his bed last night.

"You go first," he suggested.

"Okay." She paused a beat, before saying, "I looked up more about your painting. Did some research." She held up her hand as if warding off potential objections. "I know I should have checked in with you before my deep dive on the Internet, but you know how much I love art. And I've got this majorly huge feeling that your painting is rare and totally awesome." Her eyes were alight with excitement.

That's who Rosie was. She threw herself into things, whether it was playing Marco Polo in the pool with the boys, or jumping her heart out at a trampoline park, or creating an incredible painting at a museum. He was sure she'd even be enthusiastic about accounting too. Rosie would never do a half-assed job at anything.

Now it seemed she'd found a cause in him. Or at least, his painting.

He could never be angry that she'd tried to help him. "What did you find out?"

"I'm not completely sure yet," she admitted, "although my gut tells me I'm on the right track. Miguel Fernando Correa always signed his work with just his initials. And since he was born in Mexico City in 1705 and died in 1798, he had a huge body of work. Some of which could have been unaccounted for until now."

"I'm pretty sure Karmen's family came from Mexico City."

"That's good to know," she said. And then, "He did a lot of city scenes like the one at the Legion of Honor. He did tavern scenes or people in salons or churches. There was even a series of bullfights. As well as ordinary people going about their business, like women carrying water. He was a people guy, not a landscape guy."

Gideon thought back to the painting he'd seen in the museum. It had an amazing amount of detail, from the clothing to the faces, even the buildings and trees.

"He also did portraits, especially of famous people

of the time." Rosie opened her iPad and tapped to bring up a photo of a painting he hadn't seen before. "This is a portrait of Diego and Catalina Sanchez. I gather they were a prominent family, to be able to hire him."

"Karmen never said anything about prominent ancestors." Although she had been extremely wealthy. She'd told him her dad was an important business type, but it hadn't seemed significant back when making it from one day to the next was the only thing that mattered. For the first time, Gideon wondered if Karmen's distinguished roots originated much further back than two generations. How long had the painting of the angels been handed down?

"The only break in Correa's usual style was during this one period around 1775, when he did a series of religious paintings. Angels, mystical themes that represented God or Jesus looking down from the clouds. I found a photo of a huge painting of a battle between the angels and Satan called *Battle of Angels*. It's at the Metropolitan Museum of Art in New York City."

"Have you been there?"

She shook her head. "I've never been out of California."

He should have guessed that. Every penny went to raising her son, so how could she have bought a plane ticket to New York and splurged on a couple of nights at a hotel, just to go to a museum?

But he could take her there. He had the money. He could take Rosie and Jorge, book a plane and hotel for them right now if they wanted to go. If only he could suggest something like that without freaking her out, or making her think he wanted anything from her beyond friendship.

Especially because he absolutely wanted more, when he couldn't stop thinking about kissing her again, whether he deserved Rosie or not.

She tapped the iPad again, snapping him out of his crazy thoughts. "This is the one at the Met."

The painting was a masterpiece of armor-plated angels fighting Satan and his demons. Though he wasn't an art buff, Gideon could easily see the similarity in style to the portrait of Diego and Catalina Sanchez and the painting in the Legion of Honor. But what about Karmen's small painting?

Rosie zoomed and pointed. "See the initials? See how similar the flare of the letters is?" Clearly reading his mind, she added, "I know it seems crazy to think that Karmen's angels are by an artist so famous his work is in the Metropolitan Museum of Art. But look at this." She flipped to another open tab in her browser. "Here's another one from Correa's religious period."

A godlike figure with a flowing gray beard and snowy white robe reached down from his perch on a pink and gray cloud.

"It's not very big," she said. "Twelve by twelve,

like yours." Then she scrolled to the headline of the news article: *Lost Painting Discovered*. "This was just last year." She lowered her voice to whisper, "This painting sold at auction." She held her breath one long moment. "For fifty million dollars."

His stomach felt like it had dropped out of a skyscraper. *"Fifty million?"*

"I'm no expert, Gideon. You'd have to have someone authenticate the painting. More than one person, probably. But from everything I've found online, it looks like Miguel Fernando Correa's work. And," she added, pointing at the iPad, "that trademark signature of his looks just like the one on your painting."

Though he couldn't argue with any of her research, Gideon could barely wrap his head around it. "Fifty million," he repeated in a voice hoarse with disbelief.

"While all of his work is valuable, the religious paintings are even more so because they're rare. He painted eight that are known, though his journal entries pointed to the possibility of a ninth." She put her hand on his arm. "Yours could be the ninth."

He shook his head slowly, words beyond him now. For years he'd carried Karmen's painting around in his pack from one run-down apartment to another. The most he'd ever done for its safekeeping was to lock it in the cabinet of his bookshelf after he'd moved here.

Had Karmen had even an inkling of the painting's

worth? "Why would she have given it to me?" he asked in a hollow voice.

He didn't need more money. The truth was he had more than he knew what to do with. He'd banked all his re-up bonuses, invested the money. He'd lived on practically nothing since he got out, everything going into investments that he could someday use to help Ari. The truth was he could already afford a fancy car, even a fancy house. Nothing on the scale of Matt's place, but a damned fine home.

"Maybe she didn't know what it was worth. Or…" Rosie looked fit to burst as she said, "maybe she knew how many people you could help with it. You could set up scholarships for people who can't afford to go to college, or build homes for people who need them." She held her arms wide as if she were holding all the possibilities in the world.

He remembered Karmen's words: *You'll know when it's the right time to pass it on.*

For so many years, he'd been waiting for a sign. Now, he wondered if what he'd really been waiting for was Rosie. Not only to see the painting and recognize the artist, but more important, to fill him with the kind of hope he hadn't thought he'd ever feel again.

"I need to call Evan," he said. "Since art is probably part of a lot of rich people's investment portfolios, he'll likely know who to contact to find out if Correa really painted this."

And if this truly was a Miguel Fernando Correa painting, that would mean Gideon could help foster kids like Ari and Rosie and Chi had once been. He could provide aid to returning vets with terrible injuries, or those who couldn't seem to fit in anymore, the ones with PTSD. He could help the families of the soldiers who'd never come back.

You'll know when it's the right time to pass it on.

Maybe the right time was now, if the painting was worth fifty million freaking dollars.

★ ★ ★

Rosie prayed she wasn't getting Gideon's hopes up for absolutely nothing. But her gut *felt* the rightness of it.

She hadn't wanted to blindside him with the information. But she'd been so over-the-top ridiculously excited about the painting—and all the possibilities it could lead to—that she could barely sleep last night.

Of course, there'd also been the fact that she was lying in Gideon's bed. The touch of his lips crept into her dreams when she'd finally fallen asleep. And boy oh boy, were they erotic dreams.

Snuggled into his bed, she'd given more thought to how she'd steered clear of men after Jorge was born. She hadn't wanted Jorge to become attached to a man only to have him turn out to be a creep or a liar or unreliable or lacking in staying power and integrity.

But Gideon was different from any man she'd ever met. He was like the Mavericks—good, strong, caring. So while it had felt right to hit the pause button after their kiss last night, she wasn't at all sure that she needed to keep holding the button down.

She was sure of one thing. Right at this very moment, Gideon had the look of a man who'd been hit with a stun gun, his eyes a soft blue in his surprise— and budding hope.

"So...you had something to tell me too?" she prodded gently.

He nodded, his eyes changing color again, this time to a cross between faded and stormy blue. "I looked up Archie. I hope you're not upset with me."

"If you hadn't looked him up, you wouldn't be the man I—" She broke off before she could blurt out the enormity of her feelings for him. Feelings that ran far deeper than just desire or friendship. Feelings that might very well freak him out if he knew just how strong they were. "The man I've come to know these past months," she finished. "Now, tell me what you found."

The boys were still in Noah's room, working on their Lego surprise, and breakfast could wait a few more minutes.

"The deadbeat opened another Impressions in Las Vegas. It's in the Forum Shops at Caesars. He doesn't have much of a web presence—just a website with one page for contact information. And he doesn't seem to do much to promote any of his artists. From what I could find, everything he's sold has been auctioned off for huge amounts of money. And he's all over the society pages, going to galas and openings. I can't quite put together why he'd have a gallery in a mall in Vegas, instead of in LA on Rodeo Drive?"

Rosie had no clue why Archie had gone to Vegas. She'd just been glad he'd left the Bay Area. "Did you see the clip of that TV interview with his wife?"

Gideon nodded. "He's smooth. So smooth that my instincts are screaming there's something else going on beneath the surface." The same way his gut had told him to hold his team—and Karmen—back that fateful day in Ramadi. He would never ignore his gut again. "Something shady."

Rosie opened her iPad again. "Do you remember any of the artists' names? The ones you said he sold a painting for?"

He rattled off a name she didn't recognize, and Rosie tapped it in. "See, that's really odd."

"What?"

"So there's this one huge sale." She pointed to the brief article that came up. "But nothing else. Give me another name." The same conclusion came up. "It's just one sale. And it's weird that he didn't have a show for either of these artists."

"Very shady," Gideon agreed as he angled his body,

looking at her now, not the iPad. "We don't know for sure if these calls you've been getting are from him. But we need to watch out." He reached out with one finger, tipping her chin toward him. "You'll tell me if he calls again, won't you?"

Of course she could take care of herself. She had for years now. But she loved that Gideon was looking out for her too. Just as she loved the sweet sensation of his touch.

"I'll tell you," she promised.

Just then, the boys flung open Noah's door and blew like a mini tornado into the kitchen. "What's for breakfast?" Noah said.

Jorge echoed, "I'm starved."

"And when can we call Mommy?" Noah asked. "We made a huge Lego tower. I want to show her on FaceTime."

"It's for you too." Jorge smiled up at Rosie.

"Gideon can help you call while I'm making breakfast," Rosie suggested. "How about some waffles?"

As she cooked, though everything in her life seemed up in the air, Rosie's heart felt lighter for the first time in a very long time. Not only would Gideon never allow anything bad to happen to her son, but at last, the two of them were forging a relationship that felt more real than any she'd ever had before.

Chapter Seventeen

After devouring the best waffles Gideon had ever tasted, the four of them dropped the painting off with Evan. He promised to make a few calls regarding a valuation while they went to a Triple-A league baseball game featuring the Santa Clara Rockets versus the Saratoga Stallions.

Not surprisingly, the boys went wild. They cheered whenever someone crossed home plate, even though Gideon tried to get them to pick a team to root for. They ate hot dogs and popcorn and drank soda.

The lady in the seat in front of them said they made such a happy family. And that was how it felt—like they were a family, like they were happy, like nothing else mattered but the afternoon they spent together having fun.

Even with Rosie's ex and the worth of the painting still hanging over them.

For so long, darkness had shrouded everything in Gideon's life, even his longed-for homecoming with Ari. But when he was with Rosie, Jorge, and Noah, light was determined to shine through.

The only downside to the day was that Rosie didn't try to kiss him again, even though he couldn't help wishing she would. Just as he couldn't help wishing that he was worthy enough to kiss her himself.

They were just leaving the game when Evan called. "Can you swing by the house after the game?"

"Sure thing. It just finished, so we'll head there now."

"Great. Paige is making cookies for the kids. I think she's eating more dough than she's putting on the cookie sheet, though."

When Gideon first met Evan last year, the guy had been married to Paige's sister. Evil sister, actually. A more miserable guy than Evan, Gideon had never seen. But his divorce from Whitney was final, and with Paige, Evan was a new and extremely happy man.

Gideon shoved his phone back in his pocket. "Evan wants us to come by."

"Did he say anything about the painting?" Rosie asked as the boys raced ahead to the car, while he and Rosie kept their eyes trained on them.

"No. He was pretty casual, said Paige was making cookies for the boys. Doesn't sound like he's got big news. Maybe it's not what we thought." A part of him would be glad not to give up Karmen's painting just yet and thereby lose his last thread of connection to her. Yet at the same time, he'd feel a great disappointment to lose the chance of making a difference in so many lives with the proceeds from the painting's sale.

"I guess we'll know when we get there," Rosie said mildly, as though it was no big deal.

Even though they both knew it was a *huge* deal.

The drive to Evan's home in Los Altos didn't take long, and the boys were soon piling out of the car and racing up the front walk. As he and Rosie followed, Gideon desperately wanted to hold her hand. As though they truly were a happy family.

And Rosie was truly *his*.

Paige threw open the front door and gathered the boys into her arms. She was a pretty woman with auburn hair, and her face glowed as she hugged Noah and Jorge close. At the scent of freshly baked cookies wafting through the air, the boys raced into the kitchen, with Paige following, leaving Evan to invite Gideon and Rosie inside.

Like the other Mavericks, Evan was tall, fit, and good-looking, but he'd always struck Gideon as the quiet one in the bunch. Maybe it was the glasses that made him seem more studious. He was the finance guy who likely had a whole host of art appraisers on speed dial, which was why he'd felt like the best choice to bring the painting to, even though Sebastian and Charlie were both artists.

Evan shook Gideon's hand, then gave Rosie a quick hug. "Come on in."

The house Evan had lived in with his first wife had been a bona fide mansion. This place, however, was more a home than a showpiece. The rooms were big enough for entertaining, but not overwhelming. Evan took them into the living room, which had been remodeled into a library with floor-to-ceiling bookshelves. Artwork, Chinese vases, and small porcelain figurines were scattered here and there, but mostly it was books—hardbacks to paperbacks, finance tomes to mysteries, coffee table art books to biographies.

"Can I get both of you a drink?" he asked.

"Not for me, thanks," Gideon said. Whatever they learned about the painting, he wanted to have his wits fully about him.

Rosie shook her head with a smile.

They took the sofa, while Evan sat in a comfortable wing chair obviously used for reading, if the stack of books on the table beside it was any indication. The painting, sitting in the middle of the coffee table, was now wrapped in brown paper and tied with string.

"As both of you know, people like to invest in art," he began. "It makes them feel good to think they've not only got beauty, but also an appreciating asset." Evan pulled the string out of its bow and opened the flaps of the paper. "My art appraiser looked at it. He had a buddy of his look at it too. And that guy had a guy as well."

"You haven't been rushing all over town for this, have you?" Gideon hadn't meant to put Evan out, or interrupt his busy work schedule.

"Nope, all I did was make a couple of calls. Once the appraisers saw the painting, they were more than willing to drop everything for it."

Gideon's stomach did a backflip. Next to him on the couch, Rosie was as still as a cat hunting a gopher.

Evan pushed his glasses up his nose. "As far as those three experts are concerned, this is an original Miguel Fernando Correa."

"Oh my God," Rosie said on barely more than a breath.

While Gideon felt the air sucked out of his lungs, without being able to drag in a single breath.

Evan went on, "When Correa was in his seventies, he entered a period where he painted only religious subjects. That lasted exactly two years, almost to the day. No one quite knows why. But that makes his religious works extremely rare."

"And even more valuable," Rosie added.

"Exactly."

Gideon heard Evan and Rosie as if their voices were coming down a long tube. He saw their mouths moving. He heard the boys' voices drifting in from the kitchen as they begged Paige for another cookie. But it was all from a long distance. It wasn't that he hadn't believed Rosie. But he hadn't accepted the possibility of the painting being a Correa, not truly. It had been more like a weird dream. A crazy, no-way-this-could-ever-actually-happen-to-me-in-a-million-years possibility.

"As I believe both of you also know, the last one of these paintings went for fifty million dollars." Evan smoothed the paper down around the painting, as if he were afraid to actually touch it. "That was last year. As this appears to be the ninth in the series that everyone always hoped existed but could never actually prove, the interest for it is going to be *huge*. They think this might go for even more. Of course, they still need to do a technical authentication. But in a situation like this, it will get priority and shouldn't take too long. At which point, they can take it to auction almost immediately after it's been authenticated."

His words hung in the air, beating like wings over Gideon's head. "Why would Karmen give it to me?" he said aloud, more to himself than to Rosie or Evan.

Karmen had carried the painting to the Middle East in her duffel, for God's sake. And he'd been hauling it all over the country in his pack, appreciating that it was a beautiful painting from a close friend. Not a priceless work of art.

And though he knew how much good he could do with the proceeds from an auction, he suddenly wasn't sure he could part with everything the painting symbolized. His life prior to that awful day when so many of his friends had died. The man he'd been but wasn't anymore. And his feelings for Karmen, unexpressed and intangible.

"There are so many possible reasons for giving it to you," Rosie said softly. They'd discussed that Karmen might not have known the worth of the painting—or if she did, that she'd wanted him to sell it and do good with the money. "But all I can think is that most of all, Karmen wanted you to have it because it was special to her. And so were you."

* * *

Until now, Rosie hadn't really thought beyond the worth of the painting—and all that the sale of it could do for people in need. Last night the thought of fifty million dollars had seemed so exciting, so amazing, so unbelievable.

But from the look on Gideon's face, it was blindingly obvious that the painting wasn't just an artifact to him. It wasn't just a nearly priceless wonder of the art world. It didn't just carry with it all his pain, all his turmoil, all his heartache. And it wasn't simply Karmen's final gift to him either.

The painting *was* Karmen.

And no matter how much money it was worth, or what he could do with that money, or how many people it could help, for Gideon, selling it would still feel like letting Karmen go.

Rosie wanted so badly to wrap her arms around him and tell him everything would be okay. It was an instinct she had to give in to, and she was reaching for him when her phone rang. She'd been so intent on Gideon and the painting that the sound jarred her so badly, she almost jumped right off the couch.

Not wanting to disturb Gideon's train of thought in such an intense moment, she pulled her phone out of her purse and walked across the room to answer it. She didn't recognize the number, but sometimes her boss asked potential new accounting clients to contact her directly so they could discuss her methodology. "Hello?"

"Hello, Rosie. It's been a long time. Have you missed me?"

Her stomach froze. Her teeth chattered. She was suddenly so cold, her hair might break off in icicles.

"I'm in town and I thought we could get together for a nice cha—"

She stabbed *End* before he could finish.

Archie had found her.

★ ★ ★

Something was wrong. Dead wrong.

Rosie stared at her phone as though she were in a horror movie where she was the only one who could see the spiders crawling out of it.

"Excuse me a minute."

Gideon didn't hear Evan's reply. He was only vaguely aware of the boys running into the living room. When they would have raced to Gideon, Evan called them over, saying something Gideon couldn't hear, something that was enough to have them flopping down on the sofa.

Then Gideon was by Rosie's side at the far edge of the room. "What's wrong?" he asked softly, wanting to gather her up in his arms and make it all better.

"He's in town," she whispered as the phone fell to the rug from nerveless fingers. "He wants to get together to talk."

Gideon picked up her phone and shoved it in his back pocket. "We need to call the cops."

"And tell them what? That my ex wants to talk to me?"

"He's been threatening you."

"Only he hasn't—not directly, anyway. I don't even know if those calls were from him. This was a different number. And those calls were on the landline at the house, not my cell phone."

The phone call was like a one-two punch. First the painting and now this. She was in shock. Maybe they both were. But though Gideon knew Rosie was right about the cops not being able to do anything with the information they had, he still needed to make sure neither of them were hiding from the truth. Especially one that put either Jorge or Rosie at risk.

"One thing we know for sure. He's tracking you. Just like you figured, you can't assume he's going to leave you or Jorge alone the way he has for the past seven years. And even if his name isn't on the birth certificate, which I'm assuming it isn't—" She nodded. "—it's still all too easy for him to get a DNA test. Which means we've got to fight him head on to make sure he doesn't dare try to claim his parental rights."

While he spoke, Rosie kept her gaze fixed on Jorge across the room. It never wavered now. "All these years," she said softly, "I just stuck my head in the sand. I didn't even do anything about it. I just told myself that since he didn't want anything to do with Jorge as a baby, he never would. I should have gotten a lawyer and had all the legal stuff in place to make sure he didn't try to claim parental rights in the future."

Gideon reached for her hands and held them tightly. "Stop beating yourself up. You couldn't have had any idea he'd try something, after the way he kicked you to the curb." But there was something else he needed her to know. Something that could outright terrify her. "If you don't know what your foe wants, you can't fight him on level ground. That's the first step in every battle plan. Which means someone is going to have to make contact with him. And soon."

But Rosie didn't look scared. Of course she didn't. She was a fighter, brave as hell. Especially when it came to her son. She looked defiant, her mouth set, her eyes narrowed.

"You're right. I need to know exactly why he's reaching out to me, not just guess at his reasons because of that TV interview with his wife. He needs to declare himself. Then I'll know what the next move is." Her voice was strong and utterly determined as she added, "Which means I have to meet him." She looked straight at Gideon, her dark eyes blazing. "Right away."

It was exactly what he'd expected her to say. Exactly what he'd *worried* she'd say when he didn't want her in the same country as the guy, let alone the same city. "I'm coming with you."

Thankfully, she didn't argue. "You'll scare the poop out of him—even with a glance."

"That's the plan," he said. And then, "We go together, we find out what he wants. Then we neutralize him."

She took her phone from him and made the call.

Chapter Eighteen

Paige sent Jorge and Noah back into the family room located off the kitchen to watch cartoons—the housekeeper, Mrs. Mortimer, would take care of them if they needed anything—while Rosie and Gideon explained what had happened.

Worry lines creasing her forehead, Paige looked stricken by the news. "I'm so sorry you've got this huge, horrible thing hanging over you, Rosie. What can we do to help?"

"Whatever you need," Evan offered.

Rosie's stomach was tumbling so fast, it made her feel dizzy. But she had to be strong. For Jorge. "I would really appreciate it if you could keep the boys for a couple of hours. I've just set up a meeting with my ex."

Rosie wished she hadn't hung up on Archie the first time. It had been harder to call him back, almost as though she was begging for a meeting. But she'd done it because they needed to know what he really wanted. No more guessing.

"Of course. We can keep them for as long as you

need." Paige's smile was kind and warm.

"It's our pleasure," Evan agreed.

"Thank you," she said to them both. She wished she had the words to explain how much their help and support meant, though she had a feeling they already knew.

Rosie and Gideon went into the family room, and she knelt in front of Jorge. "Gideon and I have to go out alone for a little while, okay? So be good for Paige and Evan and Mrs. Mortimer."

"Okay, Mom."

Rosie stroked her son's face. The heartache she'd felt when Archie walked away all those years ago meant nothing once she'd had Jorge, with his soulful brown eyes, his dark curly hair, and his gorgeous smile.

"You are such an amazing kid," she whispered. "I love you."

"I love you too, Mom." As if he was an old soul who knew exactly what she needed, he threw his arms around her and let her hug him fiercely.

Over Jorge's shoulder, she saw Noah hug Gideon's leg. Gideon dropped his hand to the boy's head, stroking his silky hair. The unconscious gesture was so loving, so caring. So Gideon.

As Gideon led her out of the house and down the front path to his SUV, leaving her son behind where he would be safe, he wrapped her fingers in his big warm hand, held on to her, and promised her solemnly, "I won't let anything happen to him."

"I know," she said.

Gideon would keep that promise, no matter what.

* * *

Archibald Findley had chosen a posh restaurant in Saratoga, where parking was done by a valet. But Gideon didn't like having his keys out of his hand, especially when facing down a foe, so he parked the car himself in a lot across the street.

They were shown to the table by a tuxedoed maître d'. Rosie's ex was already seated, drinking something dark in a short tumbler. The tables were covered with white cloths and burgundy napkins and flickering candles, while the overhead lighting was low. The glassware glittered like crystal.

Gideon figured it was a fifty-dollar-a-plate joint. What a pompous douchebag.

Findley rose as they approached. He was over six feet, but Gideon was taller. And a hell of a lot bigger.

"Rosie, you look just as ravishing today as you did all those years ago." Findley was like an aristocrat out of a PBS *Masterpiece Theatre* series, with high-society manners and the sheen of wealth, but a cutting edge just below the surface. "And this must be your boyfriend. Or is he your bodyguard?" He smiled, oozing smarm instead of charm.

"Do I need a bodyguard?" she asked, her voice

without a trace of anxiety.

"From me?" He laid the flat of his hand against his chest as though shocked she could think such a thing. "Never. Do have a seat."

Gideon held the farthest chair out for her, then pulled his own as close to hers as possible. Throughout this ordeal, he wanted her to feel him there beside her, to know that he was there for her. No matter what Findley dished out.

A waiter appeared promptly to take their drink orders. Both Rosie and Gideon stuck with water.

Gideon took those moments to assess Archibald Findley. He was impeccably dressed in a blue suit, his shirt crisply white, his striped blue tie tacked down with a winking ruby stickpin. He'd slicked his hair back with some gel, the black shot through with streaks of gray. He gazed at Rosie out of eyes so deep they were almost black. Snake eyes.

He looked like a movie gangster hiding out in the back of his favorite Italian restaurant. Gideon half expected *The Godfather* theme to start playing.

"Tell me all that you've been up to since I last saw you," Findley requested.

You mean since you dumped her, pregnant and alone. Gideon felt a growl rise up in his throat. But on the drive over, Rosie had said she wanted to do the talking. Though he knew she was right—she needed to be in control, and he understood why—it was still difficult to keep quiet counsel when in the presence of such scum. It had to be enough for Gideon to be her muscle today. Still, if Findley so much as blinked out of turn, Gideon would destroy him.

"I got my degree in accounting," she told her ex, "and I have a good job in a CPA firm."

"I'm so glad you continued with your schooling, given how difficult it is to break into the art world. It's always good to have a backup plan. I believe you'll remember I told you that." Findley tried to pat her hand, but she pulled away before he could.

"What do you want, Archie?"

"Archibald," he corrected with an oily smile, enough to grease the wheels on a track. "I simply want to catch up with you after all this time."

"Like I said, I'm fine," Rosie said, her eyes narrowed, her nostrils slightly flared.

"And what about the child?"

"My child is fine."

Findley reached out again, on the pretense of touching her hand, when it was clear that all he really wanted was to bat her around like a feline playing with its prey before it pounces.

Again, Rosie moved out of reach, leaning back, crossing her arms and legs while also shifting her body closer to Gideon.

The waiter arrived with another whiskey for Findley, scooping up the empty glass. Her ex swirled the ice cubes in his new glass. "It must be very hard being a single mom," Archie noted.

"It's been no trouble at all." She shook her head, tossing a curl away from her temple, "No thanks to you."

"You knew I had no choice at the time," Archie said with an air of regret. Regret someone else might have believed was real had they not already been primed to see the scumbag he was. "But I've regretted the necessity every day since."

"Whatever you've done and whatever you regret make no difference to me," Rosie replied.

Archie made a little face, as though he was disappointed in both her and her response. "Whatever you say, I'm sure it's very hard to raise a child on your own. What with medical bills, child care, school fees— it must get harder all the time."

Gideon wanted to fire back by informing the slimeball that Rosie had plenty of friends to help and support her. But he couldn't do anything to jeopardize their mission—they needed to know what the guy wanted. What's more, they couldn't risk giving Findley ammunition for any plan he had in mind.

"We're fine, Archie. We've been fine since the day you left. In fact, that day was a blessing. We don't need anything from you. We never did."

He heaved a dramatic sigh. "Don't you think a child should know his father? Especially when I could be so good to the boy, give Jorge everything he's currently lacking. I'm sure you'd love to send him to a better school than the one he attends now."

Her shiver at the fact that Archie knew Jorge's name was almost imperceptible. Gideon felt it only because they were sitting so close. Thankfully, Rosie didn't give away a thing. "My child's school is just fine."

"But think of how much easier *your* life could be." He leaned in, lowered his voice. "You wouldn't have to scrimp and save." He spared a condescending glance for Gideon. "You could even go out with men of a higher quality than a beefcake bouncer."

Though Gideon could feel her stiffen at the insult, her voice remained calm as she said, "I'll repeat myself one more time, just to make sure you understand. My child has everything he needs."

But Archie clearly wasn't planning to back down so easily. "Ah, but he could need so much more in the future." He waved a hand airily. "Say, if you were to lose your job. Or your home, because you couldn't make the rental payments. Or if you suddenly found your credit rating had taken a nosedive."

Gideon wouldn't stand for another minute of this crap. "Are you threatening Rosie?"

Findley shot a sneer Gideon's way. "Nothing of the kind. I'm just talking about some of life's occasional misadventures, things that can happen to anyone, anytime."

Oh yes, he was most definitely a snake, slithering at the base of the tall grass rather than coming right out and saying what he wanted.

"It's time to tell Rosie what the hell you want." Gideon didn't succeed in completely holding back his growl. Hell, the guy was lucky he hadn't already torn him in two.

Findley ignored Gideon. "Perhaps we should meet alone, Rosie. We haven't talked about your art. You know how much I always wanted to help further your career."

"You never wanted to help her." Now that the gloves were off, Gideon couldn't keep his fury inside. "Only yourself."

Though Gideon could see Archie's skin pale slightly at the thought of a skirmish with someone so much bigger than himself, the man still didn't back off. "Ah, it sounds like Rosie has been telling stories. Only, I have to wonder if she's told you everything, the *real* story, the one only she and I know."

Gideon knew Findley was baiting him. He wanted Gideon to walk out of here and start questioning Rosie. He wanted to drive a wedge between them. What a fool her ex was not to realize that would never happen. Clearly, he'd never understood Rosie at all.

Before Gideon could reply, Rosie spoke. "*You* are the one who doesn't know the real story, Archie. And no, we won't be meeting again, alone or otherwise. Because now that I know exactly what you want, I promise you that you're *never* going to get it."

Then she stood, looped her arm through Gideon's, and walked with him to the door.

* * *

Rosie's stomach twisted with the nerves she'd done her darnedest not to show to her ex. "Do you think he can do any of that? Get me fired? Get me thrown out of my cottage? Ruin my credit?"

"Hell, no." Gideon drove like a bodyguard, his eyes front, then on the rearview mirror, then checking his sides as he kept watch for a tail. "You've got so many people who care about you and can help you. We're not going to let him hurt you." He reached out to squeeze her hand. "You did great with him, Rosie. You didn't so much as break a sweat."

"Yeah, you're right. I did do great." She still felt sick, though. "Even if I wanted to throw my water in his face."

"Yeah, well, I wanted to punch him."

What had she ever seen in Archibald Findley?

But she knew exactly what it was. He'd been so smooth, saying all the right things to a starry-eyed girl barely out of high school. He'd played her with such expertise, wining and dining her and telling her everything she wanted to hear, how great her art was, how beautiful and sexy she was, how smart, how mature for her age. If only she'd seen through his act back then the way she now saw through his fishing, his needling, his subtle threats.

After they pulled up outside Evan and Paige's home, she said, "Thank you for coming with me. I'm not sure I could have been so strong if you hadn't been there."

"Of course you would. You *are* strong. Never doubt that."

"I just wish I'd gotten more of an outright declaration of intent out of him."

"He was never going to give you that, no matter what you said or did. He's a snake, crawling through the grass, striking when you're not looking. He'll never be up front. Which is why we can't fight him up front either. We're going to have to be as sneaky as he is."

"I hate being sneaky," she said.

"I know you do. I'm sorry all of this is happening to you. But I promise, it will all be over soon. And you'll prevail. Because there's no way any of us are going to let scum like your ex win."

"Thank you, Gideon."

He'd been so wonderful during the confrontation—and so wonderful now as he worked to reassure her—that she couldn't resist placing a soft kiss on the corner of his mouth. Last night her kiss had been full of gratitude. Today, though she was even more grateful to him for all his support, her kiss was about so much more.

And when she pulled back, his eyes were the softest baby blue.

For just a moment, she considered pulling him close again, putting her mouth on his, parting her lips, tasting him, savoring him, never letting him go.

Until the front door opened…and the moment between them broke as they both climbed out of the SUV and walked up the path.

Jorge grabbed her hand. "Aunt Paige found the coolest puzzle for us to work on. Come see."

Noah dragged Gideon inside to look. The puzzle was of Big Ben in London, and they'd already finished putting together the outside pieces.

"I need to get some Lego kits," Paige said. "But for now, this was all I had."

"They love it," Rosie told her. And then to Jorge, "You two have done a really great job with this puzzle. I'm so impressed."

"Got a minute?" Gideon said to Evan.

"Sure." Evan led them back into the living room, leaving the boys in the dining room with the puzzle. "How'd it go?"

Rosie paced as she gave them the rundown on Findley's thinly veiled threats.

"I was expecting something like this." Evan shook his head gravely, settling his glasses more firmly on his face. "I've got the rest of the guys prepped. I know it's already been a long day and evening for you both, but we'd like to have a meeting ASAP to figure out the best way to handle this creep."

"I'm more than happy to play with the boys while you go meet with the other Mavericks," Paige offered. "And if there's anything else I can do to help, please let me know. I made sandwiches for them a little earlier."

"Thank you." Rosie's eyes welled up with her emotions, her fears, her gratitude. "I don't know what to say other than thank you from the bottom of my heart."

"You're one of us, Rosie." Evan gave her the gentlest of smiles. "The Mavericks take care of their own."

She'd been to their barbecues, their pool parties, their holidays, their homes. But she'd never dared to call herself one of them. She was Ari's friend, that was all.

What she hadn't counted on was how big their hearts were.

With Gideon's being the biggest of all.

"Thank you," she said, her appreciation heartfelt. "Let me just say good-bye to the kids and tell them I'll be back soon." She didn't like leaving Jorge again when she'd only just returned. But there was no choice. She had to talk with the Mavericks, had to find a way to stop Archie. "Boys," she called.

"Is it time to go?" There was something almost anxious in Jorge's voice as he scrambled off his chair and raced toward her, Noah close on his heels.

Then somehow, Jorge's feet got tangled—whether it was his shoelace or Noah's foot, she couldn't tell—and he went down with a *thunk*.

He was a tough little guy and usually he bounced right up as if he'd never fallen. But this time Jorge started to cry. Rosie was there in a moment to grab him up in her arms. "You're fine, sweetheart." She ran her hands over his legs, then stood him up on his own. "See? Nothing broken. You're fine, everything's okay." She kissed his tear-streaked face. "I'm going to go out for a little while, then we'll get you home for a story and bed, okay? I know it's been a really long day."

She said the words as much for Gideon and Noah, who stood beside them, as she did for Jorge. As though she needed to calm them all, ease their tension.

But Jorge clung to her, his voice rumbly with tears. And he had never been a clingy child. "Why do you have to go? Why can't I come with you?"

"I won't be long, I promise." She stood, smoothing her hands through his dark, curly hair.

But Jorge's tears didn't stop. He held on tight, his arms around her legs. And Rosie realized it was all too much for him. He was an intuitive child, and he felt all the undertones roiling in the room, sensed her fear, her agitation. He knew something was wrong, and in his little-boy world, he was terrified. She stroked his hair, murmured soothing, comforting sounds, but his body still shook.

She couldn't leave him like this. She just couldn't. As much as she needed to conquer Archie, her little boy's needs in this moment were more important.

She looked at Gideon, putting everything she felt into her gaze. "I need to stay."

"I'll go," he said, understanding perfectly. "You don't need to worry. Take care of Jorge. He needs you right now."

She wanted to throw her arms around Gideon, but all she could do was mouth, *Thank you.*

Then Gideon did the most wonderful thing. He wrapped his arm around Rosie's neck, hauled her in, his hand on Jorge's head. "I will fix this," he whispered into her hair. "I promise."

She had no doubt that he would. She'd never had any doubts about Gideon. He was strong, he was loyal, he was caring.

And he would protect Jorge the way her son's own biological father had never cared enough to do.

Chapter Nineteen

The meeting was held at Will's compound in the downstairs game room. His housekeeper, Mrs. Taylor, provided drinks, while outside, Harper and Jeremy attempted to train the two puppies, Flash and Duke. Jeremy had chosen the name Duke because he wanted a regal and powerful name for his puppy, while Noah had named Flash after his favorite superhero.

The room was a powerhouse of Maverick muscle—Daniel Spencer, Sebastian Montgomery, Evan Collins, and Will Franconi. The only one missing was Matt. None of them wanted to disturb his and Ari's honeymoon.

"Tell us what the guy said, Gideon." Daniel sat with legs spread, elbows on his knees.

"He knew Jorge's name and hinted that he also knew where Jorge went to school. And he has both Rosie's home and cell numbers."

"He's obviously been researching her," Will said.

"That's not the worst part," Gideon told them. "He very casually wondered what she'd do if she lost her job, her home, and her credit rating." His blood felt like it would boil over at any moment as he thought about the smarmy bastard.

"The creep is playing games," Evan noted. "Implied threats. Telling her what *might* happen. He must think he's so smooth."

"He didn't come right out and say he wanted to take Jorge away from her, did he?" Sebastian wanted to confirm.

"Nope. He simply implied that Jorge could have so many more advantages if his birth father got involved in his life. From what I could tell, he's feeling her out right now. He wants to know if it'll be easy, if there might be something she wants, or if she thinks Jorge is a burden and he can just flash a little money and she'll fold."

"Fat chance," Daniel said, the words almost a growl. "Rosie is like a mama bear with Jorge. She'll tear her ex to pieces before she'll let him near her son."

"I agree," Will said. "Jorge is everything to her. There's no way she'd fold. The guy obviously doesn't know her at all."

But, clearly, the Mavericks *did* know Rosie. Her devotion, her loyalty, her spirit, her strength. And how amazingly huge her heart was.

"If anything happens to Rosie or Jorge…" Gideon couldn't finish the thought, not when even the remotest possibility of their coming to harm destroyed him. "Thank you for coming together today, to brainstorm how we can permanently neutralize Findley. I'll find a way to repay you guys," he vowed.

"Family doesn't repay family," Evan said, "because family doesn't *owe* family."

"There's no debt here," Sebastian agreed, his features gravely serious, so unlike his usual gregarious demeanor.

"You're one of us now, Gideon," Daniel said.

Will grinned. "You and Rosie and Jorge—you're all Mavericks now, whether you like it or not."

"All for one and one for all," they said in unison.

Something unfurled deep inside Gideon. A kernel opening, starting to sprout. A seed growing.

He thought of Noah—how blood didn't matter, how Noah was his no matter what. Blood was irrelevant. What mattered was loyalty and love. That was the bond.

And now, the Mavericks had offered him that bond.

He bowed his head, fighting his innate sense of unworthiness, a sense that had been magnified by his screwup with Ari and then with his team. Ari, his men, Karmen—they were all he'd ever had.

Until now. Until Ari had come back into his life, and now the Mavericks. If he let the seed flower...could there one day also be Jorge and Rosie? Not just for two weeks, but *forever*?

When he raised his gaze again, he was no longer completely hollow inside. At long last, the dark, empty spaces inside him—gaping holes that had been carved out of his heart in Iraq—had begun to fill up with friendship. With loyalty. With trust. With gratitude. With love.

"Thanks." It was only six letters. Yet he didn't need to say anything more. Not when something told him that the Mavericks, who had each come through their own personal hell, understood.

The four other Mavericks grinned at him...and then they got to work fleshing out their plan.

Gideon started them off by running through his research. "When I went online to see what I could find about her ex, I found a couple of huge sales for artists neither Rosie nor I had ever heard of, and for whom we couldn't find another mention on the Internet. No other sales, no other art."

"Art is one of the most common ways people launder money," Evan said. "Her ex could be involved with some shady characters."

Will made a note on his phone. "Let's have Rafe dig into whether Findley could be laundering money." Gideon knew Rafe Sullivan worked as the Mavericks' investigator. "I'm guessing it has to do with why he shut down in San Francisco and opened in Las Vegas. There are probably much bigger clients to roll with in Las Vegas. Like, say, the mob."

"Having Rafe dig will be great," Gideon said. His fears were still churning on the surface, however. "We need to figure out a way to protect Rosie and Jorge *now*."

"That's easy," Daniel said. "They have to move in with you."

"Right," Sebastian agreed. "As soon as you get back to Evan's, you can't let Rosie or Jorge out of your sight."

"You've already got Noah with you," Evan added. "The boys will be ecstatic. It's perfect."

Gideon's heart felt almost too big for his chest at the thought of Rosie in his home for more than just a night. Waking up every morning to see her. Sitting next to her on the couch while they played games with the boys. Her lips pressing against his again, her curves in his arms.

Deliberately pulling himself out of his fantasies, he nodded. "Rosie and Jorge definitely need to stay with me."

But would she agree?

* * *

Rosie flew down Evan and Paige's front steps as soon as she heard the car outside. Jorge had finally settled down and was playing happily with Noah. While Gideon was gone, she'd gotten down on the floor with the kids, pulled a blanket over, cuddled up with them, and they'd all closed their eyes for a bit. It had been a long, emotional day for everyone and though the boys both denied they'd ever sleep, she'd heard their rhythmic breathing.

But Rosie definitely *hadn't* settled. And she hadn't slept. In fact, at this very moment her heart was beating so wildly she thought it might beat itself right out of her chest.

As Evan walked up to the front door where Paige waited for him, Rosie threw herself into Gideon's arms. He held her tightly to him, as though she wasn't the only one who desperately needed a hug. She wanted to hold on forever. Just close her eyes against his broad chest and pretend that everything was absolutely fine.

Finally, though, she let go and stepped back so he could tell her about his meeting with the Mavericks.

But instead of giving her an update on the plan, he asked, "How is Jorge?"

"Better." She smiled at Gideon's concern. Did he have any idea how like a parent he sounded? He would make a great dad. "I think he was just overtired. I got them both to lie down for a bit."

"Kid are perceptive," Gideon noted, echoing her earlier thoughts. "He probably picked up on some of our stress, even though he doesn't know what we're stressed about. Fortunately," he added, "kids are also incredibly resilient, as you well know."

"I do," she said, beyond warmed at how much

Gideon cared for Jorge. "Now tell me what happened at the meeting."

"Rafe Sullivan, the Mavericks' investigator, is plowing straight through Archie's life as we speak. If your ex is dirty dealing, we'll find something to make him back off."

"The Mavericks' investigator?" She felt a weight drag her stomach down to the path they stood on. "That's going to cost a lot of money."

"He's on retainer. They pay him whether he does anything or not, so he might as well do this."

She wondered if he was just trying to make her feel better. But he reached out, cupped her cheek, and all she wanted to do was savor the warmth of his hand.

"You're a Maverick now, Rosie. Jorge is too. And this is what Mavericks do for each other."

Evan had said she was one of them. But despite her appreciation for his help, despite feeling like her family had grown since she'd met the Mavericks, she hadn't realized quite what that meant. She wasn't only Ari's sister of the heart, she was also a Maverick. And God, she was grateful. She wanted to turn her face into Gideon's palm and press a kiss to it.

Instead, she asked, "How long do you think it will take for Rafe to comb through Archie's past and his business affairs?"

"We're not sure. That's why we have a plan for the meantime." Even in the darkness, she felt him tense up.

There was always another shoe to drop, always one more thing to drag her down. But only if she let it. And she never had before. "What's the plan?"

"You and Jorge need to move in with me until this is all taken care of."

"Move in with you?" Her heart was doing leapfrogs in her chest at the thought of it. "I have work and Jorge has school. There's got to be another plan." One that didn't involve Gideon sleeping mere feet away every single night.

She'd been able to hold back last night, but she wouldn't bet her savings on being able to hold out after everything he'd done for her tonight.

"I know it's not completely convenient," he agreed. "But we need to do this for Jorge."

She knew Archie had devious intentions. Just as she knew Gideon would do whatever it took, sacrifice anything and everything, to keep Jorge safe.

Still, she had to suggest, "What if we stayed at my cottage, at least?"

"I totally get why that would be easier when all your things are there," he said, "but my complex has interior hallways and fewer points of entry than your cottage." He sounded like he was securing a captured military target.

Gideon, the man of few words, was using a lot of words to convince her. And not, maybe, just to watch over their safety.

And if she were totally honest? She wanted it too, despite the feeling that her life was spinning *way* out of control. She had to agree with the plan. It would be stupid not to—and she would never be stupid about Jorge's safety.

"We should check with Ari and Matt, though. After all, you've got Noah staying with you too."

"You're right. We need to make sure they're okay with this." Gideon glanced at his watch. "What time is it over there?"

"Six in the morning. But Ari said something about getting up early for a long day hike they were planning."

The FaceTime call was short, but Ari and Matt understood the situation and were totally on board. They knew the Mavericks could handle anything and that Gideon would never allow harm to come to either of the boys or to Rosie.

The only problem now was that Rosie wasn't sure how she could be around Gideon night after night without doing something totally crazy.

Like begging him to take her to bed.

★ ★ ★

Gideon hadn't admitted how badly he'd wanted Rosie to throw herself into his arms until she did it. Just as he hadn't admitted how badly he wanted Rosie and Jorge to stay in his home until she'd started arguing with him.

Noah would be thrilled, of course. The only downside?

Keeping his hands—and his mouth—to himself day and night around Rosie was going to be the hardest thing Gideon had ever done.

After they let the boys know the new perpetual sleepover plan, Jorge looked like his old self again as he crowed, "Yay, sleepover!" then jumped up and down with Noah.

"Thank you for everything." Rosie hugged Evan, then Paige.

"Any time you need to drop off the boys with us, just let us know," Paige said. "I love having them."

"Plus, it's an excuse to make more cookies," Evan added, patting his flat stomach.

The boys barreled down the front walk toward the SUV, Rosie following, telling them to slow down. But they would never slow down. Gideon loved that about them.

He shook Evan's hand. "Thanks."

"No problem. We're here for you guys. And I'll have the auction house keep working on the painting too."

"I appreciate that," Gideon said, "but keeping Rosie and Jorge safe is my priority. All that matters is making sure that bastard can't get to Jorge."

Evan's expression turned hard. "He won't. Archibald Findley is going down."

They fist-bumped.

His new sense of kinship, of being a Maverick, meant more than Gideon could ever express. For the first time since he'd lost his team in Ramadi, he belonged to a brotherhood.

He wouldn't let any of them down.

By the time he got to the SUV, Rosie was already in the front seat, the boys in back. Just like they were a family. After a quick stop at her place to collect a bag for her and Jorge, they headed into his apartment complex. Gideon scanned the area, and when he didn't see anything unusual, he used the keycard to take them inside.

In the elevator, he found himself thinking that maybe an apartment wasn't enough anymore. He needed a house with more space, a backyard, a pool for the kids to play in, where even Noah's puppy could be included.

His stomach clenched as he realized hope was no longer just a kernel inside him.

No, he was full-on dreaming now.

"Have you eaten?" Rosie asked. "The three of us ate while you were meeting with the Mavericks, but I can make you a grilled cheese if you're hungry. Just ask Jorge—I make a fabulous grilled cheese."

"Yeah," Jorge said. "It's super yummy."

"Grilled cheese sounds great," he said as he ruffled each of the kids' heads.

He longed to touch Rosie again too. It was an ache in his bones, his skin, his heart.

While Rosie went to the kitchen, he carried Jorge's bag into Noah's room and Rosie's into his. Her flowery aroma lingered from the morning, but it was more than just her scent that made it different. Somehow his whole place felt changed. Especially when he thought about her sleeping in his bed.

And imagined lying right beside her.

Gideon could only pray they neutralized Findley soon. Because he didn't know how he'd keep his hands to himself if this went on too long. Rosie would use his shower, she would use his bed, she would be everywhere.

And he would go completely nuts.

By the time he headed back out to the kitchen, she'd finished making the grilled cheese. Just as she and Jorge had promised, it was delicious. He licked his fingers. He wanted to lick her.

"Fifteen minutes of Monopoly," Rosie offered when the boys asked to play a game, "then it's bedtime."

Despite having had a lie-down at Paige's—and falling asleep, Rosie assured him—Noah and Jorge were tired enough that they didn't complain when time was up, even though they hadn't finished the game. There was teeth-brushing, a short reading from their *Magic Tree House* story, kisses and hugs, and then it was lights out, door closed.

Then it was just Rosie and Gideon.

"We should turn in." He couldn't trust himself to be alone with her tonight. Not when unquenched desire was pushing him to the breaking point. Before she could offer to take the couch the way she had last night, he said, "I already put your bag in the bedroom. The bean bags were just fine for me last night."

But she shook her head. "You should sleep in the bed tonight." She stepped closer. "I need you to be well rested so you can be at your best as our bodyguard."

He couldn't breathe with her so close. Couldn't think straight. "I've slept in foxholes, on the ground, in the rain. It's no big deal."

"Maybe not." She stared into his eyes, mesmerizing him. He was watching her so closely that he could practically see her mind working, which was how he knew when she came to a decision. "But your bed is big enough for two."

Then she went up on her toes and pulled his head down, put her mouth on his. And as she tasted him, his entire body caught fire.

She was so sweet, so soft, so warm. He lost himself in her scent, in the delicacy of her lips, her mouth, and her body pressed to his. She felt so small in his arms. So fragile. And yet so strong. The strongest woman he'd ever known.

Then she tipped back her head and met his gaze, her eyes a rich, dark, swirling cocoa. "Come to bed with me, Gideon."

And in that moment, he knew he would follow her anywhere, anytime, for as long as she wanted.

Chapter Twenty

Gideon was good. He was honorable. He was tough. He would protect Jorge with his very life.

There was nothing more Rosie could ever need in a man. And she needed Gideon more than she'd ever needed anyone in her life.

She washed her face, brushed her teeth, and put on a long T-shirt with a kitty on the front, a birthday present from Jorge. All the while, her heart was beating like a hummingbird's wings.

That kiss.

There had never been another like it.

Rosie hadn't kissed or been intimate with anyone in seven years. But Gideon's kiss hadn't brought her back to life. How could it, when it turned out she'd never really lived? Never really known true passion until Gideon held her in his arms and kissed her?

As Gideon got ready for bed in the bathroom, she turned off the overhead light, leaving only the soft glow of one bedside lamp. She climbed under the covers on the side opposite the clock, where he obviously slept, and was plumping the pillow behind her head when Gideon came out of the bathroom wearing sweats and a T-shirt.

In her fantasies about the moment when they finally made love, they had torn each other's clothes off. But as he climbed into bed beside her, she knew real life was going to be so much sweeter and hotter than her secret middle-of-the-night fantasies—even if they weren't ripping off their clothes.

Her son's life depended on her decisions. So she had to make the right ones. And being with Gideon, she thought with a smile, was the best decision she could possibly make.

Yes, he had his demons. But who didn't? She wasn't afraid to help him vanquish those demons—just as he'd already proved he wasn't afraid to help her vanquish hers.

They turned to face each other at the same moment, and he laid his hand gently on her cheek. So tender. So warm. So sweet and yet sexy all at the same time. "I don't want to screw this up."

"You're not going to screw up anything with me." She pressed her hand over his. "But even if you did, I would forgive you. Just like I know you would forgive me."

A ghost of a smile touched his lips. "I want tonight to be unforgettable. As unforgettable—and perfect— for you as it will be for me."

"You're already perfect to me." She matched his hushed voice, aware of the boys just down the hall. "There is nothing you could do to make me think differently."

Even as she said it, she knew Gideon would need proof. His past experiences meant he would never think he was good enough. Unless she could help him believe—unless she could show him—that he was better than anyone.

"Touch me," she whispered. "I've longed for you, Gideon. I've longed for your kiss. I've dreamed of touching you, tasting you, feeling you inside me."

His eyes went smoky blue as he stroked his fingers through her hair, pushing it behind her ear. "For so long, I've wanted to bury my face in your hair. To smell you. To drink you in." He trailed his fingers around the delicate, sensitive shell of her ear, then down her neck to the hollow at her throat. "I've dreamed about licking you right here." His voice was deep and husky with need. Need for *her*.

Rosie's only other lover had been a shadow, only there to give her Jorge. In her heart, Rosie knew Gideon was the one she'd been waiting for.

He kissed the tip of her nose, then her cheek, her neck, his breath fanning across her face, his warmth following the length of her body. And as he pressed the lightest of kisses over her skin, she drank in his every feature. His long, golden-tipped eyelashes. The tiny flecks of green in the blue of his eyes. The scent and maleness of him. The rough pads of his fingers on her skin. She wanted to feel everything, remember everything, every moment, every detail.

And when he kissed her *finally*—It was fire dancing on her lips. It was need growing in her belly. It was desire heating her sex.

She coiled her fingers around the nape of his neck and pulled up her leg to curl her foot around his calf. She opened to him, her lips, her body, her heart.

Gideon devoured her, sliding his tongue against hers, going deep, overwhelming her senses, from zero to one hundred in a millisecond. She was breathing hard, her breasts begging for his touch. But instead of answering her unspoken plea, he simply held her tight against him, ravaged her mouth, stoked the flames building ever higher inside her.

She pulled back slightly, his name on her lips. *"Gideon."*

He trailed fingers of fire across her neck, down to the swell of her breasts, taking her lips again, even as he tugged up her T-shirt. Then his hand was on the bare skin of her belly, the rough texture of his fingers jangling her nerve endings and turning the switch on her body to hot-hot-hot.

"I want our first time to last forever," he said. His mouth was on her neck, his lips tasting, his tongue licking.

"I'm not sure I can go slow." She wanted it all, now, just as much as she wanted to savor every second.

"We've got all the time in the world, sweetheart."

Oh, how she loved hearing the endearment on his lips. *Sweetheart.* She moaned as his fingers found the tip of her breast, gently squeezed. And her body ignited.

"I've never wanted anyone the way I want you." She needed him to know how much he meant to her, so much more than that other man ever had.

As if he got the message, he swept her shirt over her head, baring every inch of her skin to him, except what lay beneath the triangle of silk bikini panty. His gaze was reverent as he took in her nearly naked curves. "You are so beautiful." She was glad for the soft glow of the bedside lamp revealing the smoky blue of his eyes, the desire written there, the need etched in the lines of his face. "I couldn't have imagined you more beautiful than this."

"You've imagined me?"

"Hell yes." His voice was so rough, so masculine, so sensuous as he danced one fingertip around her breast. "I imagined putting my mouth on you, right here." He bent down and licked over her skin. "Feeling you go all hot and wet. For me. All for me."

As he touched her, as he kissed her, as he drove her completely wild, she could barely think, barely do more than gasp out a needy moan.

"You captivate me, Rosie. Everything about you. You have from the moment I first saw you." Then he dipped his head and did all the things he'd only imagined—and so much more—tasting her, loving her.

She bit her lip, trapping the cry of pleasure. The boys were close by, so they had to be quiet. But while keeping quiet was hard, in so many ways, it was delicious too.

"What else have you imagined?" she asked when she could find her voice.

"Trailing my fingers down your belly like this." He slid his hand toward silk. And then lower still. Her belly quivered as he moved just inside the fabric. "And making you so hot you tear the clothes right off my body."

This was a Gideon she'd hoped would emerge. Fun and open, full of burning need and aching desire. "I can do that."

Seconds later, his clothes were flying, and then he was breathtakingly naked before her.

"*Gideon.*" He was all bronzed skin and hard muscle. Dazzling. "You're like a Roman statue."

His mouth cracked in a smile. "One with a fig leaf covering the important parts? Or one without?"

She laughed with him, loving that he felt at ease enough with her to joke. "Without the fig leaf, preferably. And preferably with all your appendages attached too." Once more, his fingers trailed her belly.

"What else have you imagined?" she asked him, her voice shaky with need.

He looked along the length of her nearly naked body, then reached down between her legs and covered her with his big, hot hand, stroking her through the silk. "I can imagine making you beg, making you whimper, making you come apart for me over and over again."

Before she could tell him she was nearly there already, he dipped deep inside the minuscule bikini panties, his hand covered by silk and lace...and found the heat of her. And as he played her, she clutched his shoulders in her hands and rode the sweet wave of sensation, building, burning, blazing in his arms.

* * *

For so long, Gideon had been convinced he wasn't good enough for Rosie, or for her son. But even that was no longer enough to keep him away. Whatever it took to be even half as good as she was, whatever he had to do or work on or change to deserve her, any sacrifice, any challenge, it was all worth the chance to be with her.

There had never been anyone like Rosie. Nothing near as sweet as the feel of her skin and the sound of her voice. He could be happy with just this, giving her endless pleasure with his hands and mouth, and never ask for anything more.

But he wanted to give *her* more, wanted to fulfill all her fantasies, wanted to make every dream she'd ever had come true.

Her eyes fluttered open, dark and dazed. "*Wow. That was even better than I imagined. And* I have an *amazing* imagination."

"It only gets better from here." He knew he sounded cocky. But he didn't care. Because he damned well intended this to be the best lovemaking she'd ever experienced.

Then she reached down between his legs, wrapped her hand around his erection, and *oh yeah*, there was so much more he wanted and so much more he wanted to give her.

"I want to taste you," she whispered. "I want to touch you. I want you inside me. And I want it all *now.*"

He would never survive her mouth on him. But Rosie was taking no prisoners as she pushed him flat on the mattress and crawled down his body. As she wrapped her fingers around him and squeezed, then took him in her mouth, he gave himself up to her. Of all the women in all the world, Rosie was the only one who filled his heart, the only woman to whom he could ever imagine feeling this connected.

He wound his fingers through the silk of her hair as she whisked him away to a world of sensation. There was just her mouth on him, her skin so soft, his heart beating crazily. When he couldn't take a moment more, fearing he'd go up in flames, he pulled her over him.

But before he made love to her, he needed her to know everything in his heart.

"You are the smartest, most beautiful, amazing, independent, sexy, strong, desirable, funny woman I have ever known. You make me feel alive again in ways I never thought I would."

For a long moment, she didn't speak. She simply stared into his eyes as if in wonder. Until, finally, she said, "You captivate me too, Gideon. Every single thing about you. The light, the dark, the gentle, the rough. I want every inch of you—heart and soul—to be mine."

His heart full, near to bursting like never before, he rolled over her, took her lips, going deep, long and lingering.

They were both breathless when he surfaced. "I want to worship your perfect body forever," he murmured against her lips. "I want to make you feel so much pleasure you can hardly stand it." He slid down to take her breast in his mouth, to pleasure her with sweet licks and tiny bites. "I want to watch you try to keep all those delicious moans inside…and finally realize you can't. Because it feels too damned good." He trailed kisses down her belly, licked around her belly button, then spread her legs. As he drew a finger down her center, he felt her shudder and squirm. "I want to make you come apart into so many beautiful pieces that you forget your name." He buried his face in her, drank in her scent, her taste, her tremors, then pushed her higher with his lips, his tongue, his fingers. Her muscles tightened, squeezed, contracted.

Then, without a sound, bliss took her over, head to toe, inside and out. He drew every ounce of pleasure out of her climax, kissed and caressed her until she was trembling all over from the aftershocks. Only then did he move slightly away from her to open the bedside drawer and grab protection. Sheathing himself, he went up on his haunches, pulled her to him, spread her legs over his, grabbed her sweet, gorgeous hips, and plunged deep.

"*Yes.*" The one word on her lips was grace. Need. And most of all, joy.

Everything about her was soft, and everything about him was hard as he stroked her slowly on the inside, making her crazy but keeping his own control. He wanted her completely wild before he let go.

But God, she felt so good wrapped around him. And there was such beauty in her rapture, her expression so open, her pleasure so complete.

The moment she started to let go again, coming apart on a gasp and a shudder, he plunged right over the edge with her.

And nothing would ever be the same.

He would never be the same.

Because he could never go on without her.

* * *

"You did it," Rosie said against the silky hair on his chest. "You actually made me forget my name. I knew it started with an *R*, but that was as far as I could get for a while there."

He had bundled her close with the covers pulled over them. She felt tired, but so good. So needed. So desired. So special.

"I don't want you to think I have women over here all the time."

What on earth? She tipped back her head to look at him. "Where did that come from?"

"The condoms in my bedside table. I haven't needed them in a long time. I had them from before and I didn't throw them away. But I don't want you to think that I—"

She reached up to put her fingers to his lips. "I didn't even think about it, Gideon. Besides, you don't have to explain anything about your past to me."

"I do," he insisted. "I want to." He stroked her cheek. "You're the only one. You need to know that."

She curled herself around him, getting closer, if that were even possible. "I do know that. And you're the only one for me too."

He nuzzled the top of her head as he said, "I've never felt like this." His deep voice sent thrill bumps across her skin.

"Neither have I."

For the first time in her life, Rosie was in love.

Chapter Twenty-One

A phone wouldn't stop ringing. It was Archie. He was after her; he was after Jorge. And she was running, trying to lose him, Jorge in her arms. Then suddenly Jorge was gone, and she was screaming his name, but no one could hear.

Her mind foggy with sleep, Rosie realized the phone on the side table was ringing. Remnants of the dream still tormenting her, she grabbed her cell, half afraid Archie was calling to say he'd stolen Jorge right out of his bed. Afraid that if she didn't answer, she would never see Jorge again.

The last thing she expected was to see Ari smiling at her.

"Who's that?" Gideon went up on one elbow beside her to peer over her shoulder at the screen.

In the moments between her nightmare and waking, Rosie had forgotten where she was. In Gideon's bed. With the kids just down the hall. She'd answered the FaceTime call without even thinking.

"Gideon? Rosie?" Ari's shock was plain to see.

Rosie slapped the phone face down on the mattress.

Ari's voice might be muffled, but it was still audible. "You can't hide. I already saw you with my brother."

Rosie raised the phone again. "Hi, Ari."

She was full-body blushing, even before Gideon slid his arm around her waist and tucked her back into his big, hard body. They were naked, for God's sake, even if she had the sheet pulled up to her neck. And her hair must look like a rat's nest.

At the same time, however, her heart swelled at what his gesture meant: He wasn't going to hide his relationship with her. There was no one else whose opinion mattered more to Gideon than Ari. So if he wanted his sister to know, he would want everyone to know.

"You have no idea how happy I am right now!" Ari exclaimed, her face bright and smiling. "Do you know how badly I've wanted you two to get together?"

Matt's face popped onto the screen beside Ari's. "It's true. She's talked endlessly about ways she could make you two see how perfect you are for each other."

"We... I..." Rosie wasn't normally lost for words.

Fortunately, Gideon picked up the slack. "Rosie has totally captivated me since the first day I saw her. I just needed some time to convince her that I was worthy to be with her and Jorge."

Rosie turned to him, the phone momentarily forgotten. "I always knew that. You never had to convince me." Himself, maybe. But never her.

The bedroom door burst open, and the boys came bounding in. And did they freak out that she and Gideon were in bed together? On the contrary, they seemed to think it was the natural order of things.

"Is that Mommy and Daddy on the phone?" Noah squeezed in to get his face into the picture, with Jorge nudging close too.

"Hey, sweetie," Ari said. "Hi, Jorge. Blow me a kiss."

As the boys puckered up and blew kisses over and over again, Ari and Matt caught the kisses and blew their own right back.

"Your daddy and I miss you so much," Ari said. "We've got so many pictures to show you."

"And presents too," Matt added with a smile.

"Yay!" the kids cried. Then Jorge said, "We've got bunches of stuff to show you too, like how Mom and Gid are totally in love now." Jorge hooked a thumb over his shoulder at them.

A week ago, Gideon would have tensed up if Jorge had said something along those lines. Especially since they hadn't actually said the four-letter word to each other. But not only was he undaunted, he actually chuckled while keeping his arm clamped firmly around her waist and the covers battened down against the two squirming boys on the bed.

"It didn't take as long to make them fall in love as I thought it would," Noah said to his parents.

"Yeah," Jorge agreed. "Noah was pretty sure they'd take the whole two weeks. But it was *way* faster."

Noah turned to Jorge. "Now you're going to be my brother."

Jorge nodded with total reverence and solemnity. "Best friend brothers."

It obviously didn't matter that Gideon was Noah's uncle—the boys had decided on the relationship they wanted and that was that.

On the phone, Matt's eyes were sparkling. "Sounds like Noah and Jorge had it all mapped out for you two."

Noah started chanting an old rhyme. "Rosie and Gideon sitting in a tree, k-i-s-s-i-n-g."

"First comes love," Jorge joined in, "then comes marriage, then comes baby in a baby carriage."

Rosie groaned. "All right, you two little matchmakers, out you go. It's time for me and Gideon to get up."

They raced out of the room, Noah calling, "Bye, Mommy! Bye, Daddy! Love you!"

"I can't believe they've been planning this all along," Gideon said. "With all their sleepovers and playdates every day."

"Little sneaks," Rosie groused good-naturedly.

Inside, she was glowing. On the outside too, actually. "We totally fell for it."

"Any updates on the ex situation?" Matt wanted to know.

"Nothing yet, but don't worry," Gideon reassured them again, "we won't let anything happen to Noah."

"We know you won't," Ari said. "You don't have to keep saying it."

He nodded, then said with a smile, "Looks like the honeymoon is treating you well."

"It really is." Ari was glowing. "But we miss all of you."

"We miss you too." Just like the kids, Rosie blew Ari and Matt a kiss.

When they hung up, the silence in the room was broken only by the hollering from the boys in the kitchen.

"I'm glad they called," Gideon said. "I want them to know about us. I want everyone to know." Then he dropped his voice and sang softly, "Rosie and Gideon lying in a bed, k-i-s-s-i-n-g," before kissing her breathless.

Chapter Twenty-Two

With his heart overflowing, the day was too glorious for Gideon to dwell on Archibald Findley—or even the past and the darkness that had been the focus of his life for so long. All he wanted was to bask in the feelings Rosie evoked in him—the wonder, the desire, the ease, the laughter, the hope. He wanted to bask in the miracle of their lovemaking. And he wanted to bask in this precious time with *her*, and with the kids.

Rosie suggested a trip across the Santa Cruz Mountains to Roaring Camp, which nestled in the redwoods next to Henry Cowell Redwoods State Park. In addition to the steam trains taking passengers high up in the mountains or down to the beach, there was face painting, gold panning, square dancing, and more. The boys were so excited, vibrating with joy even as they waited in line to pick up their boxed lunches to eat on the ride up Bear Mountain.

Rosie was beauty personified. Gideon couldn't take his eyes off her in her flowery tank top and jean shorts, her legs bronzed, her hair brilliant in the shafts of sunlight through the trees.

Noah and Jorge were ecstatic as the steam train rumbled up the mountain. They clung to the sides, leaning back in the open-air carriage to gaze all the way to the tops of the huge redwoods and Douglas firs, waving at the squirrels racing through the branches, asking the conductor a million questions about trains. After an hour and a half, as they chugged back into the station, the kids begged to have their faces painted. They insisted on Day of the Dead, while Rosie wanted to sprinkle them with flowers instead.

"Come on, Mom," Jorge groaned. "Flowers are for girls."

Rosie laughed and gave in. When the face painter was finished, Rosie snapped photos of the transformation to text to Ari and Matt. "We should take a walk through the redwood loop before we leave," she told Gideon, pointing to a path through to the state park.

"Sure. That sounds great." Everything she suggested was great. Because being with her was all he'd ever dreamed of.

Gideon still could barely believe last night had actually happened. His heart felt like it was in overdrive. Walking hand in hand with Rosie as they trailed after the two excited little boys, he knew what true happiness was. He'd experienced moments of happiness in the past; as a teenager, watching Ari jump rope, her face joyous, her laughter singing out; as a man, when he and Zach had pulled some ridiculous prank that made the guys roar with laughter; then coming home to Ari and Noah, watching them play in Matt's pool, the childish giggles, Ari's laughter. And especially Ari's wedding. So, yes, there had been moments.

But the joy in his heart as he held Rosie's hand in his—that would last a lifetime.

Their faces painted like elaborate black-and-white skulls—Rosie got her wish too, with the flowers and swirls the artist had added—the boys raced to the blacksmith to watch him work.

"We take a bar of smelted metal, and we heat it up on the forge." The man explained the process as he pulled a stick of superheated metal out of the burning coals with a pair of tongs. "Now we're going to use this hammer to beat it into shape on the anvil."

"What are you making?" Noah asked.

Older, his face grizzled, his hair a cap of gray, the man had penetrating brown eyes and strong hands. "This will be a seahorse that can hang on a barn wall as a hook to hold horse tack." He spoke in an old-fashioned accent as if he were truly a nineteenth-century blacksmith.

"Wow!" the boys exclaimed in unison.

For long moments, loud banging rang out. Then the blacksmith pondered his handiwork, saying, "Let's see where we are." He doused the still glowing seahorse in a large metal bucket, the water hissing and bubbling around it. Holding it up for the kids to see, he said, "I've got a bit more work to do yet." Though Gideon could make out the curled tail, it didn't look like a seahorse.

"How long does it take to complete the seahorse?" Rosie asked.

"Come back in a couple of hours." He smiled brightly, then held up a finger. "But I've got one in process over here." Placing the current project back in the forge, he fished out another bit of metal with his tongs. "I'll just cool it down." He let it sizzle in the bucket, then held up a beautifully formed seahorse.

"That's amazing." Rosie was as enthusiastic as the boys.

"Now we're going to bronze it up like this." Gripping the seahorse tight in his tongs, he laid it on the anvil and polished it with a metal brush. "See how the bronze comes off this brush and right onto the metal?" He held up the brush and the seahorse for the boys to see. "This little guy is still hot enough for the tines of the metal brush to melt onto it. And the seahorse shines right up."

Rosie and the boys leaned forward to watch the magic as the gray metal turned bronze beneath the brush.

"How long have you been smithing?" Gideon

asked.

The man's face wrinkled into another smile. "Oh, about ten years. I was an engineer in Silicon Valley, but when a man retires, he's got to find a hobby or he wastes away. So I took up smithing. I've been coming out here to Roaring Camp for about seven years now. Everything you see here—" He waved his hand at the array of tools behind him. "—is what was used back in the eighteen hundreds. And my wares are for sale here." He pointed to a row of seahorses for hooks and forest animals for doorstops, plus key rings, decorative door hinges, candlestick holders, elaborate crosses. Even dice.

"These are cool." Jorge picked up two. "They're heavy."

"Pure metal," the man said. "And look at this one. I made a mistake—it's got three on two sides." He tossed a die onto his heatproof glove and held it out.

The boys turned it over to see the mistake.

"You boys can have it free of charge, since it's not right."

"Wow." Jorge clutched it in his fist. "Thank you."

Gideon bought each of the boys a pair of dice, because they were fascinated by the work and because the man had spent so much time with them.

"That was a great lesson," Rosie said. "The kids really appreciated it. Thank you."

"You're welcome, ma'am," the blacksmith said as

he used his tongs on the unfinished seahorse and laid it on his anvil. "Come back if you'd like to see this one finished up."

"We will. Thank you." Gideon took Rosie's hand in his as they walked away. Touching her was as necessary as breathing.

"Can we pan for gold now?" Noah was bouncing on his toes, excitement pulsing in every cell.

"Sure," he and Rosie said at the same time. And the boys were off, leaving them to meander along.

"Can you imagine taking up a hobby like blacksmithing *after* you've retired?" Rosie looked at him, her eyebrows raised in amazement.

In the army, they'd always been busy. Busy was good, occupying your hands, your mind. "If you were able to make a living as an artist and didn't have to do accounting anymore—" It was his goal to turn life as an artist into Rosie's reality, because that was how talented she was. "—what would you choose as a hobby? Or would you paint all the time, never stopping?"

She gave it serious consideration. "I'd want a hobby too. Art can be exhausting, especially when you put your whole soul into it."

"I know exactly what you mean." Unspoken, memories of the day at the Legion of Honor passed between them.

She squeezed his hand. "I know you do." Then she

looked at him, her gaze suddenly eager. "I'd choose something like stained glass. And I'd want to make my own patterns."

The boys rushed back for money for the gold panning, while Rosie and Gideon slowly caught up. Under the trees, at four big panning tables, the enclosed pans filled with water and dirt were crowded with kids and parents alike.

"Do you want to pan?" she asked.

"No." He wanted to watch the boys' delight. And he wanted to listen to Rosie's voice, learn everything he could about her. "Stained glass seems right up your alley. I can imagine every window filled with brilliant color."

"Me too," she said. Then she laughed and added, "Or maybe I'd take cooking lessons."

"But you're a great cook. The empanadas you made for the picnic at the Legion of Honor were great." He was pretty sure he'd neglected to tell her that. He'd been in a darker world that day.

She grinned at him, her eyes alight. "I'm glad you thought so. But I'd like to try different kinds of cuisine. My papí taught me Mexican specialties, but the rest of what I make is pretty basic. I'd like to make really authentic Indian food or Chinese."

The boys whooped when they found a flake of gold. "I'm sorry," the attendant told them, "but that's pyrite. It's called fool's gold." The boys went on panning with no less enthusiasm.

"What would you do?" Rosie bumped Gideon's arm companionably. He loved the ease between them.

"When I was on a job down in Riverside, I stayed in a rooming house where the garden was filled with fruit trees. My landlady had oranges and avocadoes and plums and cherries. Plus an overflowing vegetable garden. She let me have anything I wanted. I think that's what I'd like to do. Grow my own fruits and vegetables."

"I could learn all sorts of delicious ways to prepare them."

He grinned. "I could build window frames for all your stained glass."

"What a team." She threw her arms around him, hugged him tight.

He didn't want to let her go. Holding Rosie in his arms was like holding the stars and the moon. Like holding a beautiful, amazing flower and watching it bloom.

She settled against him, his arm around her shoulders as they watched the boys. "All your hobbies are like you," he said. "Artistic, imaginative, creative."

"And yours are outdoorsy, working with your hands."

"I guess we do what we love. It would be kind of cool to make furniture too."

She pulled back to look at him. "I've never heard

you talk so much before." She stroked a hand down his face. "I love it."

"I've never had so much to say before." It was as though telling her about Karmen, about the angel painting, about that day, the worst of his life, had popped the cork out of everything he'd bottled up inside. And now it all wanted to pour out of him.

For Rosie.

* * *

It was the best day ever.

Rosie felt like she was glowing from the inside out. Last night had changed everything. The last of Gideon's walls had come crashing down. It wasn't just making love, it was everything they'd shared, everything they'd gone through. Together.

When he looked at the boys, he was the big brother Ari had always talked about, laughing, talking, loving, teaching.

And when he looked at her, he was the lover and protector she had always dreamed about, a beautiful, caring, endearing man.

Noah and Jorge raced to them, each holding a tiny baggie of gold flakes.

"Some of it's pyrite," Jorge said sagely.

"But some of it's gold," Noah said, with excitement.

Gideon ruffled his hair. "Awesome. We'll have to

save it to show your mom. Now let's take a walk through the redwood loop in the park."

The boys wanted their pictures taken inside the huge hollow of a tree, and with banana slugs, then on top of a tall tree stump. They wanted pictures of deer and squirrels and a raccoon. Their delight was never ending.

Gideon was endlessly patient, caring, interested. And during the moments the boys rushed ahead, he dropped a kiss on Rosie's hair, laced her fingers with his, or pulled her close into the shelter of his arm.

It was idyllic. It was a fantasy. It was their new reality.

Then Gideon's phone pinged. He looked at the text, looked at her. And his gaze turned a dark and stormy blue. "It's Evan. The guys have some info for us." He didn't say Archie's name. He didn't have to.

"Good. I want to be done with him. I want him gone for good." She wanted a new life with Gideon to start right now. She went up on her toes, threw her arms around him. "This has been the best day ever."

He held her tight. "Tomorrow will be even better."

It felt like a vow he was making for their future. One she was fiercely determined they would have.

Chapter Twenty-Three

Gideon's arm lay firmly around Rosie's shoulders when they rang Evan's doorbell. Jorge hung on Gideon's hand, while Noah clung to Rosie's. There could be no doubt in anyone's mind about exactly where Gideon stood: smack dab in the middle of a family.

His family.

In all the months he'd spent watching Rosie from afar, Gideon's feelings for her had always seemed like a betrayal of Karmen's memory. His friend had been good and brave, but he'd never truly allowed his budding feelings for her to grow between them. Maybe it was the place, the war, the fighting, the fear. Maybe it was because he'd been afraid he'd lose her. And his nightmare had become a reality.

He could never make up for failing to keep her from harm, or for losing his men, or for all the pain their families had suffered. But he could keep Rosie and Jorge safe.

He knew in his heart that Karmen would approve.

The scent of freshly baked cookies wafted out as

Evan opened the door. "Thanks for coming." He tipped his head toward the kitchen, smiling. "Paige has been baking again."

The Mavericks had put out the call for a meeting, and the men were assembled in Evan's living room, demolishing a large plate of chocolate chip cookies. As Evan had already briefed Paige on the situation, she took the boys into the kitchen so the adults could talk openly without worrying about upsetting them.

Gideon sat with Rosie on the couch, his arm around her. He could see on the other Mavericks' faces that they'd known all along what Rosie and Jorge meant to him.

They were absolutely *everything*.

Sebastian spoke first. "It didn't take long to ferret out your ex's dirty little secrets. Everything is in this manila folder."

Rosie opened it, sliding it closer to Gideon so they could both review the information Rafe Sullivan had pulled together. Her eyes were wide, and she was shaking her head by the time they finished reading about the scumbag's dirty dealings.

Gideon held her hand tightly, securely, lovingly in his, as she looked up at the other Mavericks. "Thank you so much for doing this, you guys." A slight hitch in her voice betrayed her emotion.

"Rosie." Will's tone was gentle. "You're Ari's sister. You're family. We take care of family."

The Mavericks were foster brothers, just as Ari, Rosie, and Chi were foster sisters. They understood better than anybody that the bond wasn't blood. The bond was love.

She blinked away tears. "I love you guys."

Evan smiled. "Ditto. And we *will* take care of this problem."

Daniel nodded. "Using this information, we can ream him a new—"

"No, wait." Rosie leaned forward. "Of course I appreciate your offer to deal directly with Archie. I know all of you only have my best interests at heart. But *I* have to do this. *I* have to face him." She gazed at each of them in turn, then came back to Gideon. "If I don't do this myself, I'll never feel truly free of him."

Just the thought of Rosie meeting with Archie again was enough to nearly stop Gideon's heart. He didn't like it. No, he *hated* it. Hated the thought of her going anywhere near the guy.

But if he didn't let her deal with Archie on her own terms, if he wrapped her in cotton wool and demanded she do things his way, *she* would hate *him*.

Though it took everything he had, he forced himself to nod. "You need to be free of him, Rosie."

She pressed a soft kiss to his mouth, then pulled out her phone. "I'm going to call him right now and set up another meeting."

★ ★ ★

It came as no surprise to anyone that Findley had been delighted at the prospect of seeing her again. Obviously, the guy thought his threats from their previous meeting had done the job and she was ready to cave to his demands. Her ex was so arrogant that he never even considered Rosie had something in store for him that would blow a mile-wide hole in his plans.

Paige was more than happy to take care of the boys for a while longer, and Rosie hugged Jorge fiercely before they left. He didn't melt down like he had last night. It was as though he knew his mother had a very important thing to do that would make him secure for the rest of his life.

Findley had chosen another posh restaurant in another posh district, this time on Santana Row. Again, they could have valet parked, but Gideon wanted his keys in his own pocket for a quick getaway.

There was nothing he wanted to do more than pound the guy's face into oblivion. Reading his mind, Rosie stopped him on the sidewalk with a hand on his cheek. "I'm not going to be alone in there, Gideon." She went up on her toes to press her mouth to his, a kiss with so much sweetness, so much emotion. "Not when I know you're going to be right here. The fact that you'll be waiting for me makes it possible for me to accomplish absolutely anything I set my mind to."

But you need me right there beside you.

His heart cried out to say the words aloud, to make her see that he *needed* to protect her and make absolutely certain she was safe.

Yet, he knew Rosie. There was no way he could stop her once she'd set her mind to something. He couldn't tie her up or drag her off. He couldn't order her to stay away from Findley. He couldn't have the Mavericks, or Ari, command her not to go either.

The weight of all the things he couldn't do crushed his chest. Suddenly, he could barely breathe.

The very same emotions had overwhelmed him the day Karmen died, the day the IED exploded and the sniper's shot rang out. If only he'd been able step in, keep everyone from getting hurt—but his team, and Karmen, had been just as determined as Rosie. There was nothing he could have done differently. Nothing but support their decisions, their choices.

"Gideon." She cupped her hands on either side of his face. "I can do this. I *need* to do this."

He understood, he really did. Rosie needed to confront the monster in her life. She needed to protect her son.

Just the way Karmen needed to walk outside the wire, to do her job, to be a soldier, to help her team.

"Please trust me, Gideon."

He wanted to trust her. Knew he needed to trust her.

But how could he let her walk into danger without

him? What if something went wrong?

He would never, ever forgive himself.

"Gideon." Rosie murmured his name again, this time against his cheek, and suddenly his heart pounded with the need to leave nothing unsaid. Not again. Never again.

He drew her close and held her tightly to him. "I'm terrified to let you go in there without me. But I also know that I have to trust you to do this your own way. On your own terms." Gideon hated the idea of Rosie facing Archie again, of talking to him, listening to his lies, even breathing the same air. But he understood why she needed to. And he would stand behind her, backing her up every step of the way as she neutralized the bastard. He leaned his forehead against hers. He'd lost Karmen without ever having acknowledged, or told her, what was in his heart. He would not let Rosie go without expressing the depth of his feelings for her. "I love you. And I will be waiting for you right here, right outside the door. I will always be here for you. So do this. And then come back to me, safe and sound."

"Oh, Gideon. I love you too." Tears flooded her voice. "So, so much."

Joy wrapped around his heart, around his entire being, around the parts that had been shrouded in darkness for so long.

Then Rosie pulled herself up, stronger and more committed now than she'd been even moments before.

"Okay, it's time to take him down."

He gave her a thumbs-up. But though he trusted her to know the right thing to do, watching her walk away—and forcing himself to let her go without running after her to keep her safe at all costs—was the hardest battle he'd ever fought.

Chapter Twenty-Four

Though she was on the precipice of the biggest confrontation of her life, Rosie wasn't scared. With all the Mavericks backing her up, she felt strong.

And most especially with Gideon waiting right outside for her.

Gideon. He was such a warrior—so tough, so immovable, until you uncovered the beautiful and gentle man beneath all his layers.

She could feel his love flowing to her down the sidewalk, tethering them together. A beam of light that couldn't be broken. She wanted to turn and run back to him, kiss him one more time, feel his arms around her one more time.

But she would save that reward for when her deed was done.

This restaurant had the same crystal glassware and fancy trappings that Archibald Findley had always needed. His table was in the back, on a raised dais surrounded by a short railing.

Archie was the same polished, entitled, arrogant

creep he'd been yesterday. He gazed out over the other diners as if they were his minions, his eyes dark and probing. Today's suit was black with pinstripes, his dark hair, with just the right amount of gray to appear distinguished, was perfectly coiffed, as if a stylist attended him every morning. His nails had always been flawlessly manicured, meticulous attention given to every detail of his appearance. From afar, he looked like he'd stepped off a movie screen to dazzle his fans. That's what Rosie hadn't understood when she was young and naïve. Archie was all about appearance and completely lacking in substance. He was all flowery words that had no real meaning. It had likely taken him years of practice to perfect his persona.

No wonder she had fallen for it. Men and women twice her age fell for that slick Archibald Findley façade. He was so smooth, suave, and sophisticated, it was difficult to see the slime.

For years she'd blamed herself for trusting him, for not seeing through him. But the truth was that she hadn't been old enough or worldly enough to recognize all the signs. Not until it was too late.

But she saw right through him now. And she would never let him harm Jorge.

Rosie smiled at the maître d' as she passed him. "No worries. I can find my own way to the table."

"I ordered a drink for you," Archie said as she sat.

Of course he had. It was the same champagne he

used to ply her with seven years ago, though she'd been underage at the time.

She set it aside, untouched. "Yesterday when I asked what you wanted from me," she said, not at all interested in beating around the bush today, "you fed me a line about wanting to help because of the burdens of being a single parent. But I know what you really want." She waited a beat. "You want to take my son."

"Take him? I would never take anything away from anyone." Archie gave her a wide-eyed look of innocence so patently false that it only enhanced the pure evil shining through. "I did my best to help your art career. Don't you remember?"

"Of course, Archie, I remember everything." She let herself enjoy the grimace on his face when she used the hated nickname. "I remember how you didn't help me at all. How you sabotaged me. How you lied to me. And how you've never done one single thing for my son, never offered one iota of help in the seven years since the day I told you he existed. I remember how you just disappeared. *Poof.*" She made a gesture with her fingers like smoke vanishing into the air. "So, no, I don't need your kind of help. Which means there's really no reason for you to call me again." She gave him one last chance to redeem himself by agreeing.

Of course, he didn't take it. She hadn't thought he would.

"Rosie." He shook his head as though she was a major disappointment to him. "Regardless of how you feel about the past, you can't deny that I can afford better schools, better health care, better opportunities, and all the important things our son truly needs."

The *our* infuriated her, but she managed to press on without throwing the champagne in his face. "But only if he comes to Las Vegas to live with you, right?"

His eyes lit. He was so sure he had her cornered. The pompous bastard. "Jorge moving in with my wife and me in Las Vegas would make things so much easier and simpler, don't you think? Of course, you can also move to town if you'd like to be closer to him."

There, finally, he'd said it. She'd known it all along, but it was vindicating to have her suspicions confirmed. But it was equally horrifying, sending bile shooting up her throat at the thought of Jorge ever living with Archie and his wife. *Never.* She would *never* let that happen.

"Actually," Rosie leaned forward, "let me tell you what will be easier and simpler. You will back off. Permanently."

He looked at her like she had fewer brain cells than a fly. "Rosie, honey, I can't, in all good conscience, do that. You know he needs me."

Forcing herself to ignore the sickening *honey*, she couldn't help but wonder where his conscience had been when he said she'd have to handle her pregnancy on her own. She could have asked him. But he would have some slick reply he'd already rehearsed. And she was done with his slick replies. Instead, she said, "He doesn't need someone like you."

Reaching into her oversize purse, she pulled out a duplicate of the file the Mavericks had put together. Setting it on the table, she left it there, closed. Like the elephant in the room. Like the bit of spinach between the teeth that no one wants to tell you about. Like a ticking bomb that was impossible to defuse in time.

Archie's gaze went right to it. Got stuck there for a few seconds. Then he looked up and smiled as if there wasn't a thing to worry about. As if nothing in a folder *she* brought could possibly hurt him.

"I believe you had a reason for going to Vegas," she said, pushing him forward. Toward a trap entirely of his own making.

"San Francisco was much too dreary." He shuddered dramatically, still cocksure, still oblivious, still thinking he had the upper hand. "Year-round sun is *far* more appealing."

"I'm sure it is," she agreed, "but I believe you also had some business partners who required you to be in closer proximity to them." She tapped the folder. "Your gallery is a sham." She didn't want a scene or eavesdroppers, so she kept her voice low enough to be masked by the buzz of lunch conversation. Leaning closer, as close as she could stand without throwing up at the smell of his overpowering cologne, she said, "To be more precise, your gallery is a shell. A front. You move paintings. You move money. And then you make that money look clean for some very bad people." She opened the file, read a name, a big, bad name, one even she'd heard of.

At last, his smile was gone. And his eyes had gone very cold and very dark. "I have no idea what you're talking about." But he swallowed hard enough to make his Adam's apple bob.

She smoothed a hand over the folder. "The evidence was quite easy to come by. In fact, it took my investigator less than twenty-four hours to put it together."

"Investigator?" He went pale beneath the Vegas tan.

"You think you know me so well, Archie. You still think I'm the naïve eighteen-year-old girl you once preyed on. But it turns out that you don't know me at all. And what you didn't figure on is that I have friends, very powerful friends. And they know exactly how to handle a weasel like you."

"What the f—" The curse word didn't come to fruition as he looked around, then lowered his voice. "I haven't done anything. You can't prove anything."

"I disagree. You've done a lot. More than I ever thought you were capable of, to be honest. It's all here." She caressed the file lovingly. "And this afternoon it's all going to the U.S. Attorney's Office."

He was breathing hard and fast at the thought of actually having to pay the price for all the dirty deals he'd done. "How dare you, you little—"

She held up a hand to stop his low-voiced rant. "Here's the thing. These cases can go one of two ways. They can go lenient. Or they can go bad. Really bad. Especially if they decide to use you as an example for all the other would-be art launderers out there."

He opened his mouth, closed it. It could be fear. Or it could be that he didn't believe she was capable of following through on her threats. But he would be so wrong.

She was very capable. She always had been.

"Now, my friends," she went on, "they know people. Powerful people. Important people. People who can make it easy on you." She shrugged. "Or they can tighten the screws until it really, really hurts."

"What the hell do you want?"

"Funny, when I asked you that yesterday, I didn't get an answer."

A worm in the grass, Archie squirmed and writhed. "What do you want?" he asked again. His words were so muted, so fraught with fear and shock, that she almost had to read his lips.

"Leave me and my son alone. He was *never* your son. You disowned him even before he was born. You denied him. You ignored him until suddenly you had a use for him. I would *never* want a man like you to be anyone's father. So don't call us, don't come near us, don't even live in the same state with us. Not ever again. For any reason."

"And if I do what you ask, you won't turn in the information?"

She snorted softly and shook her head, a slight smile on her lips. "Of course I'm going to turn it in. It's my civic duty. But knowing how slick you've always been, I'm sure you can rat out some rats, make a few deals, and probably get away with little to no jail time." She waited a beat. "If you want my friends' help, that is."

"You—" He didn't call her the name he wanted to. He was afraid now. Deeply afraid.

Was it bad to feel so good about that?

Not one bit, she decided.

"If you don't leave my son alone," she continued, "my friends will make sure you can't cut *any* deals. And you can expect an extremely long jail term. Oh look, I've been talking so much, I've forgotten my champagne." She sipped, and bubbly had never tasted better. Then she pushed the folder across the table. "You can have this, by the way. Just so you know I'm not bluffing. But the originals are going to the authorities."

He opened the folder, flipped a couple of pages, stopped, read, and then read again. Then he looked at her. His usually smug face was drawn, with deep lines that hadn't been there only minutes before. His skin was gray, and he looked ten years older. He looked once more at the papers in the folder, all the paragraphs, all the sentences, all the words that brought him down. "If I leave you both alone, you swear you'll make sure I don't go to jail?"

"If you leave me and Jorge alone and turn state's evidence, I'm sure you'll be able to make some sort of plea bargain. But that's up to you."

The truth was she had no idea how this kind of thing actually worked. A large part of her hoped the Mavericks would let him rot. It was no less than Archie deserved.

But she knew the Mavericks were men of their word, and if Archie cooperated in every way, they would keep their promise.

"All right," he said. "You win."

Goal achieved, Rosie rose and said, "Good-bye, Archie." Then she turned and walked out on him for the very last time.

She ran to Gideon, who was waiting for her in the same spot where she'd left him.

Her warrior.

Her love.

Her *forever*.

Chapter Twenty-Five

Why was the meeting taking so long?

They were the longest and worst minutes of Gideon's life. He could almost hear his watch ticking even though it was digital.

And then, there she was, running down the sidewalk to him. *Thank God.* He swung Rosie up and held her tight, not able to speak for several long moments, as profound gratitude held him in its grip.

"It was perfect," she said when he finally let her feet slide back down to the ground. "He's terrified. He'll leave us alone."

Gideon stroked a finger down her cheek, breathed in the sweet scent of her. "I'm so proud of you." They were in the middle of the sidewalk, people all around them, but she had to know—he had to tell her what he'd never admitted to another soul. "I blamed myself for not making Karmen stay inside the wire."

"I know you did." Her voice was so gentle, so understanding. "Even though no one else blamed you."

"But you know what the real problem was?" He'd finally worked it out in those long, agonizing minutes as he waited for Rosie. "I didn't trust her to take care of herself." He hadn't even trusted her enough to tell her how he felt. "We fought about it, about how I was always asking her not to go, not to do her job the way she thought best. We fought about it just before that last mission." He swallowed hard. "I know that's not why she died. But I also know she didn't die because she was careless. She died because she did what had to be done, because she was a hero, like everyone else on my team. I will always feel the ache that it was them and not me. I can't help that. But instead of arguing with her, I should have trusted Karmen to be the soldier that she was." A stranger hurrying down the sidewalk jostled Gideon closer to Rosie. "Back then, I didn't understand how strong a woman could be. But I know now, Rosie. Because you and Ari and Chi, Paige and Harper and Charlie and Tasha, all of you Mavericks, you've helped me see it. But especially you, Rosie, how you'll do anything for Jorge—yet at the same time, you don't let anyone take advantage of you either."

"I've been taking care of myself and Jorge for a long time." She wrapped her hand around his nape, pulling him even closer. "But knowing you were out here today, to back me up if I needed you, helped me stay strong in the face of evil. You and me, we're strongest *together*, Gideon. The two of us, we can do anything."

It hit him then, the true meaning of Karmen's gift. Pulling Rosie around the corner, out of the crowded street, he backed her up against the wall. "I've just figured it out, why Karmen said there was *magic* in the painting. It's about two people being the strongest they can possibly be by leaning on each other, helping each other, trusting each other."

"That really is magic," Rosie agreed. "And yet, it's so simple too."

His voice was infused with a new strength and certainty as he said, "I need to sell the painting."

Rosie studied his face for a long moment. "You're completely sure about letting Karmen's painting go now, aren't you?" It wasn't even a question. Rosie knew him inside and out, everything there was to know.

He nodded, never having felt more sure of anything, apart from how he loved Rosie and Jorge with every piece of the soul he thought he'd lost. "With the money from the painting, I can help people find the strength within themselves. The foundation we can set up will be akin to standing outside their door offering that helping hand."

"I love it, Gideon. It's so perfect. You can do so much good."

"*We*, Rosie." He stroked her cheek. "I never could have figured this out without you, when all I've done for so long is stand on the sidelines." It was what he'd been doing for ten long years, living off the grid, hiding in the shadows. Even after he'd found Ari, he hadn't truly participated, hadn't really lived, except for the times he let himself go with the boys. "Will you work with me to start a foundation where we can help vets and their families?" His mind whirled with all the possibilities. "We could help foster kids too. People like me, kids like you and Ari and Chi. We could help people who need a team to support them, bring them together. What do you say, Rosie? Will you be my team to get this off the ground?"

"Yes," she said as she held him tight. "Yes to every single one of your amazing ideas."

"I love you. I love you so damned much." He picked her up, twirling her around, making her laugh with sheer joy. "I want to keep on saying that every day for the rest of our lives. You are my heart. You are my soul. You've set me free."

* * *

Gideon was a new man. He smiled all the way up to his beautiful sky-blue eyes.

He'd always been strong. Loyal. Amazing. But now, for the first time ever, Rosie could see that he was truly happy.

As happy as she was. He would be the best father for Jorge, a man Jorge could admire, the kind of man

Jorge could strive to be. And the best life partner for her.

They truly were strong because they were together, because they gave each other strength instead of sapping it. She'd been paralyzed by those phone calls. But sharing her fear with Gideon had shown her the solution. Sharing and trusting had given her strength. Just as Gideon's sharing and trusting her with the full story of what had happened in the Middle East had given him the strength to finally forgive himself— and to risk his heart again.

The moment they got back to Evan and Paige's house, she gathered Jorge up in her arms. She hadn't realized how tense she'd been the past few days, since that first phone call. Now, as she smothered her son with kisses and knew in her very soul that he was safe, she could finally let it all go.

"Love you, sweet boy."

"Love you too, Mom." Then he raced back to the epic Lego city he and Noah were building on the dining table with the new Lego pieces Paige must have had delivered.

"I take it things went well?" Evan asked.

Her joy was written in her smile that wouldn't quit. "Absolutely. My ex is one hundred percent neutralized."

"Excellent. I'll forward all the evidence Rafe found to my contact at the U.S. Attorney's Office."

"And thank you, again." Gideon said. "For everything." He shook Evan's hand, and in the next moment they were doing one of those guy backslap hugs. It was adorable. Rosie and Paige joined in so that all four of them made one big group hug.

"Okay," Paige said, "I have the biggest favor to ask. I know you've been through a lot, and you're probably worried about not having Jorge right by your side. But is there any chance you could let us keep them for the night? It's just that we're having such a great time today. And I wanted to show them how to make ice cream with my new Ice Cream Ball." Paige oozed excitement while Evan looked on fondly. "We've got extra toothbrushes, and I promise they won't want for anything while they're here."

"Paige, you are such a doll." Rosie had needed to touch her son, kiss him, hug him. But he was safe here with Paige and Evan. Safe with his Maverick family. And he would always be safe with Gideon.

Before she answered, she looked at Gideon. After all, they were a team now. When he nodded, she smiled and gave her blessing.

"That's so wonderful." Paige clapped her hands as Evan hooked a hand around her nape and pulled her close, his expression so loving, so tender. "Evan and I will have a great time with them."

Evan nodded his agreement, then looked at Gideon. "About the painting. I don't want to rush you to make a decision—"

Gideon held up a hand. "I just need to confirm a couple of things first, but if everything works out the way I hope it will, it's a go on the auction. And when we have more time, Rosie and I would like to talk with you about using the proceeds to set up a nonprofit foundation to help veterans and foster children."

"I'd be more than happy to help however I can with setting up a nonprofit. Although, if you decided to keep some of the proceeds from the auction, no one would begrudge you that."

Gideon shook his head. "I don't need the money." He lifted Rosie's hand, kissed her knuckles. Then he looked at Jorge in the dining room, his eyes a shining sky blue. "I've already got everything I could ever want or need."

Rosie was beaming as she hugged Paige, then the boys, who gave them hugs and kisses after they found out the fun news that they were going to spend the night with Paige and Evan.

Rosie and Gideon walked hand in hand to his SUV. Once in the car, waving good-bye, Rosie said, "Paige is pregnant." After all the terrible things that Whitney, Evan's ex, had done, it would be so wonderful for Evan and Paige to finally have the family they longed for. "She's already nesting—baking cookies, buying puzzles and Legos, getting an ice cream maker, asking for a kid sleepover."

"I'm really happy for them," Gideon said. "They've both traveled a rough road before finally getting to where they're supposed to be." He turned, looking into her eyes. "Just like my road to you."

Her heart melted, even as her body heated up knowing they had a whole night to themselves.

A night in which they could be as loud as they wanted...

Chapter Twenty-Six

The moment Gideon closed the apartment door, Rosie kissed him with all the unexpressed love, all the suppressed emotion, all the pent-up need she'd felt for months now. Gideon's kiss was just as ravenous, just as desperate, his hands everywhere.

He pulled back long enough to say, "I was terrified today." Then his mouth was on hers again, stealing any response she could have given him. Until he backed off to take a breath and said, "I know you'll always do whatever needs to be done, no matter how hard. But I'm always going to go a little crazy while you're doing it."

It was a remarkable thing for such a strong man to admit. But she understood. He would always need to protect her, he would always need to protect Jorge. Just as she would always need to protect her son, and now Gideon. Their insatiable need for each other was an affirmation of all the fear as much as it was a celebration of their love.

"I'll never take foolish risks," she said. "I promise."

He framed her face with his callused hands. "I know that. But you need to know that you mean everything to me."

"I do. Because you're everything to me too. You and Jorge."

"I want to be his father," Gideon said, his face as solemn as a vow, his voice grave with meaning. "I want to be the father he's never had. The kind of father that *I* never had."

"I need that too," she replied, emotion welling up in her voice. "And more than that, Jorge needs you."

He picked her up in his arms, carried her into the bedroom, laying her on the bed, coming down against her, blanketing her body with his. "I want to make love to you every day, every night, every hour, every minute."

"Yes. Please." Because making love wasn't just about the physical. It was all the little things he would do to make her happy every day, every hour, every minute. And everything she would do to show him how loved he was.

He slid his hands under the blouse she'd worn to confront her ex. It wasn't sexy. It was utilitarian. So was the bra and everything she had on. Now she wanted everything off, shredded, gone, never to be worn again. "Tear it off, Gideon. All of it."

Taking the hem of the blouse in both hands, he ripped it apart. The buttons went flying. She laughed, loved knowing she was his now—that there was no going back. Not ever.

He made fast work of the bra's front clasp, the plastic tab cracking as he broke it apart. "You are so beautiful." It was like he was looking at her anew, making everything fresh.

As he bent down to take the peak of one breast in his mouth, she shuddered with joy, with ecstasy, with desire, with love—and with the potent knowledge that this gorgeous man, this brave man, this loyal, caring, strong man, was all hers.

* * *

She kissed him until there was only sensation. Only Rosie. She hadn't only helped him remember how to laugh, she'd brought him back to life, showing him that he was capable of loving again. That he was worthy of her love.

He'd already torn off her blouse, and as he yanked down her white jeans and threw them in a corner, he knew exactly why she'd wanted everything shredded. To destroy the last vestige of connection to her ex, even the clothes she'd worn into battle.

Then she was naked on top of him. "There hasn't been anyone for me, not since Jorge was born, and I'm on the Pill for my cycle. And since you said there hasn't been anyone for you in a long time—"

"Yes," he said, unable to let her finish the thought

when he was so completely on board. "A thousand times *yes*." Then he captured her mouth with a kiss, and together they undid his pants and tugged off his shirt.

Her skin against his, her mouth on him as she kissed every inch of bare flesh, along his jaw, down his neck, over his chest—every sensation was glorious, taking him higher, to places he'd never been. Until she took him in her hands and turned him mindless with the dangerous things she did to him, caressing, stroking, adoring.

Moments later, he flipped her onto her back so fast that she gasped. He kissed her hair, her forehead, her eyebrows, her eyelids, stopping for a long sweet kiss on the mouth before he worked his way down her beautiful body, not missing a single square inch.

And there were the parts he lingered on. That sensitive spot right below her ear. The crook of her neck. Her breasts. Her belly. And just when she must have thought—and maybe hoped and prayed—that he was finally going to taste the very center of her, he turned her over and started on her back. He loved the way she squirmed under him, loved the little sounds of pleasure she made as he followed up each kiss with a long swipe of his tongue.

"*Gideon.*"

Ah, yes, it was close enough to begging. And he gave in to her plea, slipping his hand between her legs, coming up under her to find the sweet spot. His name fell from her lips again and again as she climaxed, her voice drenched with passion and love.

When Gideon finally gathered her up in his arms and carried her into the rain shower, her beautiful features were still dazed with pleasure. It was the luxury he loved most about the place, the one thing he'd had to have. Maybe because he'd had a premonition that one day he would hold Rosie against him as he stood under the rain showerhead. The water was instantly warm, and he let her slide down his body until she was standing, her head tipped back, eyes closed, as she soaked up the rainfall cascading over her.

With his heart pounding harder than ever before—heck, *every* part of him was harder than ever before—he poured soap into his palm and lathered her body, massaging it into her neck, her back, her breasts.

Going down on his haunches, he soaped her thighs, her calves, lifting one foot to work it, then the other, while she clung to his shoulders. He rose again to wash her hair with his shampoo, wanting his scents all over her.

When he washed the soap away, she finally opened her eyes. "Your turn," her voice low and sexy and seductive.

His legs trembled as she soaped and rinsed his erection, then licked the very tip of him while she washed his legs. She stood to lather his chest, his arms, his back and shoulders.

Her touch, her kisses, pushed him to the edge. He couldn't wait a second longer, hauling her up until she wrapped her legs around his waist and her arms around his neck.

Though his body urged him to drive into her in one hard thrust, his heart knew better. Knew how sweet it would be to enter her so very slowly, so very gently, as she opened her mouth and he took her with his tongue.

And *oh*…it was pure, sweet, heady sensation. The feel of Rosie as they became one, no barriers between them, was like nothing he'd ever known, nothing he could ever imagine.

She closed her eyes, leaned her head back against the shower wall, and moaned as he took her—and she owned him in every way. Her cheeks were flushed, her nostrils flared, her lips parted as her body gripped him tight. Air puffed through his teeth as he held on to his control by only a thread. Until he felt her legs tightening, her muscles working, her skin heating.

At last, he blasted off, crying out, wrapping himself in the circle of her arms. And the soft beat of her voice, "I need you, Gideon. *All* of you."

It was all the encouragement it took, and he gave them both what they so badly needed, a ride straight up to heaven together. Always and forever together.

★ ★ ★

Gideon was so tender as he patted every drop of water from Rosie's body, then towel-dried her hair, drawing the comb through without breaking a single strand.

"I forgot to bring more clothes." She hadn't packed for an extended stay.

"What makes you think you're going to need any clothes tonight?" He wrapped her in his big fluffy robe, and she breathed in his scent, loving it. Loving him.

"Only while I make you a Rosie special for dinner," she told him. Given all the calories they'd just burned, he must be as starved as she was.

He smiled in the mirror, holding her against him, her back to his front. "What's a Rosie special?"

"You'll see. And you'll love it," she promised. Her dad had taught her a lot, but she'd had to become a decent cook for Jorge. No way was she going to let him grow up on fast food.

"Of course I will."

Behind her, he was naked. It was all she could do not to take him again right this second. Her experience with men—one man—had never been fun. She'd always been self-conscious, always worried, always judging her performance, her looks, what she said, how she said it. But Gideon let her be anything she wanted. He let her be herself. She loved him for that. And she would never stop wanting him.

"Thank you for setting me free," she said softly.

"It's the other way around, Rosie. *You* set *me* free."

The truth was that each had set the other free in different ways. He had freed her from a prison of regret for making the wrong choice with Jorge's father and the fear of risking her heart again with another wrong choice. And she had freed him from blaming himself for what had happened to Karmen and to his team.

"Now we need food." She waggled her eyebrows like a lecherous old man. "So that we have the energy to do that again. And again. And again."

When he grabbed a pair of sweatpants, as much as Rosie hated seeing him cover up all those gorgeous muscles, it was absolutely necessary if they were ever going to get food on the table.

She found spinach, bell peppers, mushrooms, cheese, eggs, and some hamburger in his fridge, which was perfect to make her special scramble. "You chop the peppers and mushrooms," she said, "and I'll grate the cheese."

"I've never cooked with anyone before." He said it with no little wonder.

For the next few minutes, they shared things they'd never done before. He had never gone for a bike ride along a river walk. Never taken a paddle boat out on a pond. Never owned a dog or a cat. And she had never been to a Sharks hockey game. Or to a race at Laguna Seca in Monterey. Or on a camping trip in Yosemite.

Together with Jorge, they would do it all. And every second they spent together would be precious.

"Can you hand me the eggs?" she asked.

He moved behind her to wash his hands at the sink, then back again, his scent tantalizing her as he passed her to open the fridge. He put the eggs beside her, then rested against her, his chin on her head, as she broke an egg into a bowl. Then another. And another.

Until he lifted the robe and stroked his fingers up the outside of her thighs. Then slipping down, along, inside. She gasped and almost tipped over the bowl of eggs.

He slid his foot between hers and pushed her legs wider. "You're doing a great job," he said in a low voice than sent a shiver of need up her spine. "Those eggs are going to be so good. I can't wait to eat them."

The next thing she knew, he was pulling her hips back, bending her over, and moving between her legs while she gripped the counter.

He pressed a kiss to the nape of her neck, his warm breath tantalizing across her skin as he said, "There's one more thing I've never done before. I've never made love. Not until you."

"*Gideon.*" She could barely get his name out as he entered her. "Neither have I."

★ ★ ★

A while later, after great food and more loving, when

he felt lazy and sated and happy with her in his arms, there was one more thing he needed her to know. Not tomorrow, but tonight. Now.

Slowly moving from her arms, he went down on one knee beside the bed. Her eyes were wide, and she sat up in surprise as he took both her hands in his. "I love you so much I ache with it. I love Jorge like he's my own child. Marry me, Rosie, and make me even happier than I ever hoped I could be."

He'd never thought he could want such a thing. He'd never thought he wouldn't fear making such a deep commitment to another person, with the risk of losing them one day the way he'd lost so many people he cared for. But Rosie had erased all his fears. Rosie had made him want this. He loved her, so much he burned with the need to make her his forever.

"Oh, Gideon." Moisture glistened in her eyes. "I swear I was just about to ask you the same thing." She tugged him back onto the bed, both of them facing each other on their knees. "Even though it's only been a week, the truth is that I've loved you from the moment Ari told me all the stories about her big, beautiful brother. Even before I met you, my heart was forever yours."

"If you're asking," he said in a voice overflowing with emotion, "I'd give anything to be your husband."

"And I want nothing more than to be your wife."

Chapter Twenty-Seven

Matt and Ari had returned from their honeymoon a week ago, and today they were taking the boys to the beach for their last summer outing before school started. It was the right time for Gideon and Rosie to drive to Bakersfield to see Mrs. Sanchez, Karmen's mother.

Gideon parked at the bottom of the long, circular drive, then put his hand over Rosie's. "Thank you for coming with me."

"Of course I'd come with you. Just like you came with me to see that man whose name I shall never say again." Then she added, "Are you sure you're okay with my coming inside?"

Before Rosie, he would have believed he needed to face everything on his own. He'd made this trip once before, not long after he'd gotten out of the army. He'd come to give Karmen's parents the photos he'd kept of her, to tell them what a brave and honorable daughter they had raised—and to confess to failing to keep their daughter safe. His gut had been clenched so tight, he'd thought he'd be sick.

But with Rosie at his side, he was ready to face anything. He would always be better, stronger, happier, with the woman he loved beside him.

"Together," he said. "That's how we do things."

Hand in hand, they walked up the drive, following the tree line as it curved, the brown paper parcel tucked under his arm. Ten years ago, he'd been overwhelmed by guilt, by regret. And he'd had no idea how the Sanchezes would receive him. Thankfully, they'd been like sponges soaking up every detail of their daughter's army life. Not only about Karmen's death, but also about her life and her friends, her bravery and her heroism. He'd had so much to tell them because Karmen had done so much, for her team, for her country. It had been his honor to help them celebrate her life and her memory. And through the letters he'd sent for several years afterward and the times he'd called her, he'd wanted to tell Mrs. Sanchez how much that day had helped him, but he'd never known how.

Flowers in planters on the front stoop bloomed beneath the portico. He lifted the heavy brass knocker, heard it reverberate inside the house. Then Karmen's mother opened the door.

She was a beautiful woman in her mid-sixties, though she barely looked older than the last time he'd seen her. She was elegantly attired in a blue dress, a strand of pearls about her neck, and he knew he was looking at the woman Karmen would have become if she'd lived.

Mrs. Sanchez held out her hands to him. "Gideon, it is so good to see you. I'm so glad you called. And you must be Rosie." Her smile was warm. "It's lovely to meet you. Please, come inside."

As soon as she shut the door behind them, he said, "Thank you again, ma'am, for helping Ariana find me." Mrs. Sanchez had been instrumental in reconnecting them.

"Please, call me Ernestina." She drew him into the house. "And it was my pleasure to help in any way I could. She wrote me a letter, you know, thanking me and letting me know that you'd come home."

Ari hadn't told him that. "I'm sorry. I should have come to see you again sooner."

"Please, Gideon, no apologies. I'm just glad you're here now. You too, Rosie. Please, tell me about yourself."

"I'm Ari's foster sister. I have a six-year-old son named Jorge. And," Rosie added with a wide smile and a squeeze of his hand, "I'm head over heels for Gideon."

"Oh, I already knew that!" Ernestina's eyes twinkled.

"We're engaged to be married," he told Karmen's mother, and Rosie held out the simple rose diamond solitaire he'd bought her after she'd accepted his proposal.

"I'm so happy for you both," Ernestina exclaimed. "Truly, this is wonderful news."

As they walked through Karmen's home, he saw that it hadn't changed. There were still large vases of cut flowers in the foyer, while potted plants, blooming with buds, hugged the corners.

"I've set coffee out in the sunroom," she said, leading them into the large lounge with windows all around. And more flowers, more green plants, more living things. A silver coffee service complete with tea sandwiches sat on the central coffee table.

"Thank you." Gideon looked at the spread before them. "But you didn't have to go to this much trouble for us."

"It's no trouble." She poured the three of them coffee. "Please sit."

He set the wrapped painting on the couch beside him, needing to express his condolences. "I'm very sorry you lost your husband."

She smiled, fondly rather than sadly. "It was a difficult time. But he and I spent our time wisely, wringing every last drop out of every last moment we had together."

Together. Mrs. Sanchez obviously knew the importance of that word, just as he and Rosie had learned. "I'm glad you could do that. He seemed like such a good man."

"He was." Her eyes glowed with the same warmth as they had the day Gideon told her everything he could about Karmen. "And hearing from you has brought back the happy memory of the day you brought us all those wonderful photos of Karmen. I look at them all the time, and they always bring me such joy."

It was obvious where Karmen's generosity had come from. And her positive outlook.

"I'm so sorry for your losses," Rosie said softly. "Karmen sounds like she was an absolutely wonderful person."

Ernestina smiled again, though her eyes looked misty now. "She truly was. And something tells me she would say the same about you."

At last, Gideon picked up the parcel. "Karmen gave this to me a couple of days before the attack." He untied the string and unwrapped the angel painting. Carefully, he removed it from the paper and laid it on the coffee table facing Ernestina.

She put a hand over her mouth. "My dear mamá's painting. It meant so much to her. She always adored Karmen."

A sharp pang of guilt needled between his ribs. "I should have told you I had it when I was here the last time. But I didn't realize—"

"Oh, no. Karmen gave it to you. That's as it should

be. The painting is meant to be passed on. And the giver is the only one who knows when and to whom it should go." She smiled with love. "She told me in one of her letters that she'd found a very special person she planned to give it to. When you came here all those years ago, I suspected that person was you. She told you the painting has a unique magic, didn't she?"

"Yes. She said whoever has it will know the right time to pass it on."

Karmen's mother gave him a knowing look. "And have you discovered that time?"

"I believe I have." He glanced down at the painting. "But there's something you might not know about it. This is an original Miguel Fernando Correa painting. Rosie is the one who discovered it."

Her expression remained serene as she nodded and said, "I believe he also painted my great-great-great-something grandparents."

"Ernestina—" He paused. "This painting is worth a lot of money."

She gave him that serene smile again. "I would be surprised if it wasn't."

"Did Karmen know that when she gave it to me?"

"Its monetary value was never important. The painting goes where it must."

"But I'm sure you wouldn't want to let it out of your family if it's been with you for generations. Especially as it was Karmen's at the end."

She was silent for a long moment. The only sound was the ticking of the grandfather clock in the hall. Finally, she said, "If the lore is correct, which I believe it to be, it's been out of the family many times. And somehow it comes back, like it did to my dear mamá."

He was afraid she still wasn't getting the whole picture. "A friend of mine recently had it authenticated and valued. It's worth at least fifty million dollars."

She put a hand to her pearls. "Oh my. Isn't that amazing."

"If you feel it belongs in the family, I want to give it back to you."

"And if I don't?" Ernestina held his gaze steadily.

"Rosie and I would use the proceeds from an art auction to fund a nonprofit foundation to help foster children, veterans, and their families."

"And we would like to do it in Karmen's name," Rosie added.

Karmen's mother was radiant in a shaft of sunlight. "She always told me you were a man with a big heart, that there wasn't anything you wouldn't do for your team. I'm not surprised that you've found in Rosie a woman with a heart just as big."

As she smiled at them both, the last of his angst, the last of his guilt seemed cleansed away.

"It's what Karmen would have wanted you to do," Ernestina said with a decisive nod. "The painting truly is magic. It has passed through many hands and saved many lives."

But it hadn't saved Karmen's.

She wagged her finger at him. "I know what you're thinking. But we are not to know its mysterious ways. All Karmen must have known was that it was time for her to pass it on and that you were the person to give it to. Somehow, she was able to see that you would use it for good and not for profit." Ernestina's smile was full of the richness of love for her daughter. "Both Karmen and the painting chose well."

"Thank you," he said, his heart full. Karmen's mother believed in him. Karmen had believed in him. And, most of all, Rosie believed in him.

"And let me tell you another secret. No matter who buys it, the painting will still find its way to the person to whom it is supposed to go. You can be sure of that."

"I am sure," he said. He now completely believed in the magic.

"Would it be helpful if I were to tell your auctioneer its history?" Ernestina asked. "At least what I know of it."

"More than helpful." Evan's contact at the auction house had said anything they could find out would surely increase the sale price.

Happiness was a warm glow on her face. "It will bring back wonderful memories of my family. We get so busy with our daily routines. But it's good to look back. And while I'm looking through all the old papers it will be as if my mamá and Karmen and her father are with me."

While Gideon had lived in misery with his memories, Ernestina lived for those memories. It was a unique, and wonderful, way of looking at life. One he would strive to remember during any rough moments the future might hold.

* * *

"She was lovely," Rosie said an hour later as he pulled onto the highway. "But I'm still amazed she gave her wholehearted blessing to your selling the painting once she heard how much it was worth."

"After losing her daughter and her husband, I think she simply wants Karmen's legacy to live on."

Rosie knew he was right. Though there were some bad people out there, in her life she'd been lucky enough to find so many good ones. Gideon had too. "Well, she was certainly excited, telling you everything she could remember about the painting."

"Evan's auctioneer will be ecstatic," he agreed, "especially if she can find documentation in her papers."

Gideon had come a long way from the man in the shadows whom she'd first gotten to know. But she still needed to remind him, "He's *your* auctioneer, Gideon. It's *you* doing this. It's *you* giving away a multimillion-dollar painting and not keeping a penny for yourself. Not Ernestina or Evan."

"I don't need the money. I know it seems like I arrived with nothing, but I've made some good financial choices since leaving the military." She could see that he was gearing up to ask her a question. "I know you're fine on your own and don't need help from anyone, but—" He raised their entwined fingers to stroke her cheek with the back of his hand. "I'd like to get Jorge some art lessons. What do you think?"

"I've been saving up." She'd always tried to do right by her son.

"I know. But will you let me pay for it so he can start lessons now?"

"Yes," she said a moment later. She'd been independent for so long, taken care of Jorge on her own, along with the help of her best friends. But now she and Gideon were a team, along with Jorge. Together, they could do anything. "Of course. He would love that. *I* would love that."

He glanced at a road sign ahead. "There's someone else I'd like you to meet. A friend over in San Luis Obispo. Zach is an old army buddy I haven't seen in a long time." He pointed. "If it's okay with you, we could take this turnoff to go see him."

Her heart swelled at the strength it took to let every single one of his walls fall. Rosie knew what a huge step this was for Gideon. First seeing Mrs. Sanchez and now Zach, both of whom were inexorably tied to his time in the army. Over the past week, Gideon had slowly revealed the rest of his history to her—the Middle East, coming home, how broken he was after he got back stateside. At the time, Gideon had insisted on going to see the families of all the guys on his team who had died. Meeting those families had been horrific for him, especially when one of his team members' wives blamed Gideon for getting her children's father killed.

"It's more than okay," she said. "Besides, I'm sure the boys are having a ball with Ari and Matt, so there's no need to rush home."

As Gideon took the exit, his mouth creased in a smile. He smiled so much more now. For so long he'd felt the need to deny the laughter, to deny any joy. She would never let that happen again.

Seeing both Zach and Mrs. Sanchez was a turning point. It meant he was healing.

And Rosie would be there for him every step of the way. She always would be, just the way he would be there for her.

Forever.

"I love you," she said.

He turned, a brief glance away from the road, and looked at her, his eyes a gorgeous sky blue. "I love you too. More than you'll ever know."

But she did know. She felt his love in every breath. Just as she knew he felt hers.

Epilogue

Today was the final barbecue and pool party of the summer at Matt and Ari's house. The boys had started first grade last Monday, and standing under the big awning over the back deck, they were regaling Susan, Bob, Daniel, Tasha, and Lyssa with every detail of their first week at school. The two puppies, Noah's Flash and Tasha's Darla, already exhausted from all the activity, were napping. The rest of the Mavericks would show up soon, along with Jeremy's Duke, and the puppy whirlwind would start all over again.

Gideon and Rosie were sitting together on deck chairs, soaking up the sun, their fingers laced together as they watched Noah and Jorge go through every single school day event with pantomimes and hand gestures.

The kids were amazing. Gideon still could hardly believe they were *his*. DNA didn't matter. Only love.

Love that filled him up from the pit of his stomach to the tips of his fingers and toes and straight back to his heart.

Unwilling to let go of Rosie, with his free hand Gideon reached into his pocket and awkwardly removed a slip of paper from his wallet, which he handed over to her to unfold.

"What's this?" She was staring at it as if she'd forgotten how to read. "Tickets to the New York Metropolitan Museum of Art?" Absolute shock hushed her voice.

"It's for Columbus Day weekend," he explained. "The Monday will be a holiday. Since Jorge has a teacher day on Friday, he'll be out of school four straight days. With the warehouses right on schedule, Daniel's got no problem with my taking a couple of days away." He smiled at her. "Do you think you could get that Friday and Monday off as well?"

But she was just staring at him. Then he realized her eyes were blurred with tears. "You remembered we wanted to go there. Especially now, to see the *Battle of Angels*."

"I remember everything you've told me," he said softly. "And I signed us up for painting lessons at the Met too."

She stared at him, unblinking. "Like *us* meaning me and Jorge?"

"Like *us* meaning all three of us."

She let out a deep breath, her eyes shining. "Oh, Gideon."

"I pulled out the painting. The one from that day at

the Legion of Honor." He'd seen where she'd stored the tube in which she'd rolled it up.

She bit her lip. "And?"

"It wasn't exactly easy to look at. And it's probably not going to be easy for me to paint again." He touched her hand. "But I'm ready to look at some of my stuff. And painting seems like a pretty damn good way to do that. Especially if you're right there beside me." He'd looked at the painting on his own, and somehow it hadn't been as traumatic as he'd feared because Rosie had already seen it. Because it hadn't horrified her. "I'm glad you didn't let me tear it up."

"I love you so much," she whispered.

"As much as I love you." He kissed her fingers. "And I was thinking that next summer, when Jorge's out of school, we'd go to Paris and see the Louvre."

She threw herself at him, hugged him tight.

"Get a room," Ari teased with a smile as she carried over two huge pitchers of margaritas. Matt followed with lemonade, plastic glasses, and a plate heaped with sandwiches. Charlie's robot fountain would be filled with the margaritas and lemonade.

"Gideon is taking Jorge and me to the Met." Rosie's voice was full of awe and wonder. As if she didn't know he'd happily take her and Jorge wherever they wanted to go. Even the moon.

Ari didn't need to ask what the Met was. She knew Rosie well enough. But she nudged Matt. "I bet Noah would love to go too."

Matt gave her a look. "What if this is some sort of romantic getaway? We'd be horning in."

Ari smiled at Gideon. "Is it a romantic getaway we'd be horning in on?"

Every moment with Rosie was romantic, whether they were filling the dishwasher or dancing beneath the fairy lights in her backyard. "It would be great if you came," he said. Truth was, Gideon was even happier about the thought of a full-on family vacation. Heck, maybe they could convince some of the other Mavericks to come too.

"Noah will love it," Ari said. "New York City is so vibrant."

"I haven't booked the plane tickets yet," Gideon said, "but I can do it for all of us."

"Or we could just keep things simple and use my plane," Matt offered.

Rosie laughed. "I vote for simple."

A year ago, neither Gideon nor Rosie would have thought they'd know someone who had his own plane, let alone that they'd fly in it.

A year ago, they didn't have each other either.

But now they had absolutely *everything*.

Jorge had started his art lessons, and Charlie and Sebastian were paving the way for Rosie to enter the art world now that she no longer had a reason to hide. Gideon was unquestionably positive that her career was going to be huge. She wouldn't be an accountant for much longer—there simply wouldn't be the time when she was so busy painting.

What's more, Jorge's bio-dad was going into Witness Protection. He'd signed over all his parental rights and agreed never to contact Jorge. At the age of eighteen, Jorge could decide whether or not he wanted to contact Findley.

Yeah, life with Rosie and Jorge was nothing short of perfect.

Gideon raised her hand to his lips. He would never get tired of touching her. "Need a margarita, sweetheart?"

"That would be marvelous, thank you, honey."

He loved the endearment. And it was with great difficulty that he managed to let go of her hand so he could retrieve the offered drink.

Ari was pouring the mixed margaritas into Charlie's amazing robot fountain.

"Let me help with that." He took the second pitcher and poured it in.

"Thanks. I was hoping you'd come over."

As she smiled at him, he realized there was a new ease between them. He'd always been so racked with guilt that he'd never truly let himself go, not even with his sister. It was another thing for which he had Rosie to thank.

"I'm so happy for you and Rosie," she said softly.

"I've waited a long time to see you like this. You deserve happiness, Gideon. You deserve Rosie. You're both the best thing for each other."

He set his pitcher on the table beside the plastic glasses, then picked up his sister's hand, squeezing it tight. "If you'd told me that a month ago, I would have said you were crazy."

"Oh, Gideon."

He shushed her with a gentle look. "But falling in love with Rosie and Jorge, and being here with you, I've learned something huge. I can finally accept that I did my best. No matter how much I might wish I'd done things differently, or that my best was better, there's no do-overs. There's just now and the future. I'm not going to waste another moment making wishes for things that can't possibly come true. Those years with you that I missed, I can never have back, just as I can never get my team back. But what I *can* do is cherish every day with Rosie and Jorge, and you and Noah, and this big family you've brought me into, from this moment on."

She gazed at him with shining eyes, a tear wobbling in the corners. "I love you, Gideon."

"Ditto, kiddo."

She hugged him fiercely. And he hugged her back with every bit of love in his heart.

When they pulled apart, she was wiping her eyes.

★ ★ ★

A few minutes later, when Rosie's margarita was finally in her hand, the rest of the Mavericks blew out onto the deck. Francine accompanied Sebastian and Charlie. Jeremy raced to the boys because he'd brought a new dump truck he wanted to show them. Right on his heels was Duke. A puppy—and kid—melee ensued on the grass. Soon, Paige and Evan arrived, then Evan's twin siblings sauntered in, along with their mother. They'd picked up Chi along the away.

There were hugs and backslaps all around. No one batted an eyelash at Gideon with his arm around Rosie. It was as if they'd known his feelings for her all along. Only Chi hugged Rosie longer than usual, saying something in her ear that made Rosie smile.

"Grandma, look at the cool dump truck Jeremy brought." Noah held it up with pride, then grabbed Susan's hand, while Jorge grabbed Bob's. They dragged them off to Noah's huge sandbox—vastly different from the sandbox from which Gideon had made it back—followed by puppies, and Jeremy gamboling along beside them like another big, happy puppy. Francine rambled after them with her walker, wanting to get in on the kid action too, probably because she was surrounded by old folks most of the time at the retirement home.

"Maybe you should go rescue your parents," Ari

said, to no Maverick in particular, as she filled margarita glasses and passed them out. Charlie was beaming because her fountain was getting use beyond the wedding.

"They're fine," Daniel said. "They love it. They're waiting for more grandchildren." Which he also said to no Maverick in particular. Or maybe to all of them.

But Gideon looked at Rosie. She smiled back. And he thought of all the fun they were having—and would continue to have—making hay on the baby front.

"In fact, since they're busy," Daniel rubbed his hands together like an evil mastermind, "this is a good time for us to plan."

Everyone gathered closer. Lyssa sat on the edge of the deck to catch the sun, her arms wrapped around her legs, Kelsey and Chi beside her.

"What's up?" Will asked.

"Dad told me the house next to theirs is up for sale," Daniel said.

The Spencers lived in Chicago. When the Mavericks had all started making money, they'd moved Bob and Susan into a big house in a really great neighborhood.

"And since our family is growing all the time—" He tugged Tasha closer. "I thought we should look into buying it."

Gideon noted that Tasha's brother Drew hadn't come today. He was a bit of an outcast, mostly of his own doing. But then Gideon had been an outcast, all his own doing, for a long time too. And he'd made it back into the fold, to the brotherhood, to family.

"No question," Sebastian agreed. "We should buy it."

"It's perfectly situated," Daniel told everyone once they'd all nodded their agreement, "with the two garages on opposite ends of the properties. I figure we can knock down the fence and build a sunroom connecting the two houses."

"We could do the work ourselves," Will said.

Bob Spencer had made sure his boys were handy with a tool belt, that was for sure. "I can help," Gideon offered, knowing his way around a hammer and saw just as well as the rest of them.

"I'm in too, if you need some welding," Charlie offered.

"When do you think the new place will be ready?" Paige asked. While everyone else was downing margaritas, she was sipping lemonade.

"We wouldn't be able to start until late spring," Daniel said.

"Late spring will be good," she said, smiling.

"Why late spring?" Will asked.

Harper was grinning as she elbowed him. "You'd better call your mother over here. I think there's an announcement coming."

Noah and Jorge got there first, then Jeremy. Bob

and Susan came with Francine, who rolled her walker up the ramp Matt had installed for her, and Charlie helped her into a comfortable, cushioned chair at the table.

"So what were you all plotting?" Susan asked.

Daniel gave her a *who, us?* look.

"It was so obvious, honey." She grinned fondly at them all. "It always is."

"Okay, since you have eyes on all sides of your head," he joked, "we might as well fess up that we'd like to buy the house next door to you guys and turn it into a guest house for all of us. We're starting to need a lot more room for our family get-togethers."

"This family is certainly multiplying." Susan looked at Gideon, then Rosie and Jorge, who had climbed onto Rosie's lap. Susan's smile was loving, welcoming, totally inclusive. "The bigger the better."

It was the perfect moment for Evan to pull Paige back against him and lay his hand over her belly. "We definitely agree."

Susan covered her mouth. "Oh my goodness. Are you—"

Paige nodded. "We are!"

Susan jumped up to hug Paige close, tears in their eyes.

"What's going on?" Jeremy asked in a big outdoor voice.

"Paige is going to have a baby," Harper told him.

"Oh *wow*." His eyes grew as big as dinner plates. "That's *awesome*."

Gideon reached out to take Rosie's hand in his, raising it to brush his lips over her knuckles.

They were a family already, him and Rosie and Jorge.

But they were also Mavericks.

And it could never hurt to add a few more.

★ ★ ★

Lyssa was thrilled for Paige and Evan. It had taken them so long to find each other and admit how much they loved one another, even though they'd first met in college. They deserved all the happiness in the world.

It was amazing to think that two years ago, there'd only been her, her brothers, and her parents. Now they were about to have the first Maverick baby since Noah was born six and a half years ago. She'd actually thought Ari would be the first. But nope, it was Paige.

The baby news made Lyssa ache to move closer to everyone. She loved being near her parents in Chicago. But the guys were all out here. And her extended family was all here too.

Rather than buy another Chicago house and extend it, she thought they should move Mom and Dad to California and out of the snow. Last winter had been grueling, cold and long, even if it had given Will and Harper a white wedding.

And if her parents were out here, there would be no reason for Lyssa to stay in Chicago. Especially not in a job she didn't like. She'd given it a year. Wasn't that long enough?

"We've got more good news," Evan said with an away-we-go flourish of his hand in Gideon's direction.

Gideon Jones. He'd been an enigma from the moment he'd shown up on the scene. Still, Lyssa had seen the writing on the wall the moment Rosie laid eyes on him—and he'd laid eyes on her. She'd known Gideon was in love with Rosie long before Rosie seemed to know it herself. Where his face used to be frozen into a perpetual scowl, now he was always smiling. And when he looked at Rosie, he got positively gooey-eyed.

Lyssa felt just the slightest flicker of something, not jealousy or envy, something more like...wistfulness.

Even though she didn't need a man right now. Not when she had her career to think about first.

Gideon was smiling as he told everyone, "With the help of Karmen's mom, Ernestina Sanchez, who found a wealth of old documents and letters in her family archives, we traced some of the painting's history. And because of the added historical value of those letters, we were able to sell the painting for..." Gideon paused for a virtual drum roll. "A whopping sixty million dollars, which was ten million more than even the auctioneers expected."

Lyssa's dad stepped forward to shake Gideon's

hand, then folded him into one of his big bear hugs. "We're so proud of you, son. Not many people would use all that money for a good cause the way you are."

"That means a lot to me, Bob," Gideon said. And then to everyone, "We're going to call our new foundation Lean on Us, dedicated in Karmen Sanchez's name. And our slogan will be—" He looked at Rosie with another of those gooey-eyed, bone-melting looks. *"Let us be your team."*

Everyone clapped.

"We're still looking for a good candidate to run the foundation," Rosie put in. "Any and all suggestions are welcome."

"What about Cal Danniger?" Will suggested.

Lyssa's heart fluttered, and she actually felt a rush of heat to her cheeks.

"He'd be a good choice, since he manages our joint ventures," Sebastian agreed. "He's a smart guy. Capable."

All her Maverick brothers were nodding agreement.

"I don't want to steal him away from you guys," Gideon said.

"I'm sure he can handle both," Matt said.

As they fell into a discussion of Cal Danniger's skills, Lyssa turned away slightly from her friends. Just in case Kelsey or Chi saw her blush and started asking questions.

Lyssa was already thinking about all the

possibilities. One person wouldn't be able to handle the whole foundation. If Cal took it on, he'd need help, especially if he was still managing her brothers' ventures as well. That was a heck of a lot of money, and he'd definitely need a good accountant.

She was a *very* good accountant. Even if her boss didn't think she could handle more than collections calls. The job had fallen far short of her expectations.

But the Lean on Us Foundation? She could do so much to help Rosie and Gideon get it off the ground. It wouldn't be nepotism—she'd never sponged off her brothers. Yes, they'd helped her by paying part of her way through college, but she'd also won scholarships and worked at the same time. Even though they'd all said she didn't need to.

Working with the foundation would be a perfect way to pay them all back.

All she had to do now was convince Cal Danniger that he needed her.

In more ways than one.

* * * * *

For news on Bella Andre's upcoming books, sign up for Bella Andre's New Release Newsletter:

BellaAndre.com/Newsletter

For news on Jennifer Skully's upcoming books, sign up for Jennifer Skully's New Release Newsletter:

bit.ly/SkullyNews

ABOUT THE AUTHORS

Having sold more than 8 million books, *New York Times* and *USA Today* bestselling author Bella Andre's novels have been #1 bestsellers around the world. Known for "sensual, empowered stories enveloped in heady romance" (*Publishers Weekly*), her books have been *Cosmopolitan* magazine "Red Hot Reads" twice and have been translated into ten languages. Winner of the Award of Excellence, *The Washington Post* has called her "One of the top digital writers in America" and she has been featured by *Entertainment Weekly*, NPR, *USA Today*, *Forbes*, *The Wall Street Journal* and, most recently, in *Time* magazine. She has given keynote speeches at publishing conferences from Copenhagen to Berlin to San Francisco, including a standing-room-only keynote at Book Expo America, on her publishing success.

Sign up for Bella's newsletter:
BellaAndre.com/Newsletter

Visit Bella's website at:
www.BellaAndre.com

Follow Bella on Twitter at:
twitter.com/bellaandre

Join Bella on Facebook at:
facebook.com/bellaandrefans

New York Times and *USA Today* bestselling author Jennifer Skully is a lover of contemporary romance, bringing you poignant tales peopled with hilarious characters that will make you laugh and make you cry. Writing as Jasmine Haynes, she's authored over 35 classy, sensual romance tales about real issues like growing older, facing divorce, starting over. Her books have passion and heart and humor and happy endings, even if they aren't always traditional. She also writes gritty, paranormal mysteries in the Max Starr series. Having penned stories since the moment she learned to write, she now lives in the Redwoods of Northern California with her husband and their adorable nuisance of a cat who totally runs the household.

Newsletter signup:
http://bit.ly/SkullyNews

Jennifer's Website:
www.jenniferskully.com

Blog:
www.jasminehaynes.blogspot.com

Facebook:
facebook.com/jasminehaynesauthor

Twitter:
twitter.com/jasminehaynes1

29030959R00196

Printed in Great Britain
by Amazon